Imperfect Cadence

Catherine Bannon

Imperfect Cadence by Catherine Bannon
copyright©2016 by Catherine Bannon

All rights reserved. No parts of this book may be used or reproduced in any manner whatsoever without written permission except in the case of brief quotations embodied in reviews.

Cover and interior designed by Ellie Searl, Publishista®

ISBN-10: 0997667508
ISBN-13: 9780997667509
LCCN: 2016912371

Tea and Crumpets Books
Marshfield, MA

Dedication

THIS BOOK IS DEDICATED TO the memory of Patty Young. If Patty hadn't asked me so many times, "Is that a Canadian, or maybe a British, expression? I've never heard it before", I would never have written the book in the first place. Rest well, my friend.

Acknowledgments

THERE ARE SO MANY PEOPLE who read my manuscript and made suggestions; offered their expertise; and just plain supported me. Many thanks are due to Maggie Brazeau, Jenna Clark, Steve Foley, Wanda Foley, Anne Marie Gruszkowski, Lori Kramer, Aaron Larson, Leslie Lay, Wendy Lester-Juhasz, Brenda Mattson-Moore, Bethani Rourke, Mitchell Stein, Bill Van Note, Michael Weschler and Brenda Wyko. Special thanks are due to Connie Bailey, Cheryl Benson, Cyn Carpenter, Kim Chalmers, Emily Corrigan, Judy Duesterhelt, Jane Gordon, Sonia Helgeson, Heather Hughes, Dannielle Jones, Nancy Jones, Gina Juras, Patti Kennedy, Ana Mirimontes, Aimee Morgan, Catherine NeSmith, Bertie Rankin, Laura Short, Isabella Soriano, Laurie Anne Steele, Anna Taylor, and Janelynn Testerman. Extra special thanks go to Michelle Dacey, Joe Dunlap, Carol Gardner, Stephanie Martinson, and Connie Pierce. Super extra special thanks for Bill and Sharon Hopkins, Janise Stanley and Pat Smith. The I-literally-could-not-have-done-it-without-you awards to go Simon Kay, Teresa and Joe Linhart, Ellie Searl, Marilyn Van Note, and of course my husband Brad! You all know what you did—thank you all so very much and I love you all!

Scituate, MA, is a real place, which is located exactly where Jillian found it; on Boston's South Shore. The elephant fountain, restaurants, churches, hotels etc. where Jillian visits are all real too, although sadly the Italian restaurant where she has her first meal in the US, as well as the farm stand she visits the day before Thanksgiving, have both closed since the book was drafted. Jillian herself, her family and friends, are all figments of my imagination. Some of Jillian's experiences as she adjusts to the US, though, actually happened to my dear friend, Teresa Linhart, and Jillian's discussion of the US with Russ and Connor was inspired by a conversation with Simon Kay. Both Teresa and Simon were quite willing to share their experiences as Brits living in the US, and for that I owe them much thanks. I am not British—I am Canadian, but the culture shock is much the same.

The Olympics that take place during this story is not supposed to represent any particular Games, but I had to include an Olympics because that is where I find the matter of divided loyalties to be the strongest—when my two countries play each other in sporting events. But while I have two countries to cheer and be excited for, I have seen and heard the attitude Jillian sees in American fans myself —so there had to be an Olympics in the book.

I can't end these acknowledgements without a brief word on how this book came to be. Even after my family moved to the US, I still was semi-immersed in a quasi-British culture. Like Jillian, I am a dual citizen, and the one thing I never really did get sorted out, and have not to this day, was idioms. A friend used to ask me, "Is that a Canadian expression? I've never heard it before," and I honestly wouldn't know. That was when I realized that even after spending most of my life in the US, I was still experiencing a form of culture shock. Jillian's story was born from that realization. We are all too prone to believe that because the US, Canada and England share a more-or-less common language and share a common history, that the cultures also overlap, and that's just not so. They are different countries, and naturally have developed different cultures and attitudes. I'm not saying one is superior to another—they're not, they're just different, and should be acknowledged and celebrated as such.

Indie authors live and die by their reviews, so if you liked the book, please leave a review on the site where you purchased it.

Prologue

"**N**ERVOUS, DEAR?"

I hadn't even noticed the older woman sitting next to me in the first class section of the plane and looked over at her in surprise. She smiled at me. "I just noticed that you kept looking at your watch," she explained. "I wondered if this was your first flight." Her accent was American, but I supposed that fully half of the passengers on this flight to London mostly likely were Americans; the other half British like myself.

I shook my head, not trusting myself to speak yet. But I didn't want to be rude, either. "No, I've flown before, it's just that..." I could feel my chin trembling and knew that if I continued to speak, I wouldn't be able to keep from crying.

"My name is Teresa," the woman said. "Is everything all right?" She seemed to be genuinely concerned.

"Jillian. I'm all right, I just..." That was when the tears spilled over and I couldn't control them any longer.

Teresa fished in her bag and handed me a tissue. I couldn't stop crying for several minutes, but finally I gained control of myself.

"What's the matter, Jillian? Can I help?"

"No, it's just...Oh, Josh." I started crying again; I couldn't help it.

"Who is Josh?" Teresa asked gently. "Your husband? Brother? Boyfriend?"

"Fiancé," I managed to choke out.

"And what's wrong with Josh?"

I poured out the whole story. I hadn't realized how much I needed to talk about it. I hadn't felt as if I could tell Joyce all the details; it wouldn't be fair to her given their relationship. I didn't know if Lori had understood, since I hadn't be able to make myself tell her all of it. But it was safe to tell a stranger, someone I would never see again, until I could get home and get advice from Pammie and Siobhan.

Teresa patted my shoulder until I was finished, and then rang for the flight attendant. "I think my young friend here could use a drink," she said. "What would you like, Jillian, dear? Wine? A mixed drink?"

I swallowed hard. "Could I have a cup of tea, please? Black, no sugar?"

Teresa chuckled. "Of course, you're British, aren't you? I should have realized. And I'll have a white wine when you get a chance, but please bring Jillian her tea first."

"Can I bring you anything else?" the flight attendant asked.

"Maybe some ibuprofen if you have it," I requested. By now I had such a bad headache from all the crying I'd done in the last few days, I could hardly see.

"I hope everything is all right," she said. "I'll bring that for you now—let me know if you need anything else."

The flight attendant brought my ibuprofen and my tea, and after I'd taken the ibuprofen and drunk the tea I was feeling a tiny bit better. "Would you mind terribly if I took a nap?" I asked Teresa. "I haven't been sleeping much the last few days."

"You go right ahead," she said, taking a book out of her bag. "You look like you could use it."

I put my seat back and closed my eyes, but I couldn't sleep here any more than I'd been able to sleep back in Scituate in my bed, last night. I kept reliving that last afternoon with Josh. I'd bollocksed the whole thing up royally. And now I would never see him again.

"Jillian, we're landing."

It was Teresa's voice, and I realized with a shock that I'd fallen asleep after all. Stiffly I sat up and stretched a little. "Thank you," I said. "How long did I sleep?"

"About four hours," Teresa said. "I'm glad, I think you needed it. You slept right through the stop at Dublin. But we'll be landing in just a few minutes."

"I didn't think I'd be able to sleep," I sighed. I was grateful that I had, though. I didn't think I'd gotten more than four hours sleep a night for the last several nights.

"You were exhausted," Teresa agreed. She handed me a slip of paper. "That's my email. Let me know what happens."

I thanked her and a few minutes later, the doors opened and we deplaned. I was home. But instead of being relieved, I was dreading going forward. I was no longer waiting for my life to start—I was right in the middle of it. And I'd ruined it forever.

Part One

"JILLIAN, IS THAT YOU?"

Pammie, my flat mate, came out of the kitchen wiping her hands on a towel. "Your mother phoned. And there's some mail for you on the hall table."

"Thanks, Pammie." Graduation was just around the corner and I had been applying for jobs. So far all I had received were rejections but there were still a few firms out there from whom I still had yet to hear. I set my textbooks down and picked up the two envelopes waiting there. "Oh, one's from Cooks! And the other from British Air!"

"Good luck!" Pammie exclaimed as I ripped open the British Air letter and scanned it. Sighing, I handed it to Pammie. It was the list I had requested; that of the requirements to be a flight attendant.

"It's the same thing Virgin Air said. They have a minimum height requirement of five foot two inches. I'm too short." I opened the Cooks letter. I'd applied for an actual position with Cooks, as a travel agent. "Maybe this will be different."

It wasn't. Though it wasn't due to being only five one, Cooks had rejected my application. I threw the letters down on the table, despondent.

"Now what are you going to do?" Pammie asked sympathetically. Of the applications I had sent out, these were the last ones to come back.

"I don't know," I responded. We moved into the main room of the flat, sitting down for a moment of relaxation. "It's not as if I had a burning desire to be a travel agent or a flight attendant." Not even to Pammie had I confided what I really wanted to do—I'd never get my parents to agree, so there was no point. Even the travel industry was pushing my luck.

"I know," Pammie sympathized.

"It's just that I want to travel and they seemed to be logical career lines to look at. I suppose now I look for some other kind of job."

"You could look for some other kind of work with the airlines," Pammie suggested helpfully.

"I might do that." Remembering, I asked, "Did my mother say what she wanted?"

Pammie shook her head. "Just to tell you that she called and that she would talk to you later."

"I'll ring her back later," I decided. It would just be more of the same conversation we'd been having for some weeks now; her attempts to convince me that I should take a post graduate degree. I was not opposed to the idea per se. But since I had no clear ideas what I wanted to do with the rest of my life, save one I knew my parents would oppose, and since the degree I had taken had limited career opportunities, I was inclined to want to take a "gap year" first. I'd need to support myself somehow that year, though; my dad had agreed to pay my share of the rent through the summer if necessary but beyond that, unless I was enrolled in school, I was on my own.

I started to stand up, but Pammie held out a hand to stop me. "Jillian—there's something I need to talk to you about."

I sat back down again. That sounded ominous. "What's wrong?"

"I had a letter from Pauline today," Pammie began.

Pauline was the younger sister of my ex-boyfriend, Colin. She and I had been good friends until I had caught Colin cheating on me. It was the same tired old cliché—I had let myself into his flat thinking to make dinner for him as a surprise, only to find him in bed with another girl. Pauline and I had agreed not to let this spoil our friendship, but we had gradually grown apart as I tried to distance myself from everything related to Colin. I looked over at Pammie warily.

"What did she want?" I asked.

Pammie looked uncomfortable. "She wants to move in with us for part of the summer and the fall term."

"What?" I looked at her, astonished. "We don't have room for her, Pammie."

Pammie and I shared the flat with two other friends, Siobhan and Maggie. It was a three bedroom flat so, since I was much the smallest, I slept on the couch pending Maggie's wedding the week after graduation, at which time I would move into Maggie's bedroom. I paid a correspondingly smaller percentage of the rent until then. Or my dad did. For this, our final year of uni, our parents were subsidizing us.

"I know but…" Pammie hesitated. "It's only for about four or five months. If you're uncomfortable having her here because of Colin, then the answer is no, of course. But if it's only the logistics of the situation, I have a suggestion."

I wasn't sure if I was uncomfortable having her there or not. "What's your suggestion?

"That we put another single bed in my room, since it's the biggest, and have you move in with me just for those few months. We've spent hundreds of nights together when we were growing up—we should be able to stand it for one term."

It was true. Pammie had been my best friend since we were in primary school. "I don't know," I hedged. "What does Siobhan think?"

"I haven't mentioned it to her yet," Pammie admitted. "I wanted to check and see if it was all right with you first."

"I'm not sure. Let me think about it for a day or so."

"Fair enough." Pammie stood up. "It's my turn to make dinner. Will you be in?"

"Where else would I be?" Since breaking up with Colin, I didn't have much of a social life. "Let me know if you need any help."

"You'll be the first person I call. You're the only one of the four of us who really knows what she's doing in the kitchen anyway." Pammie went back into the kitchen. I decided to check my email before I got to work on my paper on the Wars of the Roses.

There was an email from the favorite of my three sisters in law. Adam, the youngest of my three older brothers, and Lori lived in the States, in a small town near Boston. I had never been there but they came for Christmas every couple of years bringing their children, Kaitlyn and Jeremy. Since I had last seen them, two years ago, they'd had a third child, Beth, whom I'd never seen except in pictures. Email and Skype kept us all in contact.

"Hi, Jillian!" Lori had written. "What day is graduation again? We're so proud of you, graduating with a First. Have you decided what you're going to do next year? If you'd like to talk about it, don't hesitate to call, Skype or message me.

"We have some big news. Adam has been invited to teach for six months in Washington DC. It's a huge honor and we're very excited. The only thing we're concerned about is whether I should stay here in Scituate with the children, or whether we should close up the house for the term and we all go down with him. We might be able to rent it for the summer, at least. There are pros and cons in both directions."

She went on to discuss other family news; Kaitlyn's ballet class, her work as a substitute church organist, the football team Adam coached. Suddenly I wanted to talk to her badly. Despite being so much older than I, Lori had always been a good friend, like the older sister I never had. Maybe she could help me figure out what I wanted to do about Pauline, and about next year.

I could smell something burning in the kitchen so I put my impulse on hold. Sighing, I went back to the kitchen, turned down the gas under one pot, chopped Pammie's vegetables finer, showed her for the thousandth time how to put the food processor together, and escaped back to my room, wondering if it would be worth my while just to offer to do all the cooking. Finally I picked up my mobile and pushed the speed dial number that would connect me with the United States.

"Hello, Jillian!" Lori said enthusiastically from several thousand kilometers away. "Did you get my email?"

"I did!" I agreed. "How wonderful for Adam…are you all excited?"

"Terrifically," Lori commented. "It's a wonderful opportunity for him. Now if we could only decide what to do with the rest of us."

"How far is Washington DC from Scituate?"

"A little less than 400 miles."

"What's that in kilometers?"

"I'm not sure. Maybe 600?"

I saw their difficulty. "That is rather a long way to be going back and forth, isn't it?"

"It is," Lori acknowledged. "We've compared the relative costs of renting a house for all of us, or finding an extended stay hotel or furnished studio for just Adam, and they're not different enough to matter. Then, too, I'd have to take a semester off." Lori worked as a music teacher in the local primary school. "But we'll work it out. Adam hasn't yet asked the school about faculty housing. How about you, dear? How are things with you?"

"Confused," I admitted. I told her about Pauline, and about the rejection of my applications. "I'm not sure what I want to do. I've been so busy with my schoolwork that I haven't really had time to figure out what I want to do with my life, and there's so much pressure to make a decision right now. Lori, would you and Adam please try to help me convince Mum and Dad that I need a gap year? I'll find a job, some kind of job; I don't want to feel as if I'm sponging off them. But I truly need more time before I decide if I want to go to law school like Dad wants, or to teach like Mum wants, or something else altogether and if so what. I know I should have thought of this before I started my degree but I didn't realize how busy I was going to be."

"I can't see you in either law or teaching," Lori said decidedly. "You've never liked talking in front of others. And I'm not sure I can see you as a flight attendant, either, to be honest. A travel agent, maybe, but I think your friend Pammie is right. If you want to work in the travel industry, you might want to think about doing it behind the scenes."

"Or a tour guide," I suggested, having just thought of the idea myself. "No, maybe not. You're right, I don't like talking to large groups of people. I don't mind it one on one or smaller groups. But Lori, will you help me?"

"Of course I will," Lori declared. "In fact, I have an idea that might solve both our problems. I'll have to mention it to Adam but I can't imagine he'd have any problem with it. This is what I'm thinking…"

A few minutes later I went running into the kitchen crying, "It's okay to let Pauline come, Pammie, I'm going to spend the summer and the fall term in America with my sister in law!"

It was almost that easy. After a long, three way call with my parents, Adam, Lori and me, everyone agreed that a few months helping Lori take care of the children in Scituate while Adam was in Washington would be a good compromise, and would in fact satisfy my longing to see more of the world than just England. I promised to make a final decision about a post graduate degree and/or what line of work I wanted to take up, before the end time was up. In exchange, my father agreed to continue my allowance till the end of the year, since I would have no opportunity to earn money while I was there.

"I have to be here for Maggie's wedding," I told Lori and Adam in a call to discuss logistics. "That's on June 22nd. You have to be in Washington by July 1—why don't I come on the 26th?"

"That sounds perfect," Adam said. "I'm so glad you're able to do this, honey. I had worried about leaving Lori alone with the kids for so long, but housing in Washington is outrageous, almost worse than Boston. With you here, I can rent a studio apartment in Virginia and take the Metro into work, and leave my car here for you to drive."

"I don't drive very well," I admitted. "Living in London, I've never needed to."

"Have Dad take you out and get you more comfortable with it," Adam commanded. "You'll need a car to get around here—Scituate doesn't have the advanced public transportation you're used to. Boston does, but Scituate is far enough outside the city so that we have a commuter rail and that's about it."

"No, wait until you get here," Lori countermanded him. "You're going to need to get used to driving on the other side of the road; I'll take you out a few times when you arrive until you're more sure of yourself."

I was a bit nervous about driving on either side of the road but I trusted Lori. "I'll be sure to bring my British license with me. Can I drive on that or will I have to get an American license?"

"I'm not sure," Adam admitted. "I'll find out before you get here."

There was so much to do between that day in late May and when I left, that time went quickly. Almost before I knew it, I had graduated from uni. A few days later I wore my buttercup colored dress as one of Maggie's bridesmaids. A few days after that, more excited than I'd ever been in my life, I boarded a plane for Boston.

Eight hours later, I stepped out of the plane and walked up the ramp into Logan Airport. Lori and Adam had promised to meet me by the baggage claim, explaining that only ticketed passengers were allowed past the security checkpoint. I began following the signs to the Baggage Claim, dragging my roll-on behind me and with my purse and my laptop slung over my shoulder.

I pulled out my mobile to text them that I had arrived and would see them shortly, and was just looking down at it when I bumped into a young man who'd stopped short in front of me, also looking down at his mobile. "Oh, I'm so sorry!" I gasped, as I dropped my laptop right onto his foot.

"No matter. It was my fault." He bent over and picked up my laptop. "I should have been watching where I was going."

"So should I," I admitted.

"What part of England are you from?" he asked, smiling at me. "Is this your first visit to the US?" He was big and blond and blue-eyed and had a wonderful smile.

"London, and yes it is. My brother lives here and I'm here on a visit."

"I love London. I lived there for three years when I was in school. My grandfather still does and I visit him as often as I can." He handed me the laptop with another of those smiles. "I hope you enjoy it here."

"I'm sure I will." I adjusted the laptop strap across my shoulder and smiled shyly at him. "Are those your friends?" I motioned to a group of people, some fifty meters ahead of us, who were waving at him.

"They are and I'd better get over there. Enjoy your stay!" He flashed another smile at me and ran off towards them, calling, "I'm coming!" I noticed that he was limping and felt badly that I'd evidently done some minor damage when I dropped my laptop. I watched after him for a minute, then recalled my own excitement and turned back to find Adam and Lori.

They were there, as promised, and had the children with them. "Aunt Jill!" Kaitlyn shouted, running over to me and hugging me around the waist. "Daddy says you're coming to live with us!"

I hugged her. "I am," I told her. "Do you like that idea?"

She nodded vigorously. "I'm going to be in first grade in the fall," she informed me.

"Well, aren't you the big girl!" I took her hand and we joined her parents.

"Hi, honey!" Adam greeted me with a kiss on the cheek. "How was your flight?"

"Just fine." I hugged Lori and took Jeremy's hand. "Hello, Jeremy. Do you remember Aunt Jill?" I much preferred Jillian to Jill, but when my brother Nick's daughter Violet was learning to speak she had been unable to pronounce my whole name. So I was Aunt Jill to the children and Jillian to everyone else.

"No," my nephew said clearly, and buried his face in his mother's skirt.

"Jeremy..." Adam said warningly.

"It's all right. He hasn't seen me for two years. He'll remember me later, when he's had time." Lori was carrying Beth. "Hello, Bethie. I'm Aunt Jill."

"Jill," Beth agreed.

"She's so big! What is she now, eighteen months?"

"Sixteen," Adam corrected me. "Okay, hon, let's get your luggage and head home. We're going to get stuck in rush hour traffic—sorry."

I collected my two checked bags and followed my family out to the car park.

"You take the front seat, Jillian," Lori instructed me. "I'll sit in back with the kids." She busied herself fastening Beth into a car seat. Adam opened the boot and started loading my bags inside.

I automatically started for the passenger seat only to see the steering wheel. I reversed myself and went round to the other side. "It feels strange," I mused.

"Oh, that's right, you have right hand drive in England," Lori remembered. "I'm sorry, Jillian, there will be a lot of things you'll find different here."

"We'll stop for dinner on the way home," Adam reported, taking his seat behind the wheel. "I'm sure you're exhausted and will want to go right to bed."

He was right, I realized. It was past ten pm Greenwich time. We'd been served a meal at the appropriate time on the airplane, but I knew I should eat something just to help get myself on American time.

My first impression of America was of an endless motorway furnished with cars all on the wrong side of the road. We were moving at a crawl for the first part of the trip but after we turned onto a different motorway things picked up a bit. Adam pulled off the road at an exit and onto a secondary road and into a car park.

"This is a favorite family place," Lori explained. "I hope you like Italian. The kids—well, Kaitlyn, really—were determined to show it to you immediately. We gave in because it'll be time for Beth and Jeremy, at least, to go to bed as soon as we get home and it seemed easier than my trying to cook dinner as soon as you got in the door. I hope you don't mind; I know you must be exhausted."

"I love Italian," I promised, helping Kaitlyn out of the car. She took my hand and we walked into the restaurant together.

When we were seated at a round table in the back of the room with menus in front of us, I suddenly realized how tired I was. "Wine, Jillian?" Adam offered.

I shook my head. "Not tonight. I'd fall asleep in my plate. I'll just have water, maybe with lime." I opened the menu and was astonished at how many entrees I had to choose from.

"I want the spaghetti," Kaitlyn announced.

"What about you, Jeremy?" Lori asked, holding the children's menu where Jeremy could pretend he could read. I looked down at my own menu again, noticing that the words were blurring together.

When the waiter came over Adam indicated that I should go first, but I shook my head, still reviewing the menu. Adam ordered the drinks and the children's food first, then Lori and he made their selections. Too tired to make a decision, I went with the line of least resistance, perhaps inspired by Kaitlyn. "I'll have the spag bol," I decided.

The waiter looked startled. "I'm sorry, ma'am?"

"She means the spaghetti Bolognese," Adam translated.

The waiter went away. "You don't call it that here?" I asked.

Adam shook his head. "Not to worry, though, honey. There are a lot of things that have different names over here."

I sipped my lime water. "I imagine it will take some time to adjust."

We finished dinner and drove the rest of the way home. Lori had sent me pictures of the house but I hadn't realized how large it was until we drove into the driveway. "We got a particularly good deal on the house when we bought it six years ago," Adam explained. "Kaitlyn was a baby and we knew we wanted several children, so we went ahead and bought it." He stopped the car and came around to open the door for me.

"Your bedroom will be on the first floor—that's ground floor, to you," Lori added, picking up Beth as Kaitlyn insisted on holding my hand. "While the children are small, we wanted them upstairs with us—there are three bedrooms on the second floor and two on the first. Kaitlyn and Beth are in one upstairs room and Jeremy in another, with us in the master. Your room has its own bath so you won't have to run up and down the stairs."

"It'll be my room when I get big," Kaitlyn informed me as Adam unlocked the door. "But you can have it for now."

I smiled down at her. "Thank you, sweetie."

"Here we are." Adam held the door open. "Lori, show Jillian around while I get her bags. Poor kid looks ready to drop in her tracks."

"Maybe I could see the house tomorrow?" I suggested. "It's almost one in the morning my time and I've been up since five."

"Of course you can," Lori agreed instantly, setting Beth on the floor. "Stay here, Bethie. Mommy's just going to show Auntie Jill her room while Daddy gets her bags."

"I just need the small black one for tonight," I said. "Everything else can wait till morning."

"I'll just be a minute," Adam promised, retreating back out the door.

"Your room is pretty bare," Lori admitted. "We bought a bed and a dresser but that was about it since we weren't using the room and we rarely have overnight guests. We'll go shopping later in the week and get everything you need."

"I don't need much," I said, stifling a yawn and unutterably grateful to see Adam coming in with my overnight bag.

"Come on, Jillian." Lori led me to a door in the hallway and opened it. "The bathroom is just over there, the door on the left."

"Thank you."

She kissed my cheek. "I'm glad you're here, honey. Sleep yourself out in the morning."

She left, closing the door behind her. I looked around. The room was not as sparsely furnished as Lori had indicated. There was a white wrought iron bed with an old-fashioned wooden chest at the foot; a dresser painted white; a computer table likewise; a comfortable looking chair upholstered in dark blue. It was completely devoid of any decoration, though, which may have been what she meant. Right now, though, I didn't care what the room looked like or if the mattress was filled with rocks. I went into the bathroom and did what needed doing, then came back out and undressed.

The mattress was not filled with rocks; it was quite comfortable. I was asleep in minutes. Strangely enough, I dreamed of the young man at the airport, and they were extremely pleasant dreams.

Three days later I was more or less on Boston time and my room was decorated with light blue curtains, bedspread and runner, and braided rug. Two Monet prints were on the walls and I was beginning to feel comfortable there. Lori and I had gone out shopping while Adam stayed home with the children. "This will get you started," Lori had promised. "You can add anything you like as we go."

Adam was upstairs packing with Lori's help and I was keeping an eye on the children while having a cup of tea when there was a light tap on the kitchen door. A moment later the door opened and a pretty red-haired girl about my own age peeked in. "Hi," she greeted me. "I'm Joyce Ryan from next door. You must be Jillian."

"Joyce! Joyce!" Kaitlyn and Jeremy both ran to her, obviously pleased to see her. "Joyce, this is Aunt Jill!" Kaitlyn continued, taking her hand and dragging her over.

"Have a seat," I invited. Clearly she was very familiar with the children.

"Thanks." Joyce sat down at the table across from me. "I've been the kids' babysitter since Kaitlyn was born, and I'm giving her ballet lessons."

"I thought she took lessons at a studio." I was confused.

"She does," Joyce explained. "I teach there, and every once in a while I come in and just work with her a little. I'm a dance major, specializing in ballet, and I get college credit for it." She pulled Kaitlyn up on her lap. "Don't I, kitten?"

Kaitlyn nodded, while I reminded myself that college meant something slightly different in the US than it did in England. I stood up. "Would you like some tea?"

"I'd love some, if it isn't too much trouble," Joyce responded. "Is Lori around?"

"They're both upstairs," I explained, refreshing my tea and pouring a cup for Joyce. I handed it to her, sat down, and picked up Jeremy, who was looking pouty. "I can call them for you."

Joyce shook her head. "I'm in no hurry, if you don't mind my sitting here."

"Not at all." I sipped my tea, studying the girl across from me. She was quite pretty, with the most amazing green eyes I'd ever seen.

"Are you liking it here?" Joyce asked, adding a little sugar to her tea.

I nodded. "I'm still getting used to a lot of things that are different, but I'm enjoying myself."

"I'm so glad you were able to come visit," Joyce said with obvious sincerity. "Kaitlyn's been so excited about your coming, haven't you, punkin?"

Kaitlyn nodded vehemently. "I love Aunt Jill." Then, with a child's quick change of subject, she demanded, "Joyce, will you dance the Sugar Plum Fairy?"

"Not this morning, punkin, I didn't bring my shoes with me this time," Joyce explained. "But if you'll go tell your Mommy I'm here, I'll do a barefoot dance for you now, and bring my shoes tonight."

Kaitlyn scrambled off her lap and ran for the stairs. "Mommy! Joyce is here!" we could hear her calling all the way up.

Joyce and I looked at each other and laughed. I liked her. "I'm going to keep an eye on the kids tonight for the first part of the party," Joyce explained. "Then I'll come down and join you all."

Tonight was a going away party for Adam; a few of his fellow teachers from the university in Boston as well as some neighbors. Lori and I had been cooking for two days getting ready. It was to be informal, with finger food and drinks rather than a sit down dinner, and I'd been having a wonderful time with the preparations. I loved party planning.

"I know Lori plans to keep them up from their naps this afternoon so they'll be tired enough to go to sleep early," I told her. "So you won't have to spend too much time upstairs."

Lori came down just in time to hear this. "Absolutely," she agreed. "Most of the guests will be arriving between 7:30 and 8:00 and I hope the kids will be down right about that time. So you won't miss much of anything. Are you bringing Kenneth with you?" She sat down next to me and Jeremy immediately scrambled down and climbed onto her lap instead.

"Kenneth's my boyfriend," Joyce explained to me. "No, he has a family event of his own to go to." She looked over at me. "But if you don't have plans for the Fourth, some of my friends and I are planning a cookout in my backyard, and later we'll probably go down to the beach to watch the fireworks. We'd love to have you join us."

I looked over at Lori. "Do we have plans?"

She shook her head, smiling. "Not a one. The kids and I will stay home and watch the Pops on TV. You go with Joyce and have a good time."

"What are the Pops?" I asked.

"The Boston Pops Orchestra. It's a subset of the Boston Symphony that plays lighter music than the BSO. They traditionally play a concert on the Boston Esplanade every July 4 which is nationally televised," Lori explained. "I'll record it for you—you'll enjoy it."

"Be sure to bring your swim things," Joyce told me. "My parents put a pool in a few years ago."

"We don't swim at the beach?" I asked, surprised.

Joyce shook her head vehemently. "Much too cold this early. We might wade, and some of the guys will decide to be macho and swim, but the water isn't really comfortable till August."

Lori nodded agreement. "The water's not much warmer here than it would be for you at Brighton or Blackpool, despite being so much further south."

I nodded understanding. "Can I bring anything to the cookout? I love to cook—I could make a salad or some starters."

"That would be lovely. Whatever you care to bring—I'm not much of a cook myself." Joyce hesitated slightly.

"What time is the party? And where are you?"

"I live in the house on the corner, next door to the left," Joyce said. "Why don't you come over about mid afternoon? And I'll see you before then—I'll see you tonight, in fact." She shifted Kaitlyn off her lap. "You've been a very good girl waiting for the grownups to stop talking," she told the little girl. "I have to go pretty soon, but I'll dance for you now."

"I was good too!" Jeremy objected from Lori's lap.

"Yes, you were," Joyce agreed. "Can we all go in the family room now, and I'll dance for everyone."

We moved into the family room, Joyce clearly familiar with the house. She took off her shoes and performed a ballet routine in her bare feet to Lori's piano accompaniment. I was not a student of ballet but any friend of Maggie's couldn't help picking up something, so I could tell that the various combinations were not difficult. However, the way she moved and the ease with which she took her positions told me that she was very good.

Kaitlyn sat rapt, watching her. Jeremy wriggled a little, less interested. Joyce finished her routine and sat down to put her shoes back on.

"Did you like that?" she asked Kaitlyn.

Kaitlyn nodded vigorously. "When is my next lesson?" she asked Lori.

Lori consulted a calendar. "Saturday afternoon," she said. "Will it be with you, Joyce?"

Joyce looked uncertain. "If it's early in the afternoon it will be with Miss Sophie," she admitted. "My other job is kind of in the way."

"What's your other job?" I asked.

"I work at the local hotel as a housekeeper," Joyce explained. "It's just a summer job—I work at the ballet studio year round; I have since I was fourteen. But I only do that Saturdays and holidays for most of the year. During the school year; I have a campus job in one of the libraries during the week. During the summer I pick up as many hours as I can whenever Sophie has too many students for one class, and then work at the hotel since the studio doesn't pay much to student interns."

"I should get a job," I mused. "Don't you think, Lori?"

I'd never had a job. My parents hadn't wanted me to work during the school year, and in the hols my mother had always had so many volunteer projects she needed my help with that I never had time for a job. "You don't need to work, princess," my dad had always said. "You'll have plenty of time to work after you graduate." Well, now I had graduated and I had no experience at all, while a girl my own age or even younger was working two jobs and going to school as well.

"If you'd like to," Lori said. "Or you could take some classes somewhere. The kids will keep us busy during the summer but once school starts in September I'm afraid you'll be bored. But I'd wait, Jillian. There aren't a lot of job openings this time of year and I think you need a little more time to adjust to the US."

"Can you work?" Joyce asked. "I don't mean to be rude, but aren't you on a visa?"

"I'm half-American," I explained. "My dad is an American citizen and when I was born he registered me with the Embassy, the same as he did my brothers. But my mom is British; I was born in England and I've lived there all my life."

"I'd love to see England," Joyce said enviously. "I'm going to apply to grad school there." She stood up. "I've got to go. Lori, my mom wanted me to see if she could borrow your big lobster pot. She's going to try making jam for the first time tomorrow and she doesn't want to invest in a canner until she sees how it goes."

"Of course she can," Lori said, rummaging under the counter and coming out with a big pot. "Tell her to let me know how it goes—I may try it myself this summer."

"Put something down inside the pot," I suggested. "A cake rack or something. Don't put the jars right down on the bottom—they'll break and it's a dreadful mess."

They both looked at me. "Do you know how to can?" Joyce breathed.

I nodded. "I've done a lot of canning with my mother, and we've often had to do makeshift arrangements in church kitchens or when we had more fruit than our equipment could hold." I hesitated. "I don't want to be pushy, but I'd be happy to come over and help if she'd like."

"She'd love it," Joyce said promptly. "I'll tell her to call you. See you tonight!" She kissed Kaitlyn and Jeremy on the tops of their heads and left.

"She's such a nice girl," Lori told me. "She's been our sitter ever since Kaitlyn was born."

"So she told me," I responded. "I liked her. I hope we can be good friends."

Joyce's mother did call, and I agreed to go over and help with the jam the next day. Joyce came over as agreed and she and I put the children down for bed just as the first of the guests arrived.

"I'm so glad you're coming to the party on the Fourth," she told me. "It won't be a terribly large group. A couple of my cousins; some of Kenneth's family; some of my friends and some of his. It's a mixed group and not everyone knows everyone so you won't be the only one."

"I'm looking forward to it," I said. It would be nice to make some friends right off. I tended to be shy and didn't make friends easily—I'd known Pammie since Primary School and Maggie and Siobhan since we entered Year 2. We'd all grown up together. As long as it wasn't too large a crowd I'd have a good time, I was sure.

Adam left for Washington the next day. After comforting the children, who didn't really comprehend that Daddy would be back the following weekend, I went next door to help Ruth Ryan with her first attempt at strawberry jam. She was a warm and friendly woman and I was comfortable with her, just as I had been with Joyce. Joyce herself was there but as she had said, did not appear to be very experienced with cooking.

We were sitting at the table waiting out the slow boil when there was a light tap on the door and a young man walked in. "Hello, Mrs.

Ryan," he said politely. "Hi, babe." He kissed Joyce lightly on the cheek and looked over at me, a sudden shock expressed in his face.

"This is my boyfriend Kenneth Aldrich," Joyce introduced us. "Kenneth, this is Jillian Munroe, Adam's sister. Remember I told you she was coming?"

"Hi, Jillian," Kenneth said, sitting down across from me. "Welcome to Scituate." He continued to look at me as if confused.

"Hello, Kenneth." Kenneth was of medium height and slender, though his shoulders and upper arms were well muscled. He was not the type I fancied, having dark hair and eyes while I tended towards blue eyed blonds. He was undeniably handsome, however, and I liked his shy smile.

"I'm sorry, Jillian," he said suddenly. "I'm being rude and staring. It's not you, you just remind me of someone."

Joyce was looking confused as well—whoever it was that I reminded him of, she didn't know that person. But I knew the feeling—Kenneth was reminding me of someone as well, though I couldn't think who.

"I had a cousin who was killed in an auto accident a few years ago," Kenneth explained. "You don't really look like her, not at a closer look. But at first glance, the passing resemblance is startling."

"I'm not seeing it, but then I didn't know Janey as well as some of your cousins. Do you really see a resemblance?" Joyce asked softly, taking his hand.

He nodded. "As long as you take into consideration that Janey was only thirteen when she died," he added. "Now, let's talk about something else. We—I—must be making Jillian uncomfortable. I'm sorry, Jillian."

"Jillian's coming to the party on the 4th," Joyce told him. "We'll have to add her to the count."

Kenneth looked over at me again. "That's great!" He smiled at me. "The more the merrier. If Jillian doesn't mind our talking about people she doesn't know for a few minutes, there are a couple of things we need to discuss."

"She'll know them on Thursday," Joyce interrupted with a smile.

"I don't mind," I promised.

"Well then. Ben has to work till six. He'll join us then. Susannah's coming, though—she won't wait for him. Harry will be here with Sonia. Rachel says she wouldn't miss it and can she bring her new boyfriend."

"Of course she can."

"I already told her that. Russ will be here after all; Colleen has to work, though. And Josh will be here."

"Josh is back already?" Joyce sounded surprised. "I thought he was going to be gone all summer."

Kenneth shook his head. "They said until the regular guy was medically cleared to play, which could be all summer. But he flew out to meet them a couple days ago, and Josh got home the other night."

"Is he disappointed?"

Kenneth shrugged. "You never know with Josh. He's more interested in composing than playing, anyway. He said when he called the other night that he had six great weeks but he wouldn't mind a quiet summer at home." He looked at me. "We're talking my older brother, who was subbing as keyboardist for a rock singer on tour—Neil Donavan."

"Your brother was playing on Neil Donavan's tour?" I was truly impressed. "He's wonderful."

"I'm sure he'll tell you all about it," Kenneth said with one of those smiles. Who did he remind me of? "He's a quiet guy, our Josh, but he's a real musician and he never minds talking about music."

"I'll want to hear too," Joyce said. "Is Randi coming?"

Kenneth nodded. "Sorry, I almost forgot. She'll be here." I could have been mistaken, but I got the impression he'd have been just as happy if Randi, whoever Randi was, would stay home.

"So that's eleven to start and Ben later, plus Vicki and Zach, Alice and Tyler; fifteen, sixteen total. That's manageable."

"What about your family?"

"I think just Peter and Carol."

It sounded absolutely terrifying to me but I forced back my natural shyness. I liked both Joyce and Kenneth; there was no reason to think I wouldn't like their friends.

"Jillian, does this look right?" Mrs. Ryan asked suddenly.

I got up and looked at the spoonful of jam on the cold plate. "It's fine. It needs a little more time but it's looking very good. Give it another ten minutes or so."

"Thanks, dear." She smiled at me. "I'm glad you offered to help—I was nervous about trying it on my own."

"I love cooking," I told her. I washed the plate and put it back in the freezer. I sat back down at the table with Joyce and Kenneth.

"There's just one thing," Kenneth said, looking a bit uncomfortable. "I have to work tomorrow and Wednesday after all, and there may be overtime both nights. I'll still get the beer and wine, since I'm legal and you're not, but you'd better not count on me to help with the grocery shopping."

Joyce looked stricken. "I don't even know what to buy!"

"Get some hot dogs, hamburgers, chicken and stuff," Kenneth advised. He pulled out his wallet and passed her several bills. "That's my contribution. Josh said he'd get the stuff at the packie if I got held up so you don't need to worry about that."

"What's legal age in America?" I asked. "It's eighteen in England. And what's a packie?"

"That's New England for liquor store. Legal drinking age is twenty-one here," Joyce said. "I'll be twenty next month, but Kenneth is twenty two."

"I'm twenty-one," I contributed. "If you need me to do anything…"

Joyce looked hopeful. "You know about cooking. Would you help me grocery shop?"

"I'd love to!" I was delighted to be asked. "When would you like to go?"

"I guess Wednesday morning," Joyce said, obviously unsure. "I have to work tomorrow but I'm off Wednesday."

"I still have all day Thursday off," Kenneth assured her.

Joyce grimaced. "I have to work Thursday morning, but hopefully it won't take too long."

"We told people not until 4:00," Kenneth reminded her. "You should be through long before then." He stood up and kissed her gently. "I have to go, babe. I'm on an errand for my Aunt Rosemary and need to get to the garden center before they close."

"Love you." Joyce returned his kiss. "See you tonight?"

"You bet. Bye, Mrs. Ryan. Bye, Jillian, good to meet you." Kenneth was gone.

"He's such a good boy," Mrs. Ryan said. She pulled the cold plate out of the freezer. "Shall we try again, Jillian?"

I went home later that afternoon with two jars of strawberry jam that Mrs. Ryan insisted on giving me.

"Did you have a nice time?" Lori asked as I let myself in.

"I had a lovely time," I told her. "I like Joyce so much, and I met her boyfriend too."

"Kenneth's a sweet boy," Lori agreed. "I know he and his mother from the church choir. His aunt is the regular organist."

"I liked him," I said. "He reminds me of someone, but I haven't been able to figure out who."

"I'm sure you'll figure it out eventually," Lori said a bit vaguely, looking in the pantry for a box of pasta. "I'm going to make mac and cheese for the kids if that's okay with you."

"Fine," I said. "Do you want me to make it?"

"No, you've done enough today." Before going to the Ryan's I had vacuumed and dusted the downstairs, done laundry and watched the kids while Lori ran errands. "You relax while I make dinner."

Wednesday came and I joined Joyce for grocery shopping. "Where are you going?" Mrs. Ryan asked as we put the final touches on our shopping list, sitting once again in the Ryan's kitchen.

"Just out to the market in the village," Joyce replied. "I don't think there's anything we can't get there."

"Have fun," her mother told us, as we went out to Joyce's little blue compact car.

"Don't mind the car," Joyce said as I slid into what I was beginning to be accustomed to as the passenger seat. "It's thirteen years old, but it still gets me where I'm going."

"Adam left me his car to use," I said. "But he doesn't want me to take it out alone until I'm a little more accustomed to driving on what is, for me, the wrong side of the road."

"Oh, Kenneth will take you out," Joyce said immediately, pulling out of the driveway and into the street. "He taught me to drive a stick shift, since that's what he drives. You can use my car, since this is an automatic, and you can get some practice driving with him."

"That's very nice of you both. Thank you."

"The market's not far," Joyce told me. "Have you been there with Lori?"

I shook my head. "When she's gone marketing, I've stayed home with the children," I explained. It suddenly struck me. "You won't be getting any babysitting while I'm here! I'm so sorry."

Joyce laughed. "It's quite all right. I'm not going to have much time this year. I'm in my third year of the Boston Conservatory and taking extra ballet classes on the side and this coming school year my training gets even more rigorous. I'd have to pull back from babysitting much anyway."

"That's good. You'll have to tell me about your dancing. One of my flat mates at home takes ballet courses, but she isn't planning on a career in dance."

Joyce looked at me curiously. "Why not? I've never wanted anything but to be a professional dancer."

"She says she isn't good enough. She loves it, but she says she doesn't have the drive that you need to be a professional."

"I do," Joyce said, taking a right hand fork and slowing the car. "I'm going to be a professional dancer no matter what. Jillian, look over there. Those are the Scituate elephants."

She pointed to a small bronze statue of three dancing elephants, sitting in the middle of a small common.

"How adorable!" I cried. "Is it a fountain?"

Joyce nodded. "A local sign of spring is when the elephants come out of their winter box." She started the car again. "We'll come back another time so you can take pictures, if you like."

"I'd love to."

"I'll take you down to the lighthouse, too. There's a great true story about it—during the War of 1812, the lighthouse keeper had two daughters, Abigail and Rebecca. They were home alone one day when they heard the British troops approaching. So they took their brothers' fife and drum, and went out on the rocks where there was a good echo, and began to play. The soldiers assumed it was the town militia approaching, and they retreated!"

I was enchanted.

A few minutes later Joyce pulled into a car park outside a market. "It's just a small one," she said apologetically. "When we need a big market, we go down to the one in Marshfield, or up to Cohasset."

"It looks big enough to me," I said. "Our Tescos are huge, but we have plenty of the small markets as well."

"We have the huge ones too," Joyce said. "Just not in Scituate."

Joyce took a shopping cart and looked over at me. "I know we made a list, but I still don't really know what to get, other than what we need for the grill."

"Start with that," I suggested. "Then we'll build from there. You said there'll be about eighteen people?"

Joyce nodded. "More or less. Eighteen who responded. There might be a few more dropping by—Kenneth and I decided we should plan food for about twenty or twenty-two. Better to have too much than not enough, and some of the guys eat like three men apiece."

"I have three brothers, so I know what you mean," I said with a smile. "The other day, Kenneth said chicken, hamburger and hot dogs, right? Let's start with that."

We loaded up the cart with packages of chicken and ground beef. I was surprised to see hot dogs in plastic packages. "They come in cans in England," I told Joyce. She shuddered a little.

"I guess we'll need rolls for the dogs and burgers," she said. "And some sliced cheese—some people are sure to want cheeseburgers."

"And condiments," I reminded her. "Mustard, pickles, relish and so on."

I was astounded as Joyce chose two kinds of mustard, three kinds of relish, four kinds of pickles, mayonnaise, two large bottles of ketchup, and a large bottle of olives. "That's one of the widest selections I've ever seen," I marveled. "What do you have in the big stores?"

"I'll take you to the big Stop N Shop sometime," Joyce answered, reaching for a jar of barbecue sauce. She selected two and dropped them into the basket. "People will want barbecue sauce on their chicken, won't they?"

"I imagine so." I turned around to see a display of produce. I selected a couple heads of lettuce, some tomatoes and onions. "You'll want these too."

"You're right." Joyce looked helplessly at me. "What else?"

"What do you want for sides? Starters? Dessert?"

"Chips, I guess. And maybe some dips. And we could get some salads at the deli counter."

When I looked at the salads at the deli counter I shuddered. "Let's not do that. Let's make our own."

"I don't know how."

"I do." I smiled at her. "It's easy. I'll show you."

"Take over then." Joyce's face brightened. "I didn't really think this through. I never really thought about what I needed or how the food would actually get there. Kenneth's not a great cook but he's better than I am. I guess I was counting on him too much."

I was thinking furiously. "Potato salad," I said. "A cold vegetable plate with dips. I don't know about chips—it would be hard to keep them hot."

Joyce looked confused, and then her face cleared. "I'm talking about what I think you call crisps," she said.

"Oh, that makes more sense." I thought a little longer. "Deviled eggs. Cole slaw. Macaroni salad. I'll make you a whole raft of starters if you like. And for dessert, fruit dipped in melted chocolate."

"Won't that be an awful amount of work for you?"

"This is fun for me," I told her. "But I won't do anything you don't want me to. It's your party."

"Oh, I didn't mean I didn't want you to," Joyce said hastily. "I just don't want to put you out."

"I promise you, I'll have a smashing time." I looked around. "We're blocking the way here. Shall I go ahead?"

"Please do!" Joyce's face was enthusiastic. "I'll leave it all in your hands. Just tell me what you want me to do and I'll help."

I began loading the cart with vegetables, shrimp, scallops, bacon, cheeses and crackers, chicken wings, additional mayonnaise, eggs, sour cream, sausage meat, fruit and chocolate. I added a few bags of crisps for Joyce's sake.

"Maybe we could have s'mores on the beach," Joyce suggested.

"What are s'mores?"

"Graham crackers with chocolate and marshmallow in the middle. You melt the chocolate with the toasted marshmallow and they're really good." I must have made something of a face because she added. "I know, they sound horrible. But they're good."

I decided to defer judgment. "I need macaroni for the salad, and then I think we're good to go."

It was the boxes of pasta that finally defeated me. I looked at the boxes and boxes of various shapes in differing packaging. "You'll have to tell me," I said. "What ones do I choose?"

"Any shape you like," Joyce told me. "But I think this is the brand name my mother uses." She pointed. With relief, I found what I wanted in that brand.

"I think I have everything," I said finally.

"We can come back if we've missed anything," Joyce promised. "Let's check out and go home."

Loaded down with reusable cloth bags, we returned to Joyce's house where I started eggs, potatoes and pasta boiling while Joyce and

I chopped vegetables and her mother found the appropriates pots, pans, and other equipment that we needed.

"I'll clean everything up, I promise, Mrs. Ryan," I assured her.

"Indeed you won't," Mrs. Ryan said emphatically. "I'm delighted that someone has finally interested Joyce in cooking." Joyce and I shared a quick glance, both of us smothering grins.

"We have a rule in this house—whoever cooks doesn't have to clean up," Mrs. Ryan continued. "That applies no matter who is cooking."

By the time I left that afternoon, we had the vegetables cut, the dips mixed and chilling in the fridge, the chicken wings marinating, the fruit washed and where necessary cut, and as much prep work as possible done ahead.

"I should be home from work somewhere between two and three o'clock," Joyce told me. "Everyone's coming around four-thirty or five; how much time will you need to get everything else done?"

I looked at Mrs. Ryan. "Would it be all right if I came over about two-thirty or three?"

"Of course, dear. Come over as early as you like. I'll be here even if Joyce is at work." She looked at her daughter. "Is Kenneth working tomorrow?"

"No, he has the whole day off," Joyce said happily. "He'll be over tonight after dinner—he's going to stop on the way and get the propane for the grill and the alcohol."

"I'm glad to hear it. He works too hard."

"He's trying to work as many hours as he can this summer because once school starts in the fall he won't have much time," Joyce explained.

"I know. But he should take some time to relax, even so."

"Where does Kenneth work?" I asked, finishing up the process of putting chopped vegetables in covered bowls to keep them fresh.

"He works for a construction company. During the school year he works in the office but in the summers he works as a laborer's helper on the job sites," Joyce explained. "He wants to be an architect and he'll need the experience before he graduates."

I stood up. "I'll be over early tomorrow afternoon to finish up, then, if that's all right."

We made the arrangements and I went home.

The next day I arrived at the Ryan's about one. "Joyce is running late," her mother reported. "She was assigned to laundry today and she's got the last load in the washer."

"I'll try to have everything ready for her," I promised.

By the time Joyce got home at three fifteen, I had the salads compounded, the ground beef seasoned and shaped into patties, the shrimp cooked, marinated and on skewers, the scallops wrapped in bacon and ready for the broiler, the devilled eggs made, the bruschetta mixed, the Scotch eggs ready for frying and the vegetable trays set up. "You've done so much!" Joyce exclaimed, amazed.

"The chocolate for the fruit is melting right now," I said, "and I'm about to start grilling the bread for the bruschetta."

"I just need to take a quick shower and change, and then I'll be back right down to help," Joyce promised. "Kenneth will be here in about half an hour to get the grill started."

"Would you like me to start putting these chips in bowls?" Mrs. Ryan asked from the stove where she was stirring the chocolate while I sliced baguettes of French bread.

"Joyce can do that when she comes down," I suggested. "The chocolate should be stirred continuously. Or I can do it in a minute once I get this bread ready."

I arranged the bread in a skillet with melted butter and a little garlic powder and brought it over to the stove. "I can stir the chocolate while this browns," I said.

By the time Joyce came back down, her brilliant red hair still a bit damp, the crisps were in the bowls, the bread was browned and in a basket, and the food was set out on the serving trays in an attractive display, ready to be carried outside. It was the work of only a few minutes to dip the strawberries, apple, apricot and pear slices, and raspberries into the melted chocolate and arrange them on a tray. "I'll just pop them in the fridge to keep cool," I said. "I just have to get the dips and condiments ready."

Joyce looked on with amazement as I pulled out disposable muffin tins, lined each one with a paper liner, and began to fill them. Mustard, Dijon, mayonnaise, ketchup, and two kinds of relish in one tin; pickles, olives and chopped onion in another; the various dips in a third.

"What a clever idea!" Mrs. Ryan exclaimed.

I duplicated a second set for the other side of the table. "Easily refillable and even easier to clean," I pointed out.

It was then that Kenneth came in without knocking. "The grill's all set," he said. "Any time you want me to start grilling, just let me know." He looked at the food display. "That looks wonderful," he added with an easy smile. "Joyce told me what you were doing, Jillian. Thank you for helping us."

"I had a wonderful time," I told them. "Any time you want to give a party, I'll happily cater for you."

"Are you wearing your swim suit under your clothes?" Joyce asked.

I looked at here, startled. "I completely forgot it!" I admitted.

Joyce gave me a friendly little push between my shoulder blades. "Go home and get it," she ordered. "Everyone will be arriving soon; you've worked so hard, you don't want to miss the fun!"

I motioned to the table. "That was fun, for me," I told them. "I'll be back in just a few minutes."

Back at home, I grabbed my bright blue bikini and pulled it on. Joyce had been wearing a pair of denim shorts over her suit and a shirt open over the top, so I found my light blue shorts and a matching shirt. I put a beach towel, my jeans and a light sweater into my beach bag along with a hairbrush and a change of knickers. I didn't know how cold it would be on the beach and I wanted to be prepared.

When I got back to the Ryans' there were about a dozen of Kenneth's and Joyce's friends present. Two male figures dived side by side into the pool just as I reached the patio, to shouts of encouragement and the occasional catcall. The two figures turned in the water and headed back to the other side of the pool, one of them considerably ahead of the other. The faster swimmer popped up out of the water and I saw that it was Kenneth.

"Who's next?" he called, as the two of them pulled themselves out of the water.

"I am," responded a tall black chap, and the two of them dived in at the sound of a whistle blown by one of the girls. Kenneth won easily again and lined up for a third competition.

"Oh, Jillian, you're back!" Joyce exclaimed, coming over and leading me to the rest of her guests. "This is Jillian Munroe, everyone," she added. "This is Vickie, Alice, Rachel, Tyler, Will, Sam, Randi, Harry, Russ, Susannah and Sonia."

"There'll be a quiz later," quipped a male voice. I stole a quick look. The speaker looked enough like Kenneth to be his brother.

"But I'll help you study," commented someone else.

By concentrating, I managed to tie a few names to faces. The young man who, it turned out, was Kenneth's cousin, was Russ. A tall girl with the most beautiful long blonde hair I'd ever seen was Rachel. Alice and Tyler were black, so they were easy to remember. Randi bore a faint resemblance to Kenneth and Russ. The rest blended together.

"Jillian's responsible for the food," Joyce continued. "So you'll know who to thank."

"Then I need to sit next to Jillian," Russ announced. "Come, Jillian, and let me talk to the woman who created that lovely buffet I see before me." Before I could respond he led me by the hand to a chair by the side of the pool while the guys continued their swimming meet. I caught Joyce's eye and she smiled encouragingly.

"These guys are always trying to beat my cousin at swimming," Russ commented. "It's never going to happen. He swam competitively for four years of high school and two years of college, and he's good. He only quit the team his last two years because he thought his grades were slipping—from A plusses to A's."

"He's a nice guy," I said a bit vaguely. Russ and Kenneth had a strong family resemblance with the same build, wavy dark hair and slender stature, but their eyes were different—instead of Kenneth's dark eyes, Russ's were deep blue. I had the same strange feeling of familiarity with him that I had with Kenneth, but I still couldn't think who they reminded me of. "He and Joyce have been really nice to me since I arrived."

"How long have you been here?" Russ sat down beside me.

"Just over a week. I'll be staying here till Christmas with my brother's family, next door." I leaned back into the chair, enjoying the feel of the sun.

"How are you liking it?"

"I hardly know yet," I admitted. "There's been a lot to get used to, and I don't think I've even scratched the surface yet."

"My girlfriend and I will be happy to take you around and show you some of the sights," Russ offered. "I work full time but it's not a 9-5 job; I sometimes work evenings and have days free. And there's always weekends; I rarely work weekends. Not never, but it's unusual. We can take Kenneth and Joyce with us sometimes if they're free.

Colleen's a nurse and she works 3-11, but what days of the weeks she works can vary."

"That would be nice, thank you." I smiled at him. "I'd like that. I'm here to help my sister in law with the children while my brother is away, but I'll still have lots of free time. I'd like to meet your girlfriend sometime."

We exchanged getting-to-know-you information casually, until finally Kenneth called out, "Hey, Russ, it's your turn!"

"Not me, squirt," Russ called back. "I haven't been able to beat you in a swimming race since you were sixteen—no reason to think I will today."

"Yeah, but you give me a fair fight," Kenneth complained. "Not like the rest of these losers. I can beat them with one arm tied behind me—at least with you I have to use two."

"All right, all right," Russ gave in as Kenneth was bombarded by friendly insults. "I'm coming. Jillian, watch my space." He stood up and joined Kenneth at the pool. They dived in and, as expected, Kenneth won easily. I realized that this might be part of the reason for Kenneth's broader shoulders and well-muscled chest, despite his generally slender frame. Between swimming and working in a construction job, he'd naturally develop a lot of upper body strength. He climbed out of the water, donned a pair of glasses I didn't remember seeing him in before, and sat down next to Joyce, an arm around her shoulders.

Rachel came and sat down beside me, and I realized that she also looked somewhat familiar, even though she didn't resemble Kenneth or Russ in the slightest. "I just wanted to welcome you," she said. "I hope you like it here, and if I can help you with anything I hope you'll call me."

"Thank you so much," I answered, pleased. "So far I like it, at least I think I do."

"I love England," Rachel told me, smiling. "My grandfather lives there so I've visited a few times." She hesitated. "You look somewhat familiar. Have I met you before somewhere? Maybe in England?"

I shook my head. "I don't know. You look familiar too, but Kenneth says I look like a cousin of his who was killed a few years ago."

Rachel's face cleared. "That must be it," she said. "He's right, you do look like Janey at first glance."

"You knew her?"

Rachel nodded. "She was my cousin too," she explained. "I'm not related by blood to Kenneth and Russ, but my Uncle Dan married their Aunt Beth, and Janey was their child. So while we aren't cousins to each other, we have mutual cousins. Uncle Dan and Aunt Beth were killed too—it was a very hard time for both families."

"I'm so sorry."

"Thanks." Rachel smiled at me. "It was a long time ago, but it still hurts."

"Let's talk about something else," I suggested. "What about you? Are you a dancer like Joyce?"

"Not me. I'm training to be an physical therapist. Vickie and Alice are both dancers, though—they go to the Conservatory with Joyce. Do you dance?"

I shook my head. "I took lessons when I was little but I never really took to it. I like to cook, and sew, and decorate."

"And she cooks really well," Joyce said from behind us. "Come on, ladies, let's get some food before the boys eat it all."

I hadn't realized that Americans were not familiar with Scotch eggs. Kenneth had eaten them before—"My dad's job took us to England for a year when I was about thirteen or fourteen," he explained—but no one else had ever seen them before. Everything else was disappearing quickly but the Scotch eggs weren't finding much of a market. I was about to take them back to the kitchen when I heard a male voice call out, "Hey, are those real English Scotch eggs?" and I put the platter back down. I looked up into a pair of wide blue eyes over a smile I immediately recognized. It was the young man from the airport.

"Well, if it isn't my friend from the airport!" he exclaimed. "You were just arriving when I was on my way home, remember?"

I nodded. "I remember. How are you?"

"You've met before?" Joyce demanded.

The young man explained. "My name's Josh. I'm Ken's brother. Sorry I'm late, Joyce—traffic." He looked at me.

"Jillian Munroe. I'm visiting my brother and sister in law—they live next door."

"What a strange coincidence!" Joyce commented. "Josh, help yourself to anything you can find. Kenneth, put something on for Josh, he just got here." Kenneth, across the pool, nodded obediently and stood up.

"Come have a seat," Josh invited, loading up his plate with Scotch eggs, chicken wings, salads and vegetables. "Tell me about your visit. How are you liking America? You said this was your first visit, didn't you?"

I sat down on the edge of the pool beside him and we chatted lightly. I couldn't get over the coincidence of his turning out to be Kenneth's brother. He'd been in my dreams several times—he had had that much impact on me. And now he was right here, beside me.

"I know there's a lot to get used to," Josh was saying. "I remember when I first went to London, it was overwhelming. But I grew to love it. I almost didn't want to come home."

"You said you were there for school?" I remembered.

"Yes. I got my undergraduate degree at the London College of Music," Josh told me. There was a shadow in his eyes and I wondered what was wrong.

"Kenneth said something about living there."

"Yes, the whole family was there for a year, and I stayed when they went home," Josh explained. "My grandfather had moved over there a few years before and I stayed with him for the rest of my course. I graduated and came back home for grad school."

"Josh, your burger is ready!" Kenneth called.

Josh stood up. "Excuse me, Jillian, I'll be right back." He walked around the pool to the grill and I saw that he still was limping. I knew that no matter how firmly my laptop had landed on his foot the other day, he wouldn't still be limping—the laptop just wasn't that heavy. So it must have been something else. I was glad of that—I didn't want to be responsible.

"Did you have a good time?" Lori asked when I got home that night. She was relaxing in the family room, the TV softly playing music. I sat down across from her.

"I had a wonderful time," I enthused. "We swam and talked and played games and ate until it got dark, and then we all drove to the beach. The guys built a fire and we toasted marshmallows and some of the guys even roasted some of the hot dogs that hadn't gotten eaten before. Kenneth and his brother and cousin had all brought guitars, and they played and we all sang. I didn't know all their songs but I taught them one or two English folk songs they didn't know. The night was so clear we could see the fireworks over the water…I guess from Boston. It was lovely."

"I'm glad, honey." Lori stretched. "Have a glass of wine. I don't usually hear you talk so much—you must have really enjoyed yourself."

"I did. No thanks on the wine; I had a couple glasses of Sangria. I'll make myself some tea in a minute. They all really liked my raspberry lemonade."

"I've met some of Joyce's friends. Were you comfortable with them? I know you're shy in groups sometimes."

"I was to start with," I confessed, twisting the handle of my beach bag through my fingers. "But they were all so friendly. Except one girl. Randi. She's a cousin of Kenneth's, and she was a bit…unfriendly. She asked me if we had July 4th in England." I stopped.

"What did you say?" Lori prompted.

"I said that we did; it fell between the 3rd and the 5th. Everyone laughed at her, and Josh…Kenneth's brother…"

Lori nodded.

"He said to her, 'That's an American holiday, Randi. Why would the English celebrate our independence?' And she turned red and wouldn't answer. Someone else said, 'Maybe they celebrate getting rid of us hotheads', and the conversation went another way. But after that I could sort of feel her not liking me, if you know what I mean." I sighed. "But Josh told me afterwards that she's a bit like that to everyone, and that I shouldn't take it personally."

Lori nodded. "That would be Randi Bradford. Her mother is the church organist, and Randi is in the choir. She walks around with a perpetual chip on her shoulder, at least around me. I think she resents the fact that she wasn't asked to substitute when her mother was out or on vacation, though she isn't really an organist and she often wouldn't be available if her mother isn't, anyway. Rosemary Bradford is a lovely woman—I don't know where Randi gets it."

"Everyone else was so friendly," I confirmed. "Josh and Joyce and Kenneth are going to take me to Plymouth this weekend, and a girl named Rachel wants to take me to Boston next week and show me some of the historic sites there. Josh and Kenneth's cousin Russ offered too, but he already has a girlfriend and he sort of withdrew when he saw that I was taken care of."

"You'll enjoy that," Lori said. "I was going to offer to take you with the kids, but you'll enjoy it more with your friends."

"Maybe we can do some things again with the kids," I suggested, standing up. "I'm going to get myself some tea. Can I get you anything?"

"No thanks. The concert is just about over and I'm going to bed." Lori stood up too and turned off the telly. "I'll see you in the morning, dear. Have a nice night."

I made my tea and took it into my bedroom, sipping it and thinking back over how much fun I'd had. Rachel might turn out to be a good friend. I still liked Joyce best and was glad she lived next door. But Josh... The thought of him sent little shivers all through me, and I had very pleasant dreams all night.

Adam came home for the weekend and the kids went wild over seeing him. When we'd finally gotten them to bed, we sat down with glasses of wine and dessert.

"How's everything going?" he asked me after we'd finished the topic of his new job and studio apartment.

"A little strange," I answered. "I don't think I was prepared for quite so many things to be different."

Adam nodded. "I never really had to go through that," he acknowledged. "Dad was stationed in Washington, DC for a little while when we boys were little—well, Nick and I were little; Phil would have been in high school by the time we went back to England.

But I remembered enough so that it was relatively familiar when I came over here for university."

"Are you finding it difficult, dear?" Lori asked with a motherly attitude that I found at once soothing and irritating.

"In some ways, but I'll adjust. The whole idea was to see another part of the world. And Dad liked the idea of my spending some time here—he said I was the most British of his children and he was glad that I would be seeing the other part of my heritage."

"In that regard, I think you should come to Washington DC some weekend when Lori brings the kids down," Adam said. "Or maybe you should come down with me one week. There's a lot to see; certainly a lot to interest a history major."

"I'd like that," I said, and we starting making plans.

On Sunday we went to church. I was fascinated to learn that the church was one of the oldest in the US.

"The current building dates from the early 19th century," Adam told me as we entered, "but the church was first founded in 1634." Evidently that qualified as very old in America.

It was a picture-postcard church both outside and inside. We took our seats in a white-painted, red-cushioned pew, and I was pleased to see Joyce sitting with her mother and a big, craggy man I assumed to be her father, across the aisle. To my surprise, when the pastor entered from a side door at the front, he was followed not only by a middle aged woman who took her seat at the organ, but also by Kenneth, who had his guitar in his hand.

"Oh, good, Kenneth's going to sing," Lori said quietly. "He's very good."

He was. He had a deep baritone voice and for the first piece he sang, after the first reading, he accompanied himself on the guitar. He sang again as the offering was taken, and for this the woman at the organ moved to a piano.

"The whole family is musical," Lori said quietly. "I believe there's a cousin or brother, I'm not sure which, who's a composer."

"That would be Josh," I told her. "That's him, in the pew up front."

I was impressed. Josh and Kenneth had both played guitar on the beach but I hadn't heard Kenneth's singing voice clearly. I loved music. I hoped he would sing again.

"Oh, he will," Lori promised when I said so after the service. "He sings usually two or three times every summer. The choir takes a break during the summer and various choir members sing solos or small groups. Kenneth hasn't been able to sing with the choir very much for the last few years while he's been in school, but he still comes back in the summer. Maybe you should join the choir in the fall—we can always use another alto."

"Is Josh a member?" I asked as casually as I could.

Lori's eyes twinkled at me. "Why, yes, he is."

"I'll think about it," I said with dignity. Lori smiled knowingly.

Lori and Adam went to retrieve the children from the nursery and I went over to join Kenneth, Joyce and the senior Ryans.

"You sounded wonderful," I told Kenneth after we'd all exchanged greetings. "You have a lovely voice."

Kenneth blushed. "Thank you," he said, almost shyly. "I'm not as good as my brother."

"Josh?" I asked.

"That's right. He's around here somewhere."

"I'm right here," came Josh's voice, and his hand landed on my shoulder. "You're plenty good, bro. My voice isn't any better than yours is, and if I'm better on guitar it's only because you don't practice enough. If you played more often you could play rings around me."

"I'm not any good on piano, though," Kenneth disclaimed.

Josh cuffed him lightly. "Quit fishing for compliments," he told his brother affectionately. "Next time you sing, I'll do a duet with you if you want. Maybe get Randi and do a trio. You sing, don't you, Jillian?"

"Just glee club singing," I said. "But I love it. My sister in law just invited me to join the choir in the fall, and I think I'm going to do it."

"Oh, good!" Joyce exclaimed. "I'm a second soprano—what do you sing?"

"Alto," I told her.

Josh looked enthusiastic. "That would be great, if you joined," he told me. "Kenneth, what do you think—a quartet?"

"I'm willing to do duets, quartets, trios, whatever anyone else wants," Kenneth promised.

"Jillian, will you join us for dinner this noon?" Mrs. Ryan asked. "Lori, Adam and the children too, of course. And Josh, you must come as well. I want to hear about your travels."

"Why, I'd love to," I said, as Josh offered his acceptance as well. "Let me check with Lori."

Lori agreed, delighted. "Just let me get the children into play clothes," she told Mrs. Ryan. "What time would you like us?"

"About noon. Take your time."

"Can we bring anything?" I asked, to Lori's approving look.

"If you'd like to bring something for dessert, that would be lovely."

Back at home, Lori and Adam got the children changed while I reviewed the pantry shelves. I had over an hour so I decided on a trifle. I quickly changed my own clothes and put an apron while I mixed a sponge cake and set it in a low oven. While it baked I sliced strawberries, mixed them with raspberries and blueberries, and threw together a custard. Finally I whipped cream. By then the cake was ready so I took it out and let it cool slightly before I poured sherry over it. I layered the cake, custard and mixed berries, topped the whole thing with the whipped cream and sprinkled more berries and slivered almonds over the top.

"Jillian, that looks beautiful," Lori said, coming into the kitchen with Beth on her hip. "Come on, Kaitlyn. Jeremy, take Daddy's hand. Let's go see Joyce."

Mrs. Ryan had cooked a leg of lamb with rosemary and garlic, and she and I and Lori had a wonderful time comparing recipes. Josh proved to be interested in cooking as well and had several comments to offer. After dinner Joyce and Kenneth, who had stayed as well, invited me to join them for a drive. I had no wish to intrude on their private time so I declined, after agreeing to join them, and Josh, for a visit to Plymouth the following day. Josh, too, decided to stay behind.

"Come take a walk with me," Josh invited me.

We walked down to the beach and stood watching the water. We didn't talk much—we didn't need to. We were comfortable together in silence. Finally Josh sighed.

"I'm glad you came to Scituate," he said softly. "I hope you like it here."

"I do," I told him. "It's strange. There's a lot to get used to. But I'm glad I came."

"I'll help in any way I can," Josh promised. "I want to spend a lot of time with you this summer."

"I'd like that." We sat down on the sand and talked for almost an hour, before we realized that we needed to get back.

"Jillian, that was a wonderful trifle," Lori said as we walked back home across the yards. "Have you ever thought about going to culinary school? I think you'd be much happier doing that, than you would with any of the professions Mother and Dad are trying to coax you into."

I looked at her in amazement. "That's exactly what I want to do," I exclaimed. "I haven't mentioned it because I knew what Mum and Dad would say, but I'd love to do that, and then start a little business doing event planning."

"That sounds much more like you than teaching or law," Adam agreed, unlocking the door and leading us into the house. "Let Lori and me just settle Beth and Jeremy for their naps and we'll talk about it."

When she came back downstairs, Kaitlyn happily settled with her dolls in the corner, I'd set up a tea tray and poured three cups. "Do you think I could ever talk Mum and Dad into it?" I asked.

"I think you might," Lori said, taking her tea and leaning back in her chair. "They only want you to be happy, honey."

"I'd love to cook for a living," I said. "Not in a restaurant, even as a chef, but running catering events. Planning parties. Preparing special foods for special events. I'm good at that, Lori, I know I am. I imagine I'd have to take a couple of business courses to learn how to best manage a business, but I know I could do a good job with this, and I'd enjoy it so much."

"I'll back you up," Adam promised. "In the fall, I'll stand you to a cooking class if you'd like. I'm sure there are several we could find. If you enjoy them, and if you're still of the same mind afterwards, I'll help you talk to Mother and Dad at Christmas."

"Remember our conversation about singing quartets?" Josh said when Lori passed me the phone a week or so later. "Kenneth signed us up to sing two weeks from now. We'd love to do a quartet if you're interested."

"I'd like to try," I said thoughtfully. "I haven't sung in a choir since secondary school but I used to love it."

"How's your sight reading?" Josh asked cheerfully. "Do you want to see the music ahead of time?"

"I'd better," I admitted. "My sight reading is only so-so." I relaxed into a chair, enjoying the sound of his voice. I'd been dreaming about him almost every night since I arrived in America, even before I'd officially met him, and talking with him made me feel warm and tingly.

"I'll send it over with Kenneth next time he goes to see Joyce," Josh promised. "It's not difficult but it's familiar to the rest of us."

"Who's our soprano?" I asked. "Joyce?"

"No, Joyce doesn't like singing solos or small groups," Josh said. "It'll be my cousin Randi."

I hesitated, but didn't say anything. "All right. When do we rehearse?"

He provided me with the rehearsal times, with the first one being two nights away. "Then tomorrow night, how would you like to go out to dinner and a movie?"

"I'd love to!"

"Great! Would you mind meeting me down on Front Street? I don't have a car at the moment—I'll explain later. About six or so?"

"I'm sure Lori won't mind giving me a lift," I agreed. "But how will we get back?"

"I'll work that out," he promised. We settled on a meeting place and time. "I'll see you tomorrow."

"I'm looking forward to it." I hung up the phone and went out to the kitchen. "Lori, can you drop me off tomorrow at 6:00 on Front Street?"

"It might be a bit awkward, but I think we can manage it if it's important," Lori agreed with a smile. "Do you have a date with Josh?"

I nodded. "He said he didn't have a car at the moment and he'd explain."

"We'll find a way. Maybe Joyce can stay with the kids for just a few minutes."

But when Kenneth dropped off the music later that evening, he had another solution. "Joyce and I have a date just about that same time tomorrow," he offered. "We'll pick you up, drop you off and go ahead with our plans. Then at the end of the evening, we'll come get you and I'll bring you both home. Josh lives within walking distance of where you're going; you can wait there with him if we're not ready when you are. We won't be out late—we both have to work the next day."

"If you're sure I won't be in the way," I said hesitantly.

Kenneth waved a hand in dismissal. "We're going that direction anyway, both ways, and I'll drop you off first so Joyce and I will still have privacy for me to kiss her goodnight, if that's what you're concerned with." His dark eyes twinkled at me.

I couldn't help smiling at him. "In that case, I'll accept your offer."

I was becoming very fond of Kenneth, in a sisterly sort of way. He was so obviously head over heels in love with Joyce, and he was not at all shy about letting anyone in the vicinity know it. Most chaps I knew would rather lose a finger than use the L word but Kenneth was very frank about his adoration for my red-haired friend. Yet he was always ready to include me, or go out of his way to help smooth the way.

Lori rehearsed me in the alto part of the two pieces, which as Josh had said were not difficult. I was feeling fairly confident by the time Kenneth and Joyce knocked at the door and escorted me out to Kenneth's little red Honda. It was only a few minutes to Front Street and Josh was standing in the lobby of the theater where he'd promised to be.

"Have a great time," Kenneth said, coming around to open the door for me. "Don't forget, you're going back to Josh's condo after your movie; Joyce and I will come back and have a drink with both of you before we come to take you home."

Josh thanked his younger brother and took my hand. "Shall we go to the early showing of the movie and then take our time over dinner, or would you rather eat first and go to a later showing?"

We decided to go to the early showing and relax over dinner. The movie was a comedy that had us both laughing, something Josh solemnly declared later was very important. "We laugh at the same jokes—that's a big step towards compatibility," he told me. But what I found more important, and somewhat distracting, was the way he took my hand during the movie and played with my fingers.

Dinner was lovely; a north Italian menu with superb wines. I couldn't face dessert, although I did have a glass of amaretto while Josh devoured a piece of chocolate raspberry cake. "Feel free to try it," he encouraged me.

I took a single bite. "It's wonderful," I said. "But I couldn't even finish my chicken. I'll be having it for lunch, for two days."

After dinner we took a short walk along the water before Josh led me back to his condo in the same complex as the theatre. "Can I pour you a glass of wine?"

I shook my head. "I think I've had enough alcohol for this evening," I decided. "But I wouldn't mind a cup of tea, if such a thing can be found in a bachelor establishment."

Josh's eyes twinkled. "Oh ye of little faith," he said, and walked me over to the small kitchen. He opened a cupboard and showed me several varieties of tea. Delighted, I chose one and Josh set a teakettle on the stove.

"Now, aren't you sorry you made such a discriminating statement?" Josh teased me, settling down beside me with a cup for each of us and the tea made the proper way in a pot, not bags dipped in cups of hot water.

"I'd forgotten that you lived in England for three years," I admitted, sipping the tea. It tasted good.

"Want the grand tour?" Josh asked, seeing me looking around the room. It was a pleasant sitting room papered in a soft beige, with a well-equipped, if tiny, kitchen to the right and a single bedroom beyond with a bathroom attached. The sitting room had a small couch covered in dark brown corduroy and two apricot throw pillows. Two overstuffed chairs were covered in a brown and apricot print; carpet and curtains were dark gold. A large desk on one wall was in walnut, as were the coffee table and end tables. There was a large mahogany hutch on the wall by the kitchen. A non-working fireplace was on the wall across from the door, with a spinet piano in front of it. The bedroom had a huge bed of golden oak, with two large chests of drawers and a nightstand on either side, to match. The curtains and bedspread were of the same gold as the curtains in the sitting room. Opening a door that I thought would be a closet, after a nod of permission from Josh, I found a small washer and dryer.

"I like the colors," I said as we came back into the sitting room. "Did you do it all?"

"Sort of," he answered, motioning me back into my seat. "A lot of the furniture is family stuff. My Aunt Elaine helped me pick out the rest. I'm a guy—I don't get decoration." He picked up his tea.

"And you live here alone?"

He nodded. "Why, were you wondering if I had another woman hidden away?" he teased.

"Well, some chaps have roommates, or so I'm told," I retorted, pouring myself another cup of tea.

He grinned at me. "You can check under the bed if you like," he said. "Seriously, angel, one bedroom place."

I flushed. "Of course, I'm sorry." I tingled as much as hearing him use an endearment as embarrassment at my mistake.

"No need to be." He smiled at me. "Seriously, I'm something of a loner and I'm not always easy to live with. I'm on the list for a two-bedroom place when there's one available, and at that point I'll invite Kenneth to join me here so he and Joyce can have a little more privacy."

"That's nice of you."

"I'd have gotten the two-bedroom place initially but Kenneth had just started college, Joyce was still in high school and Kenneth thought it would make things too hard until she got a little older," Josh explained. "Too much temptation. But she's an adult now, and Kenneth and I get along well. Not everyone would be able to live with me but he can."

"I don't believe you're that hard to deal with," I protested.

"Believe it, angel. Not all the time, but I'm…moody. Especially when I'm deep in the music."

"Are you trying to scare me off?" I asked semi-seriously.

He shook his head and reached out to take my hand. "I don't want to scare you off," he swore. "But I do want you to know what you're getting into if you start a relationship with me."

"I'll take my chances," I promised. I paused. "You were going to tell me why you don't have a car."

Josh was quiet for a minute. "Kenneth said he told you about Janey…" His voice cracked a bit.

I was instantly sorry I'd raised the subject. "You don't have to…" I started.

His smile was sad and gentle. "It's all right. What Kenneth may not have told you is that I was in the car too, and was the only survivor other than the driver of the truck that hit us. I developed something of a phobia and haven't been able to make myself drive. I can ride in the car as a passenger, but I can't force myself to drive."

I squeezed his hand. "I'm so sorry, Josh."

He squeezed my hand back and didn't answer. Finally he asked, "Scare you away yet?"

"Not a chance."

We sat in silence for a few minutes until there was a knock at the door. "That'll be Ken and Joyce," Josh said. "I gave him a key but he's being polite." He called loudly, "It's okay, you can come in!"

The door opened and the two of them came in, flushed and laughing. They had gone to an amateur comedy club at the high school, a fundraiser to send a group of students on a trip to build houses with Habitat for Humanity. A friend of Joyce's had been appearing in a stand-up act and they both appeared to have enjoyed themselves hugely.

"You met Susannah at my cookout," Joyce reminded me, dropping into a chair across from me. Kenneth sat on the floor at her feet and she massaged his shoulders.

"I remember," I said. "Medium height, light brown curly hair, green shirt."

"That's Susannah. Her younger brother is one of the kids we're trying to send to New Jersey."

"Doesn't Habitat for Humanity have local projects?" I asked. "I thought that's what I remember from their European presence."

Joyce nodded. "They do, but the kids chose to volunteer with a group that's doing repair and rebuilding after Super Storm Sandy a couple years ago."

I remembered. "I didn't realize you were still doing cleanup."

"That's going to take a long time to complete," Josh said. "I didn't realize that was tonight, Joyce. I thought it was next week."

"It was originally going to be next week," Kenneth said, "but there was a problem with availability of the gym. I'm sorry, I thought you knew." He stood up, kissed the palm of Joyce's hand, and sat down on the arm of her chair.

"If you have another fundraiser, Jillian and I will go," Josh promised. "Can I get either of you a drink?"

"Is that tea I see on the table there?" Joyce asked. "I'd like tea, if there's enough."

"There's plenty." Josh went to the kitchen and got another cup. "What about you, Ken?"

"Would you mind if I just made myself a cup of coffee?" Kenneth asked.

"I'll make it." Josh busied himself with the coffee maker for a few minutes and came out with a full cup of coffee, which he handed to Kenneth, and an empty cup into which he poured tea for Joyce. "Do you want sugar or milk?" he asked her.

"Nothing, thanks."

He handed it to her. We chatted our way through two cups each before Kenneth stood up and stretched. "Well, ladies and gentleman, I'm having a good time but I also have to be at work at seven am tomorrow. It's about time I took my girl…my girls home and got myself some sleep."

"Hey, one of your girls is my girl," Josh protested.

"I'll let you keep the little brunette," Kenneth conceded. "I'm keeping the redhead for myself." He held out his hand to Joyce and pulled her to her feet. I stood up as well and to my surprise Josh did as well. Kenneth seemed to expect this, however, and the four of us went down to his car.

Kenneth drove me home first and Josh got out with me. "I have to take my girl home," he declared. "But we'll give Kenneth a chance to kiss Joyce goodnight in privacy."

In fact, we had enough time for another cup of tea apiece before Kenneth appeared at the kitchen door. Silently Josh handed him a handkerchief and he wiped Joyce's lip gloss from the corner of his mouth without any indication of embarrassment.

"Good night, angel," Josh said softly. "We'll pick you up tomorrow night for the rehearsal."

The rehearsal was held at the church so we could get used to the sound. Josh played the piano for us as well as singing tenor. "When we rehearse again next week, my Aunt Rosemary will play for us," he promised. "For now, you'll just have to put up with me." His eyes twinkled at me.

We were rehearsing two pieces. In the first one, Randi and I, soprano and alto, opened in unison. After a few measures the men, also in unison, joined us; a few measures still later we broke into four parts. Almost immediately Randi stopped us.

"Not quite, Jillian. Like this." She sang the alto part for me a capella. I didn't hear anything different than I had been singing, but I was not a musician so I listened carefully, thanked her and we started up again.

She stopped me again at the same place. With continued kind condescension, Randi corrected me again. The third time, though, Kenneth spoke up.

"That sounded perfectly fine to me," he said. 'What are you hearing that you think she's doing wrong, Randi?"

"Her A flat isn't quite…steady, I guess you'd call it," Randi responded, smiling sweetly at me.

"Her A flat is perfectly fine," Josh said irritably. "Randi, we've been here fifteen minutes and we haven't gotten through the first verse yet. We've got two songs to go through. It's not doing any of us any good to have you interrupting us every three seconds." He looked at me. "Ready to go on?"

Lori, who taught music for a living, had gone through both pieces with me in very careful detail. I had a good ear and was pretty sure I was right. Then again, I understood what the men didn't; that this was Randi's way of making sure I knew who was the dominant female here. "Absolutely ready."

"Then let's start from the beginning and keep going." Josh played an introduction and Randi and I came in on cue.

Randi didn't quite dare interrupt us again at the same point but once we were firmly in the chorus, she stopped us again. "Jillian, dear, do you think you could put a little more swing in it?"

"Randi," Josh said politely but with an edge to his voice, "since I'm the professional musician in this group, why don't I run the rehearsal? Otherwise we'll never get done."

"Hear, hear," Kenneth muttered.

"I was only..." Randi began.

Josh held up a hand. "Ken, is Joyce home tonight?"

"She is."

"Call her and tell her to get over here—we need another soprano. Randi clearly isn't interested in singing with us."

"I never said that," Randi said hastily.

"Then I don't want to hear another word out of you unless it's written in the music. Is that clear?" Josh's jaw was set firmly and his eyes were cold. Randi nodded, very obviously not saying a word. Clearly she would listen to Josh. I wondered what he had on her.

We got through the rest of the rehearsal without incident. When we were driving home, Josh said to me, "I hope Randi didn't upset you."

"She confused me," I admitted. "I was pretty sure I was right."

"You were right," Kenneth agreed, taking a turn with a little more force than necessary. "I don't know what got into her tonight. But then she's always had it out for anyone—any girl, that is—that she thought Josh was interested in."

Josh flushed. "Don't be silly, Ken."

"I'm not. Ask Joyce. Ask Russ. Ask Rachel. We've all noticed it." Kenneth turned into Adam and Lori's driveway. "It's been pretty obvious."

"Then it's a good thing I don't date much," Josh said, clearly trying to close the subject. "I'll be right back, Kenneth."

"I'll be right here. Don't mind me." Kenneth leaned back in the seat and turned the key sufficiently to provide power to the radio.

Josh walked me to the door. "When we rehearse again next week, my Aunt Rosemary will be there. She's the regular organist and Randi's mom—she'll keep her in line."

"I thought you kept her in line pretty well," I reassured him. "Don't worry. As long as you and Kenneth are satisfied with my performance, Randi won't bother me."

"That's good." Josh hesitated a bit, then he bent down and kissed me very, very lightly. Even though his lips barely touched mine in a butterfly kiss, the shock waves that ran through me almost knocked me off my feet. "Have dinner with me tomorrow?"

I nodded. "I'd love to."

"I'll call you in the morning." He squeezed my hand. "Good night, angel."

I hardly slept that night and when I did, my sleep was filled with dreams that almost embarrassed me, they were so vivid.

The second rehearsal did go much more smoothly, as Josh had promised. Mrs. Bradford simply paid no attention to any of Randi's theatrics. "Nonsense, Jillian sounds perfect," she said the first time. "Her voice blends beautifully with yours. Jillian, don't change a thing, dear. Kenneth, you cut that last phrase off just a bit soon, do you think you could hold it about a beat longer, dear? Thank you. Josh, you're wonderful as always. You're all wonderful. You're going to sound marvelous on Sunday. Let's pick up from letter B, shall we?"

After that, Randi at least managed to hold it down to a dull roar. If looks could kill, I'd be—well, maybe not dead but at least unconscious on the floor, but she didn't say anything more after that.

Things went smoothly on Sunday during the service and both pieces were well received. I noticed something in the program that I hadn't known before—Josh and Kenneth had different last names. Kenneth's name was listed as Aldrich, which is the name I knew him by, but Josh was listed as Whittaker. I assumed that Kenneth was the product of a second marriage. No reason why either of them should have mentioned it but I was still somewhat surprised. I filed the information away for future consideration and concentrated on the service.

I still was thinking seriously about a career in event management. The fact that Lori and Adam supported the idea gave me more courage to consider raising the subject with my parents. One afternoon, at lunch with Joyce and Rachel, I raised the question with them. "What would you think if I were to go to culinary school and then open my own catering business?"

"I'd wonder why you think you need culinary school," Joyce answered promptly. "I'd hire you to put on any event I was planning right now."

"So would I," Rachel chimed in. She closed her menu with a sigh. "I guess I'll have the clam roll."

"Fish chowder and a Greek salad," Joyce said.

"I think the chicken salad wrap special," I said. "So you think it would be a good idea? I'm trying to think of a way to convince my parents."

"I can't imagine why they'd object," Joyce declared. "You did such a wonderful job with my picnic. And that trifle you brought for dessert that Sunday was magnificent."

"I don't know why you need your parents' agreement to begin with," Rachel added. "You're over twenty-one and have graduated from college."

I stopped myself from saying, 'University'.

"I understand," Joyce commented. "Even though you don't need their permission to do what you want, you still want them to approve of what you're doing."

"Lori and Adam think it's a good idea," I acknowledged. "They're going to help me talk to Mum and Dad."

"Then you don't need to worry about it," Joyce concluded. "They may fight you for a bit, but they'll come to realize what a good idea it is. I wouldn't worry."

"Me either," Rachel agreed.

I picked up my iced tea and took a cautious sip. Joyce giggled.

"It's okay, Jillian, they don't serve sweetened tea here."

"Good," I said emphatically.

Rachel looked at me, curious. "What are you talking about?"

"You should have seen her face the first time Jillian tasted sweetened tea," Joyce teased. "You'd have thought the world was coming to an end."

I grinned sheepishly. "It was enough to put one into a diabetic coma. What kind of heathen puts sweetener into an innocent glass of tea?"

"And tea is sacred to you Brits, isn't it?" Joyce prompted.

"Too bloody right." Both my friends burst into laughter, and a moment later I joined them.

"What are your plans for Labor Day?" Rachel asked when we sobered.

"What's Labor Day?" I asked.

The girls looked a bit vague. "If I remember correctly, it relates most closely to your May Bank Holiday," Rachel said. "It's the first Monday in September. School in the US generally starts that week. Your sister in law will probably have plans for that weekend."

I considered. Adam flew home every weekend to spend time with the family. They'd dropped the idea of having Lori alternate weekends down—after the first try they'd realized the difficulties of traveling with three children. Still, they'd encouraged me to consider their house my own when it came to inviting my friends over. "She hasn't mentioned anything in particular. I think it's the week before Labor Day that Adam wants me to go to DC with him for a week."

Both girls had been to DC and they told me what I needed to see the most, until the waitress put our food down in front of us. I looked at my sandwich. "What's this?" I asked.

"Chicken salad," Joyce said, surprised. "What you asked for."

"This is what you call chicken salad in America?" I looked down at it curiously.

Rachel nodded and bit into her sandwich. "What would you call chicken salad?"

"Sliced chicken with lettuce and tomato," I responded, peering more closely at the mix of chicken, celery, green onion and mayonnaise. Cautiously I took a bite. "It's good, though," I added with relief.

The American experience was in some ways proving more than I bargained for.

Plans for the week in DC proceeded. Adam reserved a hotel room for me not far from his studio apartment. "There simply isn't room for you," he admitted. "It's barely big enough for me. But this is comfortable and inexpensive and it's an easy walk to the Metro. Why don't you ask Joyce to come with you? I'll be able to spend some time with you, but I'll be teaching during the day."

I invited Joyce on the trip that evening, when we were at dinner with Josh and Kenneth. The two men had gone up to the bar to renew our drinks and it seemed an appropriate time.

"I'd love to," Joyce said promptly. "We can share a hotel room and we'll have a wonderful time. I love DC."

"It will be smashing." I was a bit relieved. While I was not unaccustomed big cities in general, I knew my way around London. I had been frightened of the idea of making my way around the capitol city of a nation as large as the US, all by myself. It would be a help to have someone there who at least understood the monetary system. Yes, I understood that the dollar was the basis and that the smaller coins were in decimal fractions thereof, but without understanding the exchange from a dollar to a pound, I was left not knowing if I was being cheated or if I had a good deal. We shall not even discuss the issue of tax at the register. Barbarism.

"When do we leave?"

Josh and Kenneth arrived just then with our drinks. "Daiquiri for the little lady," Josh said with a smile, setting it down and sliding into the seat beside me.

"And a virgin margarita for the birthday girl," Kenneth finished, taking his seat beside Joyce.

"I didn't know it was your birthday!" I exclaimed.

"It's actually tomorrow," Joyce said.

"Happy birthday," Josh said. "What are your plans?"

"Quiet dinner at home, then Kenneth has something up his sleeve that he won't tell me about," Joyce said with a teasing smile.

"And I'm not going to, either, so stop fishing," Kenneth retorted. He lifted his glass and proposed a toast. "To Joyce."

We drank to Joyce, who blushed and smiled. "One more year and I'm finally legal," she said.

"And we'll have the biggest party ever seen," Kenneth promised. "Jillian can cater it."

It suddenly struck me that when Joyce's twenty first birthday came around, I'd be back in England. "I'll have to come back for it," I promised.

Josh put his hand over mine, and I realized we were both thinking the same thing.

Joyce, mercifully, re-directed my thoughts. "When do we leave, Jillian?" She explained to the men, "Jillian's invited me to go to DC with her later in the month."

"The week before Labor Day," I explained. "We'll leave with Adam Sunday night, and come back with him the following Friday afternoon just before the holiday weekend."

"You'll enjoy DC," Josh said. "It's a great city. I've played there."

"Josh does fill-in keyboard for a lot of bands and orchestras," Kenneth explained as I looked puzzled. Then I remembered that Josh had been coming back from a tour when I first met him.

"I thought you were primarily a composer," I said, looking at him.

"Primarily I am," Josh agreed. "But I minored in keyboard performance and I get a call every so often when someone's rehearsal accompanist gets sick or when schedules conflict."

"Any chance you'll get called to DC while we're there?" Joyce suggested.

He smiled. "Probably not. Mostly I get called locally. But while I was traveling with Neil Donavan this past spring, we did three concerts in DC."

"What are the must-sees there?" I asked. "We'll have the better part of five days."

"You can see a lot in that time," Kenneth told me. "You should see the White House, the Capitol, and the monuments. After that, it's whatever interests you."

"I'll bet Jillian would like to visit the Library of Congress," Josh suggested. "And the American History museum."

"You were a history major, weren't you?" Joyce asked.

"English and history," I said, putting down my menu as the waitress approached us. "But I read mostly English history. I did my thesis on the Plantagenets. I've got a lot to learn about American history."

"I know something else you need to learn about," Josh said with a gleam in his eye. "Baseball."

Kenneth groaned out loud. "Run now while you still can," he advised me.

We ordered, then I looked at Josh. "I've been here for about five weeks," I tallied. "During that time I have been made vaguely aware that there is such a game as baseball, and that most of the city seems to be going crackers over it. So I imagine that there is some necessity for my learning the basics. But Kenneth seems to think that I'm in danger learning it from you. So . . ." I turned teasingly to Kenneth. "What should I know that I don't?"

"Josh is a baseball addict," his brother told me. "Run, before you get sucked in."

"Like you're not just as serious a Red Sox fan as I am," Josh retorted. "Jillian, do you have any plans for tomorrow?"

I thought. "Not unless Lori has something in mind that I don't know about. It's a Friday, so Adam will be home."

"Would Lori mind your taking the entire day off?"

"No, of course not. She's told me often just to let her know when I have something planned. She's adamant that I'm not to feel that I'm tied to the house and the children—that I'm here to learn about the other side of my heritage as well."

"Then you and I are going to a minor league baseball game," Josh concluded. "Kenneth, would you mind dropping us at the commuter rail station on your way to work in the morning?"

"If he can't, I can," Joyce promised.

"Bring stuff for overnight just in case," Josh warned me. "The trains to Portland, Maine, where we're going, don't run very often. We'll try to get back tomorrow night but it's a good thing to be prepared."

"Don't get me wrong, I love the Sea Dogs," Kenneth broke in. "But if you want to teach her about baseball, why don't you take her to Fenway?"

"A couple of reasons," Josh explained, sitting back so the waitress could put down his soup. "First, Fenway is awfully loud. She's going to need a lot of explanations, and she can hear me better at Hadlock than at Fenway. Secondly, I think she'll like the relaxed, family friendly atmosphere at Hadlock. And finally, she should have some idea of the game before she goes to a major league game. I'll take her to Fenway later in the summer—you and Joyce, too. But Hadlock will be better for a first attempt."

"Good points, all of them," Kenneth admitted. "I don't suppose I could talk you into waiting till Saturday so Joyce and I could come with you. I can drive us up, instead of being reliant on the train. I have to work till noon, but the game isn't till six, we'll have plenty of time."

"Sure, that would be fine, if Joyce doesn't have to work," Josh said, applying himself to his soup. "What does your schedule look like, Joyce?"

"I have to work until two," Joyce said. "Would that give us enough time, if you picked me up right from work?"

"It's only a three-hour drive; we should have plenty of time," Josh said. He looked at me. "Is that all right with you?"

"It's fine," I replied. "I'm completely at your mercy. Should I still bring overnight things?"

Josh and Kenneth looked at each other. "Game starts at 6:00, over by 9:00 or 9:30, three-hour drive home..." Kenneth counted up. "Probably wouldn't hurt to have your toothbrush handy, just to be safe. If we're all still wound up and adrenalized from the game, we can drive back home and be in shortly after midnight. If we're all exhausted, there's a small hotel within walking distance of the ball park."

"Sounds good to me," Joyce said. "Jillian, you'll have a wonderful time, even if you don't know baseball very well."

"I don't know baseball at all," I confirmed. "But if this is something important to my understanding of America, I'll pay attention."

Saturday evening found us all sitting in a small baseball field that Josh told me was modeled after the famous Fenway Park in Boston. "Fenway is both the oldest and the smallest major league field in the US," he told me. "This is a minor league park so it's even smaller, but it's designed to look like Fenway."

"You're going to have to start me at the beginning," I complained. "Define, major league and minor league."

"I'll do it," Kenneth told Josh. "I know you like to watch batting practice. I don't care enough about it." He began to explain the major league farm team system and the various levels of minor league play. Joyce chimed in on occasion.

By concentrating, and asking a lot of questions, I managed to follow the major part of the game. Baseball was certainly a complicated sport. Josh explained every detail patiently, multiple times if necessary, until I finally had something of an idea how the game was played. To be honest, I found the fan contests between the innings to be more enjoyable.

"American marketing," Josh explained dryly. "The sponsors get mention, and the team gets money, and everyone is happy."

"They're adorable," I said, watching two small girls attempting to sing an advertising jingle.

"You won't see this sort of thing in major league ball," Kenneth told me, smiling at the two little girls. "In fact, I think this is about the highest level of professional ball that has them. But it's cute and it's family fun."

At one point, the batter hit the ball out of the park; there was a loud horn blast and a fountain of lights sprayed forward from behind the center field wall. A lighthouse moved up from behind the wall, slowly, to the wild applause of the fans.

"Home run!" Josh shouted, as the lighthouse slowly moved back down again.

"I take it that's a good thing?" I inquired, taking his hand.

He smiled. "Definitely. Did you like the lighthouse?"

"I'm not quite sure I followed the significance of it—does it lighthouse every time someone hits a home run?"

"I like that; lighthouse as a verb," Josh decided. "Yes, every time a Sea Dogs player hits a home run, it lighthouses."

I giggled.

"Are you having fun?" he asked.

I was, I decided, and told him. "I can't say I fully understand what's going on, but I'm enjoying myself."

"I'm glad." He squeezed my hand.

The game was over, successfully in my friends' viewpoint, around a quarter past nine. "Do we want to drive home tonight?" Josh asked Kenneth, the driver, as the game entered the top of the ninth inning.

"I'm willing," Kenneth said, but there was a touch of weariness in his face at the thought, and I remembered that he and Joyce had been out late the night before celebrating her 20th birthday at a folk rock concert, and both had worked at physically demanding jobs during the morning. I looked at their clasped hands and realized that, with both of them living at home with their parents to save money for their future, a whole night alone together was a rare thing that they had probably been looking forward to.

"Why don't we find out if there are rooms available?" I suggested. Kenneth looked at me with relief in his face.

"That's a good idea," he agreed. "It's been a long day."

Josh's eyes followed mine and comprehension dawned. "Sure, we can stay," he agreed. "Sorry, kid, I didn't mean to be insensitive."

Kenneth pulled out his mobile phone. "I'll call." He dialed a pre-programmed number. "Hi, do you have any vacancies for tonight?" He listened. "Four of us. We can make do with that. Thanks, we'll take them. Aldrich. We'll be there in between fifteen minutes, half an hour." He closed his phone.

"They have three rooms vacant. Two of us can share, can't we?" He couldn't quite suppress the grin.

"I think we can manage that," Josh said, grinning back at his younger brother, who ignored him in favor of watching Joyce.

"I don't object," Joyce said in a small voice, blushing pinkly.

"I don't either," Kenneth said, finally letting loose with a broad grin.

Josh looked at me. "Are you all right with staying over?"

"I'm fine. It was my idea." I looked teasingly over at Joyce. "Joyce and I won't mind sharing, will we?"

She turned an even brighter red and I stopped teasing her.

The game came to an end and we walked up to where we'd left the car. The hotel was only a block away, with a car park behind. Kenneth parked the car; we each found our overnight bags, and we walked up to the main street and into the building.

The lobby was small, but quite lovely. Deep leather chairs beckoned invitingly, and a gas fire burned even on a summer night. Josh checked the four of us in while Joyce, Kenneth and I all sent text messages to our respective families that we were staying the night and would chaperone each other. I didn't imagine anyone would be fooled; the appearances, however, must be preserved at all costs.

One room was on the first floor; the other two on the ground floor. "First and second floor," Josh corrected me. "If no one minds, I'm going to take one of the rooms on the lower floor. Those steps are a bit steep for me."

"Joyce and I will take the upstairs room," Kenneth agreed.

The two of them, bags in hand, disappeared up the stairs. Josh and I looked at each other and Josh opened the door assigned to me, just off the lobby. My eyes widened. The room was huge, with a king bed, and an en suite bath to the side.

"Are all American hotel rooms like this?" I asked. In England, hotel rooms with king beds are rare.

Josh laughed. "No, angel," he said. "American hotel rooms come in all shapes, sizes and qualities, just like English ones do. This is a particularly nice hotel of its kind; an independent house, relatively low priced. But even here in this hotel, other rooms are much smaller than this one. The room Joyce and Kenneth are in, for example, has a queen sized bed, a dresser, a table and two chairs, and not much room beyond that. The bath is so small that the sink is outside in the main room. But I don't think they'll mind."

"You've stayed here before?"

He nodded. "Often. I've come up here to see baseball games several times a year. I prefer rooms on this floor—the stairs are a bit steep and I find them hard to manage. But once in a while I've had a room on the second floor—first floor to you—and I'm pretty sure I recognize the room they're in."

He sat down in a chair by the window. "Sit down," he invited. "Are you sure you're all right with staying over? And with my visiting you for a while?"

I nodded. "Of course it is. It would have been cruel to take the night together away from Kenneth and Joyce."

"They've loved each other since they were babies, those two," Josh told me. "I think Kenneth was five when he first started day dreaming about the pretty little girl in his Sunday School class. He didn't start dating till she was old enough for her parents to let her go out with him, and I don't think either one of them has ever dated anyone else."

"Are they engaged?" I didn't think so; I was sure Joyce would have told me. But I wondered why not.

"Not officially," Josh said, stretching. "They each have two more years of school ahead of them; then Kenneth has a three-year internship before he can take his licensing exam and officially call himself an architect. Assuming he passes the first try—a lot of people don't. Kenneth, as you may have already gathered, is ultra-responsible and won't ask Joyce to marry him until he's closer to being in a position to support a wife. But no one has questioned for years but that they'll marry eventually." He settled back down in the chair and smiled at me. I sat down in the other chair.

"That's sweet," I said. "I like them both so much."

"I just hope it doesn't put you in a bad position, our staying here. Her folks are a bit overprotective."

"No reason why it should," I said.

Josh stood up. "I'll go now," he said. "It's been a long day. He leaned over and kissed me softly, then more deeply, then finally with a deep sigh pulled away. "Good night, angel. Sleep well."

This was far, far different from the light butterfly kisses we had shared before. I stared at him and he smiled at me. "Didn't you realize I was falling in love with you?"

I wanted to cry suddenly. He saw, and took me in his arms.

"I wasn't going to tell you yet," he said gently. "It's too soon. We've only known each other a month, give or take, and you're only in this country for a few months. But I love you, Jillian." He kissed my forehead. "All I'm going to ask you now, is whether or not you think there's any chance that someday you might love me back. I'm not putting any pressure on you and I'm not asking you to carve anything in stone. Just, maybe, someday."

I nodded. "I think, maybe, someday. Maybe even now." In fact, ever since he had arrived at Joyce's party it was as if the entire world were in black and white and only Josh in color.

His whole face glowed. "I'll let you go sleep now, then, angel. I'm afraid if I stayed any longer, feeling the way I do right now, I might be tempted to take an undue liberty." His voice was teasing, but there was a seriousness behind it. I nestled into his shoulder for a moment and then pulled away.

"Good night, Josh. I...I love you."

It took me a while to get to sleep that night.

The sun was streaming in the windows when I woke. I showered, dressed and packed my overnight bag again before venturing out into the lobby. Josh was already seated there, reading a newspaper and drinking a cup of coffee. "Good morning, sunshine!" he greeted me.

"You're an early riser," I told him sleepily.

"Not really. It's a quarter to nine."

"Really? I must have been more tired than I realized. Do I have time for a cup of tea?"

"You have all the time you need. You don't really imagine that Kenneth and Joyce will be up early, do you?" Josh teased. "Seriously, we're not in any rush. We don't have to check out till noon, and if Joyce had to work today she'd have said so yesterday."

"True. And if she did, we'd have had to be on the road long before now to get her there on time." I saw the tea bags and hot water and began steeping myself some tea. I'd never really gotten used to tea bags.

"They don't have much in the way of breakfast," Josh told me. "Just rolls and fruit and cereal."

"That's plenty for me," I said. "I may be English, but I only want a full breakfast about four times a year. Today isn't one of the four days."

"I'm a big breakfast eater," Josh admitted. "This will hold me for now, but when the others get up I'll take us all out for breakfast or brunch somewhere."

"You're a lot bigger than I am," I pointed out. "You need more fuel. How tall are you, anyway?"

"Just a hair under six foot four. Two hundred twenty pounds. What about you, small fry?" His teasing smile was still gentle. "Five foot even?"

"Five foot one, I'll have you know. Roughly seven stone."

He took my tea out of my hand, put it down on the counter and took me in his arms, heedless of other guests and staff in the vicinity. "I wasn't expecting you," he murmured into my hair. "I wasn't planning on falling in love for a few years yet, not till I had my career a little more firmly established. Then you came along and that was the end of that. I was a goner."

"I certainly wasn't planning on falling in love with an American," I said. "I'm only going to be here till Christmas. Not even all the way till Christmas. Adam's finished in DC about the middle of December and I go home then. What am I going to do?"

"We'll find a way," Josh declared firmly. "I love you, angel. I'm not going to let you out of my life."

I leaned back against his shoulder, loving the feel of him. He buried his face in my hair; then let me go. "Don't want to scare the neighbors," he said, giving me my tea again. "After all, we are in public here."

We didn't speak until a few minutes later when Kenneth and Joyce came downstairs, carrying their overnight bags, holding hands and both of them looking radiant. Kenneth was wearing his glasses.

"Forget to take your contacts out, last night, bro?" Josh asked with an affectionate grin.

"Are you both ready to go?" Kenneth asked, ignoring him, but grinning back.

Josh nodded. "Let us just get our bags," he said, and picked up both of them. "Let's go check out, and then I want to find more to eat than they have here."

"I know where to find the best breakfast in Portland," Kenneth advised, picking up Joyce's bag as well as his own and leading the way to the front desk. "

"And that will be a good American experience for Jillian," Josh agreed. "Checking out, please."

We settled into the car and Kenneth drove us down to the waterfront to a 50's style diner, of the sort I'd seen in movies and hadn't realized existed any more. "There aren't a lot of them," Josh admitted, "but there are a few. Good food, too."

We sat in a booth rather than at the counter. "The counter is pure Americana," Josh admitted, "but I have more room to stretch out my leg here."

Both men ordered large breakfasts. I toyed with a single slice of raisin bread French toast and a couple rashers of bacon. Joyce, the dancer, concerned with her weight, pushed some fruit around on her plate and ignored the bowl of hot cereal in front of her.

"Eat," Kenneth commanded.

Joyce shook her head. "I thought we should let Jillian see a bit more of the town, and maybe introduce her to Maine lobster. I'm saving my calories for that."

Kenneth took a banana, sliced it into her cereal, and put a spoon firmly into her hand. "Six bites and I'll shut up."

Joyce made a face at him but she obediently put the spoon into the bowl and took a bite.

"Joyce has a good point," Josh conceded. "Jillian's over here at all because she wanted to travel. Let's do a little sightseeing and have some lobster before we head home. No one's in any kind of rush, are they? We'll be home in time for dinner."

We all agreed, and so it was that I came to see Portland's waterfront, the Victorian mansion, a second hand bookstore that made me ache for Charing Cross Road and its bookstores, and finally settled down for lunch at a seafood restaurant. I realized that none of us wanted to break the spell; Josh and I were still wrapped in the rosy cloud of realizing we were falling in love; Joyce and Kenneth with their glimpse of a future when they would be together always. Finally, we drove back home, arriving about four o'clock.

Josh walked me to the door and kissed me. "I'll see you tomorrow, angel," he whispered. "I love you."

"I love you," I repeated, and reluctantly entered the house.

"Aunt Jill!" Kaitlyn cried immediately. "You came home!"

Adam and Lori came out of the family room. "So you finally made it home," Adam said sternly, but with a teasing light in his eye. "Does Big Brother have to go get the rifle?"

I raised my hands in protest. "Little Sister's virtue is still intact," I promised. "It was after nine when the game ended, and poor Kenneth was tired—it didn't seem fair to make him drive three hours home. So we stayed over. I had my own room, not to worry. No illicit visits."

"I trust you, honey," Adam said, giving me a one-armed hug. "It's the nature of older brothers to be over protective. Your relationship with Josh is your own business."

"Did you have a good time?" Lori asked, leading us both back into the family room.

"I had a wonderful time. I'm not sure I really get the point of baseball, but we had fun anyway." I told them about the game, and the morning touring Portland. "It was brilliant." I looked at my big brother. "Why are you still here?"

"I don't have to be in DC till mid-morning tomorrow so I'm staying over tonight and will take an early shuttle tomorrow," Adam told me. "Why, am I not welcome?" He smiled. "Do you need some girl talk? I can take the kids for a drive, pick up some pizza or hamburgers, and be back in a couple of hours. Would that do?"

I nodded. Even though he was ten years older, Adam and I had always understood each other. "Thanks, Adam."

When he and the children had left, I told Lori everything. Well, not quite everything—I kept the room arrangements to myself. I had promised Joyce I would be discreet about that. "My parents know we're sleeping together," she'd admitted, "but we've promised to be discreet about it so my father can pretend he doesn't know." But about Josh and me and our feelings for each other, my concern about my eventual return to England while Josh was here, all came pouring out.

Lori listened quietly, and then hugged me. "If you and Josh are meant to be together, there'll be a way," she promised me. "You're an American citizen—you can stay here if you want to. Or, it sounds as if Josh was comfortable in England—he may be willing to relocate there."

"I hope so," I breathed.

Lori looked sympathetic. "Do you hate it here, honey?"

I shook my head vehemently. "Oh, no! I'm having a good time, I really am. I'm so glad to be spending more time with you and Adam and the kids, and I really like Joyce and Kenneth. And Josh…I'd never have met Josh otherwise. I love it here. I'm just not sure I want to stay here forever—England is home."

"That's understandable." Lori stood up. "Adam said he'd bring dinner home, but why don't we start planning menus for the week. Get your mind off your worries and onto something that makes you feel secure."

I was stunned at her words, which immediately settled in as if I'd always known their truth. "Is that what it is?"

"Of course it is. Think, honey. You're very much the youngest, with three older brothers in high powered jobs; a dad in a high powered job and a mother with strong management skills. Which you have inherited, by the way, but which you're only just learning to use to their full extent. Even your close friends, if I remember Pamela Keller properly, tend to treat you like a cuddly pet. You're well past the age when you should be struggling to stand up for yourself as an independent adult but you're only just starting to do that as well. You know you're a good cook, so it's when you're cooking or meal planning that you feel confident. For the rest of life, you're all too inclined to let everyone else tell you what to do."

I had never thought of it that way, but Lori was right. This was going to take some pondering.

August moved on. Josh and I spent as much time together as possible, and he reassured me about our potential future together. "You remember that my grandfather lives in London," he told me. "It probably wouldn't be a bad idea for someone in the family to be over there; he's getting older. I'm perfectly comfortable over there, and I can write music anywhere. I told you that before."

"I can live here without any paperwork," I objected. "Even though I've lived all my life in England, I'm an American citizen too. In terms of the bureaucracy, it would be easier for me to make the move than for you to."

Josh's eyes twinkled at me. "You can't really tell me you wouldn't be more comfortable back home than here, can you?"

In truth, I couldn't. I was starting to get a little homesick. But I loved Josh and was willing to make the adjustment for his sake.

It seemed like no time before the week that Joyce and I were to spend with Adam in Washington. "You'll be on your own a lot of the time," he warned us. "I'll be working during the day. But you two will have more fun on your own than with me, anyway, and we can visit in the evenings."

The flight to DC was uneventful. Adam went with us to the hotel and made sure we were comfortable and knew how to get to the Metro from there. "I know you're used to a big city," he said ruefully. "But you're my little sister, and I worry."

"We'll be fine," I promised.

And we were. Washington was remarkably easy to find our way around. The Metro was clean and the maps were easy to read. Joyce had been there before and remembered more than she had thought she would. We toured all the monuments, the White House and the Capitol the first day, then went on to the museums.

I had not realized that the Smithsonian was not a single museum, but a number of them. Since I was looking for the American experience, we started with the Air and Space Museum—the United States had far more to do with air and space travel than the United Kingdom. I had seen clips of the moon landing, and I saw the movie *Apollo 13*, but beyond that I didn't know much. We spent a couple of hours there before moving on to the American History museum.

"I suppose you think it's pretty silly, having a exhibit of past advertising campaigns," Joyce said as we studied the brand labels from past years.

"Not at all. We have the Museum of Brands in London; it's very similar. But why don't we move on to the fashion exhibit?"

On our way there we passed a military exhibit and Joyce looked a bit uncomfortable. "I'm not very interested in the military, either," I said. "We don't have to go there."

"It isn't that, though I'm glad you don't want to go," Joyce answered, walking quickly past the arrow as if afraid I would change my mind. "It's…well, we used to belong to your country, and we broke away, and I'm not sure what you think about that."

"I think there was right and wrong on both sides," I told her honestly. "Of course I studied it from the British side but I don't think either side was completely in the right."

Joyce considered. "Boston is really a better city to study the Revolutionary War," she told me. "Maybe one day we should go in and do the Freedom Trail."

"I'd like that. Let's plan on it."

Wednesday night we met Adam for dinner earlier than usual, and he was in something of a hurry that night. "I've got a conference call tonight," he told us. "Let's just get dinner at the hotel quickly. Can you girls amuse yourselves this evening?"

"Of course we can. We don't want to be any trouble," Joyce said immediately. I agreed.

"Thanks." Adam turned the corner that would lead us to the hotel and stopped to pull out his mobile phone. "You ladies go ahead—I'll be right with you."

We walked into the lobby and we both stopped short as Josh and Kenneth stood up and turned towards us, both of them grinning like fools.

"Josh!" I exclaimed as Joyce threw herself into Kenneth's arms. "What are you doing here? I'm so glad to see you?" I stopped and let myself melt into his embrace, accepting his kiss.

"I missed you," he said. "I had this all planned with Adam weeks ago." I stepped back to see my brother coming in, smiling.

"You knew all about this," I accused him.

"Of course I did. Josh and I planned it together." Adam smiled at us.

"There was a mix up with Kenneth's reservation, though," Josh explained. "They overbooked and he got bumped. So he's going to stay in my room with me tonight. Then tomorrow they'll have a room for him."

"Is there anything I can do?" Adam asked.

Josh shook his head. "They tracked it down—a large party stayed longer than their initial reservation and it threw their computations off. They've already put a cot in my room—we'll be fine."

"If you're sure. Then I'll get out of the way and leave you to the festivities."

Festivities?

"Where are we going?" I asked.

"Should we change?" Joyce added.

"We're going to the Kennedy Center," Josh told us. "We'll wait for you to put on your pretties but don't take too long, okay?"

Adam pointed at the elevator. "Fifteen minutes, girls."

"Do I have time to take a shower?" Joyce asked as we exited the elevator and made our way as quickly as possible down the corridor to the room we shared.

"Go in and take one quickly," I suggested. "If we keep track of the time, we should both be able to squeeze one in."

By rushing, we both managed a quick shower and a change to the nicest outfits we'd brought with us. Cotton frocks both; pale blue two piece for me and a lilac sun dress for Joyce. My hair was still a bit damp when I spritzed myself with my favorite perfume and slid my feet into white sandals, while Joyce slid a pair of silver dangle earrings into her ears and looped a matching necklace and bracelet over her neck and wrist. We made down only five minutes over the arbitrary fifteen Adam had allotted us. Not that it mattered as he had already left.

"You look absolutely beautiful," Josh said admiringly, looking me up and down. Kenneth said nothing but the expression on his face when he looked at Joyce made it clear that he agreed. He put an arm around her shoulders and led her to the door. Josh took my hand and we followed.

"I'm treating us to a taxi," Josh said, and hailed one. "Kennedy Center," he told the driver, and we took off back into the District, as I had learned to call the city in the last couple of days.

"So, what are we going to see at the Kennedy Center?" I asked.

"Gregory James is playing," Josh said, his excitement evident.

"And who is Gregory James when he's at home?"

"Josh's hero," Kenneth quipped, holding tightly to Joyce's hand and running his fingers through her copper hair.

"He's a classical pianist," Josh explained. "He's a young guy, probably not more than five or six years older than I am, but he's one of the best in the world. He's an absolute genius and can make a piano do things I didn't even know were legal."

"Do you know him?" I asked curiously.

"No, but…" Josh stopped abruptly. "I'll tell you that part later," he decided. "I don't know him, but he went to school the same place I got my graduate degree, and the place was still talking about him while I was there. The keyboard professors practically genuflected when his name was mentioned. My undergraduate degree is in piano and I just hope that eventually I might be as good as he was when he was twelve."

"What kind of music is he playing tonight?"

"It's a varied program," Kenneth said. "A little Baroque, a little Classical, a little Romantic. I'm not sure if there's any 20th century or not; maybe Josh knows."

"Some ragtime, I think. Joplin."

"Isn't it a bit early in the season for the National Symphony?" Joyce asked.

"It's not a symphony concert. It's a one man show." Josh was all but on the edge of his seat.

We decided to just grab a quick bite to hold us and then have a leisurely dinner after the concert. This proved to be a good idea because we had only just settled into our seats when the lights lowered and the curtain rose to a grand piano with the top raised. The applause began as a young man, probably in his early 30's, strolled out, bowed, and took his seat at the piano.

I was totally astonished at the variety in the concert. Bach, Beethoven, Chopin, Rachmaninoff, Liszt, and finally Joplin; all of it handled precisely, but with enough emotion to make me laugh and cry, often at the same time. It was absolutely brilliant. He was brought back for three encores (Beethoven, Grieg and Joplin again) but finally the curtain stayed firmly shut.

"That was magnificent," I raved as we left the hall.

"It's moments like this when I wish I'd continued as an instrumentalist," Josh said quietly, but with an intensity that made us all look at him.

"No, you don't," Kenneth informed him as we reached the street. "You love composing and song writing. Now me; it makes me want to go back and get back in practice on the piano again. And maybe I will."

"He was really good," Joyce agreed.

We found a restaurant a block or two away and went in for dinner. My mouth fell open a little at the prices, to the point where I wondered if I was just misunderstanding the exchange again. But the looks on Joyce's and Kenneth's faces confirmed that it really was as costly as I thought.

"The sky's the limit tonight," Josh declared. "It's on me. Anything anyone wants—wine, cocktails, appetizers through dessert. Have everything on the menu if you want. It's all covered."

I looked at him. He was terribly excited about something, and it was more than just the music. There was something he wasn't telling us.

When the sommelier came, Josh ordered a bottle of wine for the table, and Joyce, Kenneth and I all produced our ID. "I borrowed my cousin Carol's for the week," Joyce whispered to me. "No one ever looks past our red hair." When we'd given the order for our starters to the waiter, Josh held up his hand.

"Before anyone says anything, I have a very special announcement to make," he said. "I told my family before we left this morning, so Kenneth already knows. I've known for months that this was possible, but I only found out that it was certain today.

"During the last week of April next, the Boston Symphony Orchestra will be showcasing an original piece of music to be played by Gregory James, and which was written by…none other than Joshua Daniel Whittaker."

It took a moment to sink in and then I couldn't help myself—I squealed with delight. "I'm so proud of you! Oh, Josh, that's wonderful! Brilliant!"

"Josh, that's such great news!" Joyce exclaimed.

I reached over to kiss his cheek. Joyce did likewise from the other side. Kenneth extended a hand across the table.

"I know I congratulated you this morning," he said, "but this news is worth a second round."

"April?" It sank in. "I'll be back in England."

"You'll have to come back for it," Josh insisted. "I'll buy your plane ticket but I have to have you with me then."

"And I have to be here." I was already planning in my mind how I would explain this to my parents. But job, school, or whatever I was doing in April, I had to be in Boston for something like that.

"Tell me about the piece," I demanded. Josh complied, happily. It was a piano concerto, and it had been his music school contacts that arranged it; that was most of what I got out of it. Josh was getting much too deep into music theory for anyone but Kenneth to follow, and even Kenneth's eyes glazed over occasionally. But he was so happy and excited, none of us would have dreamed of interrupting him.

The waiter brought our starters and took our dinner orders. Josh took a deep breath and smiled around the table. "That's enough out of me," he said. "Jillian, love, how are you enjoying DC?"

We talked about other things for the rest of the meal; then finally went out into the street. "I know it's getting late," Josh said, "but I'm still a bit too wired to settle down. Who wants to go for a walk?"

Kenneth and Joyce looked at each other and shook their heads. "It's been a long day," Joyce admitted. "I think I'm ready to go back to the hotel."

Josh reached into his wallet and handed Kenneth some cash. "Take a taxi back," he instructed. "It's late, and it's safer that way. We'll be about half an hour behind you."

A taxi pulled up and Joyce and Kenneth got into it. A second one pulled up, and Josh took my hand and opened the door. "Take us on a round of the monuments," he suggested. "Stop in front of each one for a few minutes. Then we'll be heading back to Virginia."

There was a lot of romance in seeing the monuments by moonlight, and I was feeling all soft and dreamy by the time we pulled up in front of the hotel. Josh paid the driver, giving him a generous tip, and opened the door for me. We went into the lobby and Josh walked me to my door.

"Good night, angel," he whispered, and kissed me deeply. Reluctantly I slid the key card into the door slot, and opened the door.

While the light was off, the sounds coming from inside the room made it immediately obvious that my presence was neither necessary nor desired. I shut the door and turned, stricken, to Josh.

He smothered a grin. "That means there's no one in our room," he commented. "We're just a few doors down. C'mon, love, we'll wait them out."

I wasn't altogether sure I was comfortable going to Josh's room the way I was feeling right now. I wasn't at all sure I was ready to surrender my virtue yet but I was so warm and smooshy inside and Josh had never stopped setting off fireworks in my hormones. But there didn't seem to be any other solution so I followed him down to his room.

He opened the door and let me precede him into the room. It looked just like Joyce's and mine, except that instead of our double queen beds there was a single king, with a cot, still folded, against the wall. This idea of having king and queen beds, let alone multiple king and queen beds, in the same hotel room was still surprising to me, but then Americans did seem to live on the high end, at least from what I could see. At least the Americans I knew.

"That's not entirely true," Josh was to tell me later. "There are Americans at all points of the scale from abject poverty to wealth beyond absurdity. You happen to know Americans at the 'more than comfortable' position on the scale. And don't ever let anyone tell you that the US is a classless society. We claim to be but we're just as much class oriented as the British. You're right, though, that as a nation we tend to look for as much luxury as we can afford from our respective locations on that scale. There are individual exceptions, but we're very much aware of our privileges as Americans as a whole."

Now, Josh sat down on the end of the bed and pulled his shoes off. "I hope my kid brother brought condoms."

I knew that Joyce was on the pill. I did not know if that was information she wanted disseminated. I kept quiet.

"Sit down, relax," Josh invited. "They're going to be at least half an hour, I would guess."

I perched on the edge of the chair, then slowly leaned back and slipped my shoes off as well. "I had a really good time tonight, Josh. That was a wonderful concert. I'm so proud of you, getting your concerto played by such a major symphony." Even I knew that the BSO was one of the most prestigious in the entire US. "Did you always want to be a composer?"

His smile was sad. "When I was growing up, I wanted to be a professional baseball player. Even though I was only a junior, I was on the varsity baseball team before the accident, and I was good enough so that there were scouts watching me. Then the accident happened, and that dream was gone for good. I'll admit that I was starting to outgrow it anyway, but it would have been nice to have a choice."

I looked at him curiously. "That was the accident that killed your cousin Janey, wasn't it? Is that how your leg was hurt?"

He looked startled, then realization dawned. "Jillian, angel, Janey was my sister."

"But . . . Kenneth said she was his cousin, and you're his brother . . ." I was confused.

"Kenneth and I are foster brothers. Genetically we're first cousins. When my parents and Janey were killed, I was in the hospital for almost a year, and when I got out, Kenneth's parents took me to live with them. His mother, my Aunt Deborah, was my mother's twin sister. Ken's dad, my Uncle Scott, had just gotten a promotion that would take him to England for a year. I was offered a choice; I could go with them to England, or I could stay in Scituate with my Aunt

Rosemary or my Uncle James or my Aunt Julia. I chose England—away from my memories. They were too painful yet."

His blue eyes looked backwards into the past. "I'd always loved music as well as baseball. In the hospital I couldn't work on the piano, and for the first few months I couldn't work at the guitar, so that's when I started composing. Well, started it seriously—I wrote my first song when I was twelve. The accident had taken my family away from me, not to mention baseball; I was going to be damned if it was going to take music away, too."

He sighed. "I'm sorry, love, I should have explained. I suppose I thought you realized because of my last name. I'm a Whittaker, not an Aldrich."

"I do vaguely remember that," I admitted. "I guess I thought you and Kenneth were half-brothers and had different fathers."

"In one sense that's even true. My mother and Ken's were identical twins, so they shared the same DNA." He reached out his arms. "Come here, angel. I want to make out with my girl."

He needed distraction from the memories, I realized. I went into his arms and willingly gave him my lips. Soon we were on the bed, our hands exploring each other, our lips fused together. Eventually he pulled away, breathing hard.

"If this is as far as we're going to go tonight," he said through his ragged breathing, "then I think this is as far as we're going to go tonight."

He stood up and walked to the window, obviously trying to control his breathing. My own was coming pretty hard and fast as well. I stood up too, straightening my clothes. We'd only just gotten ourselves back together again and had seated ourselves in separate chairs, when we heard the lock click and Kenneth came in.

His face reddened as he saw me. "Sorry," he mumbled, but the extremely satisfied grin on his face was enough to tell us that he wasn't, really. Quite honestly, I wasn't either.

"That's all right. I'll see you both tomorrow." I leaned over and kissed Josh lightly on the cheek. "Good night, my love. I'm proud of you."

He squeezed my hand. "I love you too."

Back in my own room, Joyce had changed into her night things. Her bed was rumpled, but she was still up, sitting at the table leaning her chin on her hand. "Jillian, we're engaged," she whispered. "He asked me. We're going to be married the June after we both graduate."

"Joyce, that's smashing! I'm so happy for you!" I hugged my friend. "That's incredible news. I couldn't be more pleased for you."

"Will you be one of my bridesmaids? I want you and Vickie and Alice and Rachel. And my friend Susannah from high school."

I was overwhelmed. "Of course I will. Thank you, Joyce, I'd be honored."

"I don't want a terribly big wedding, but I do want all of you up there with me. Kenneth is going to ask Josh to be his best man, and then his friends Ben and Harry and Stephen, and his cousin Russ. You've met Russ, haven't you?"

"Of course I have. I met him at your party."

"He's a nice guy." Joyce sighed happily. "Kenneth's going to take me out to find a ring tomorrow. Do you mind?"

I hugged her again. "Of course not. You and Kenneth go off and do whatever you want; I'll spend the day with Josh. And Joyce, tomorrow night, I don't expect you to stay here. When Kenneth has his own room, of course you'll want to be there with him."

"Thanks, Jillian." She stood up and stretched. "I don't know if I can sleep tonight, but I'm going to try."

"I'll only be a few minutes," I promised. I quickly changed into my night things and slid into my own bed. I had plenty to think about myself.

"Where do you want to spend your final in full day in Washington?" Josh asked me the next morning as we met in the lobby. "Kenneth and Joyce are going engagement ring shopping, and then to the Octagon Museum. Where would you like to go?"

"I saw something about a boat ride down the Potomac to Mount Vernon," I said hesitantly. "I think I'd like to try something like that. Could we do that?"

"Of course we could. I like that idea." Josh smiled. "Let me get a brochure so I can see about times and docks."

With a little help from the front desk we found what we needed and soon were on a comfortable boat heading down the river. "If you like this sort of thing I should take you down to Plimoth Plantation, or out to Sturbridge," Josh said. "Lori and the children will be back in school soon, won't they? We could go on a week day when it isn't so crowded."

"I know what Plimoth Plantation is since we went to Plymouth earlier in the summer, but what is Sturbridge?" I asked.

"Sturbridge is a historical village demonstrating New England life in the late eighteenth, early 19th centuries, I forget the exact years," Josh explained.

"How would it differ from life in Old England in the same time period?"

Josh grinned. "Probably very little, if at all. But it's interesting and worth seeing. We'll have to take Joyce and Kenneth with us, or get my cousin Russ and his girlfriend Colleen to come; it's hard to get there except by car, and that's a long way for you to drive when I know you're not very comfortable driving on the right."

"I don't mind having Joyce and Kenneth with us," I told him. "I like them. Russ too—I don't know Colleen. How long a drive is it?"

"About an hour and a half, two hours." He hesitated. "The only problem is, I guess we'd have to go on a weekend at that since Kenneth and Joyce will have school starting next week. Russ and Colleen both work odd hours so I suppose we might possibly find a time when they could go during the week, but a weekend will probably be easiest."

"I can drive," I promised. "Sooner or later I have to start learning to drive further than just between Scituate and Marshfield."

"Only if you're absolutely sure you're comfortable," Josh insisted. "I don't want my phobia to force you into doing something you're not secure with."

There was that word again. Lori had used it too. "I'm only just realizing," I said slowly, thinking it through as I went, "how much I've been relying on other people to do everything hard for me. Or at least to make my decisions for me. Lori said the other day that I was well past the age when I should be an independent adult, and I'm not one. If I never do anything that's hard for me, how am I going to learn?"

I saw admiration in Josh's blue eyes. "I'm proud of you," he said. Then the eyes shadowed again. "Maybe one of these days I'll learn that too."

He took my hand and led me to a bench. We sat down together and he turned to face me. "There's something I need to tell you, if you're going to be going out with me," he said seriously. "I talked a little about this before. I'm not the easiest person to be with. Ever since the accident I've been clinically depressed. I take anti-depressants; maybe you've noticed that I don't drink a lot. I shouldn't drink at all but I allow myself one cocktail or a glass of wine when it's a special occasion, like last night. But sometimes if my meds get out of whack I fall into a black pit of depression and I don't seem to be able to find my way out of it. It can sometimes take months before I get back on track, and I'm not going to claim I'm easy to live with during those times. I'm moody and I just crawl into a little hole inside myself until I'm feeling better. Winters are worse than summers.

"Then there are other times when I'm just fine, but I get lost in the music in my head and can't find my way out until I get it written down, at least in rough. Those times aren't so bad—they usually last only a matter of hours, or at least days, rather than weeks or months. But I won't hear anything that's said to me while that's going on."

I held tightly to his hand. "I'll stay with you," I promised. "You won't drive me away."

He squeezed my hand back. "That's all I ask, angel. I'll try—I promise to try."

He thought for a minute. "Here I'm talking about trips to Plimoth and Sturbridge and I haven't asked you—do you even want to go? You don't have to."

"Of course I do! I came to America in the first place because I wanted to travel. I was even applying for jobs with airlines and travel agencies in the hopes of seeing more of the world than England. I've never even been to Ireland. I want to see as much as I can in the short time I'm here."

Josh's eyes regained some of their sparkle. "I'll take you anywhere you want to go," he promised. "Mystic, Connecticut. Newport, RI. New York. Philadelphia. Los Angeles, even."

"That would get awfully expensive," I demurred.

He squeezed my hand again. "Angel, I live mostly on the income from my songwriting," he explained. "But I made a heck of a lot of money on that tour I did last spring, and I've also got a significant amount put away. When my folks died, my aunts and uncles filed and won a wrongful death claim on my behalf, and they also sold my parents' house and put all the money away for me. Finally, I was the beneficiary of their life insurance and 401k funds."

I thought about interrupting to ask what a 401k fund was but stopped myself.

"And my dad's life insurance had a double indemnity clause. All of it put together, I have a little bit north of five million in the bank, not even counting my tour money."

I felt my jaw drop. I tried to speak and couldn't.

He chuckled. "You weren't expecting that, were you?"

I shook my head. "How…how much is that in pounds? Or Euros?"

"I don't know the exchange offhand. Probably a little over three million pounds, maybe about four million Euros or so. I have that all put away, though. I haven't touched the capital. I occasionally make use of some of the interest. I make a reasonably good income with my music and that's what I live on primarily. Even with just that, I live pretty comfortably."

I had seen the flat in Scituate where he lived, within walking distance of downtown so he had easy access to banks, stores, groceries, etc. without needing a car. I had no idea what the real estate market was like in America but I didn't imagine that it had come cheaply. I nodded weakly.

His voice was gentle. "Did you know you were falling in love with a rich man?"

I shook my head. I still wasn't certain I could trust my voice.

"Does it matter?" Softly.

"Not to me," I finally managed. "I love you either way."

"The wrongful death settlement included the payment of my medical bills, free and clear, until I was twenty-one, separate from the financial settlement. So I didn't have to pay out the entire amount to the hospital." Josh sighed. "Let's change the subject, angel girl, I don't want to start getting depressed again. Not when I'm so happy I have you."

"Tell me more about where we're going," I suggested.

Josh obeyed and told me all about George Washington and his effect on American history until we arrived at Mt. Vernon. We confirmed the time of our return trip and began our tour of the grounds and the exhibits.

After a few hours it was clear that Josh's bad leg was beginning to tire, so we made our way back to the boat. "I'm sorry," he apologized.

"No need," I told him. "It's been a long day for both of us."

We spent the boat ride back planning various places we could visit together. I was ready to attempt driving, but Adam put a halt to that idea when the five of us gathered for dinner that night.

"I'm very proud of my little sister for being brave enough to try," he said. "You're finally growing up, honey. But I don't know that my insurance will cover it, if something were to happen while you were driving to Plimoth or Sturbridge, especially without Lori or me in the car. Just puddling around Scituate and the immediate area shouldn't be a problem but I wouldn't want to give the insurance company an excuse to deny a claim. Then, too, Massachusetts will let you drive, for a few months at least, on your British license but I can't speak for Connecticut and Rhode Island. You're not used to having to deal with both state and Federal laws, but just because Mass allows it doesn't mean the others will."

"Go on weekends," Kenneth said. "During the school year both Joyce and I are usually done with work or class by noon Saturday—I work mostly in the office September through April, and Joyce's extra ballet classes, at least for the fall term, are in the morning. I'll drive you, happily. We can leave from work, go wherever we're going, see the sights and come back late Sunday. We'll miss choir, but I don't imagine we'll be going every week."

We all looked at each other. I held Adam's eye.

"Jillian, you're an adult," he said. "You don't need Big Brother's permission to go traveling with your friends."

"Would you please tell my parents that?" Joyce said with a laugh. "I know I'm younger than Jillian but I am over eighteen."

Adam smiled at her. "That's a conversation you're going to have to have with them all on your own, honey."

"There's another conversation I'm going to have to have with them a lot sooner than that one," Joyce said, holding up her left hand with the emerald ring she had shown us earlier. She smiled impishly at us.

"Let me see it again," I said.

Joyce held her hand out in my direction. It was a beautiful ring; small, but I knew that Kenneth probably couldn't afford much while he was still a student. It was nonetheless a lovely ring—I wouldn't want a particularly large stone either. The main stone was emerald cut, with two small side stones, both diamonds, set in white gold. "It's just beautiful, Joyce."

Joyce and Kenneth both beamed.

"Why an emerald?" Adam asked. "Why not a diamond?"

"Every Thomasina, Dianne and Harriet has diamonds," Joyce pointed out. "I like being a little different from the mainstream."

"Besides, I always think of emeralds with relation to Joyce," Kenneth said. "Just because of her eyes."

"I love the idea," I said. "Maybe I'll do something similar when I get engaged. Not emeralds, though. Sapphires?"

"You can have anything you want," Josh said quietly, a hand on my shoulder.

Joyce laughed with delight. "Maybe I'll start a trend!"

We finished dinner and went back to the hotel. Adam ostentatiously watched Joyce and me go into the room assigned to us, then left, winking at us both.

I looked around the room. Joyce's things were already gone. "Are you sure you don't mind my spending tonight in Kenneth's room?" Joyce asked wistfully.

I looked at her in surprise. "Of course not. Why would I? You're engaged to him; of course you want to be with him."

"I think Josh would like it if you shared his room," Joyce confided, looking around the room for anything she may have forgotten.

"We're not at that stage yet," I told her. "But I will go back out and spend some time with him."

We both went back out and down to the lobby. Josh and Kenneth were waiting for us. "What do we want to do tonight?" Josh asked the group as a whole, then laughed affectionately as Kenneth and Joyce looked at each other.

"All right," he agreed. "You two go do whatever it is you have in mind, and Jillian and I will pretend we don't know what it is. We'll go off on our own." With grateful smiles, they disappeared down the hall.

"What would you like to do?" Josh asked me.

I considered. "I don't think I want to go back into the District. Is there anything we can do locally?"

"We'll take a taxi to Old Town," Josh decided. "We can walk along the waterfront, and maybe stop somewhere for an after dinner drink."

Old Town was delightful. It was still early enough for us to watch the sunset over the water, sitting on a bench with Josh's arm around my shoulders. He kissed my cheek lightly.

"Are you warm enough?" he asked.

I leaned into him and put my head on his shoulder. "I'm fine. I'm a Northern girl, remember? This is quite comfortable—it's during the day that it's much too hot for me."

We sat there until the stars began to come out; then we found a restaurant that had live piano music and went in. After consulting with me, Josh ordered us cordials—amaretto for me and frangelico for him. The piano music was soft and romantic, and the drinks made me feel soft and dreamy. We walked back up to the main road after a while and found another taxi to take us back to our hotel.

At my door, Josh kissed me long and deeply. "May I come in for a few minutes?" he whispered.

"I wish you would," I answered longingly. At that point I wanted him desperately, and wasn't at all sure whether I wanted to stop, or to let everything happen that could happen.

But it was Josh, sometime later, who groaned and pulled away. "I don't want to push you," he said softly into my ear, "but if I don't stop now, I won't be able to stop."

For a moment I longed to tell him not to stop, to take me to bed and make love to me, but he was already standing up and pulling on that clothing that had somehow been discarded in our recent activities. I sat up and pulled on my nightgown—no sense getting dressed again when I would not be leaving the room. He whimpered slightly.

"You're so beautiful," he moaned. "I don't want to leave you."

I clung to him for a few minutes until he kissed my cheek and drew away. "I'll see you tomorrow," he whispered.

It took a long, long time before I fell asleep.

Adam was in class the next day until two, so we had reservations on the four o'clock shuttle. Kenneth told Joyce to pick out something she wanted as an engagement gift, so the two of them wandered off. "What would you like?" Josh asked me. "I'd like to buy you a souvenir of the trip."

I considered. "I'm not sure," I admitted. "Can we look around?"

In a small art gallery we found a painting by a local artist of the Washington Monument and the Reflecting Pool. It was very well executed and something about it struck at my emotions. "This is what

I want," I said decidedly. "That is, if it's not too expensive and if it can be shipped to my flat in London."

"It's not expensive at all," Josh said, looking at the discreet label. "In fact, I'd say the artist is undervaluing himself, if he's the one who determined the price. We can ask the gallery about shipping."

The gallery was delighted to ship the painting to London for me so we made those arrangements. We left and started down the street but I stopped at a different gallery and looked in the window at some miniature portraits displayed in the window.

"Josh, look at these," I pointed.

He came back and looked. They were quite well executed. "I wonder who does those," he mused. We went into the gallery.

"May I help you?" the young man at a table in the corner asked.

"What can you tell me about the miniatures in the window?" I asked.

"They're acrylic on wood," he told us. "They're mostly done from photographs. Occasionally I have someone sit for one but usually I work from photos so people don't have to hang around sitting still."

"You're the artist?" Josh asked.

He nodded.

"How much would it cost for you to do one for me of my girl here?"

The artist studied me for a few minutes and then named a price. Josh nodded.

"Let's do it," he said. "If that's okay with you, angel?"

I was thrilled. The artist pulled a digital camera out of a drawer and had me sit down. He took several shots of me from different angles and discussed colors with Josh. Josh paid him in advance and smiled at me. "And now," he said, "you and I had better meet up with the others, have some lunch, and think about getting to the airport. It's the Friday of a long weekend and it's going to be crowded; we should get there early." He thanked the artist and we left.

When we got to Reagan National airport, I could see what he meant. With texting, we finally agreed to meet Adam at the gate; we had our boarding passes so even if we didn't see him till we were on the plane, we'd be all right. He caught up with us before the flight began to board, however, and it was only then that we realized that Josh had called ahead, more than two weeks ago, and upgraded us all to business class.

"It's nothing," he disclaimed, when Adam tried to thank him. "I'm too big to fit in the average airline seat comfortably, and I didn't want to sit alone."

"Even so," Adam insisted. "Thank you, Josh."

"You're very welcome."

So we traveled home in style. Kenneth and Joyce, of course, sat together; Josh and I sat together across from them, with Adam sitting just ahead of us. "I know it's very short notice," Josh said to me quietly, "but do you think that working together, we could manage to put together a small party for Monday? It's supposed to rain, unfortunately, but maybe an indoor picnic at my condo?"

"How many people?" I asked. "If we plan a menu now, on the plane, and go shopping together tomorrow, I don't see why we couldn't manage by Monday. As long as we don't get too elaborate."

"I'm thinking maybe thirty people," Josh said. "Just my family and their significant others, and your brother and sister in law, with the kids. Joyce's parents. My cousin Doug has already left for college, and my cousin Stephen lives in New York, but I think the rest of them are home. I know that this weekend Colleen has off work, and Russ took vacation time."

"Cold chicken pieces," I said. "Sandwiches. Lots of different salads. Devilled eggs. The cold vegetable plate I did for Joyce's party. Cheese and crackers. A whole lot of starters. Almost all finger food, except for the salads. For dessert, a selection of fairy cakes."

"That sounds marvelous," Josh declared. "I'll help. I think it would be fun to do it together, don't you?"

We started putting together a grocery list and made plans to shop the next day. The small market where Joyce had taken me the first day was within walking distance of Josh's condo, but just to be safe I leaned forward. "Adam, do you suppose I could use one of the cars tomorrow to go up to the larger market in Marshfield if we need to?"

"I don't know why not," Adam said. "I don't have any plans. What are you two plotting?"

We told him, and he nodded approval. "There's a shop in downtown Scituate that I believe does cooking classes," he said. "You should sign up for that, Jillian. It's six or eight weeks, one night a week. Lori and I will have some kind of party while you're here that you can help Lori organize; the more of that you do, the easier it will be to convince Dad to let you go to culinary school. I don't think Mother will be too hard to convince."

Joyce leaned across the aisle. "My mother will want to have an engagement party for us—I'm sure she'll be willing to let you help her with it."

"I'd love to," I said promptly. "Tell her to call me."

We reached Boston, and took the MBTA into South Station. "I told Lori not to even try coming in to get us," Adam explained. "Where it's right before a holiday, I didn't want her driving into the city. We'll take the commuter rail to Greenbush and she can collect us there."

"I'll text my mom to pick us up there, too," Joyce said, and got out her mobile phone.

"I can walk from Greenbush," Josh said.

"No, you won't," Adam said firmly. "It's over two miles into the village from the station. We'll drop you off."

Josh didn't argue. I knew that the walking we had done had taken more of a toll on his bad leg than he was willing to admit.

We had a wonderful time the next two days creating food for Josh's party. Josh was, himself, an excellent cook. "I was in bed for months after the accident," he told me. "I was still in high school, but I finished all my graduation credits early since I didn't have much to do but study. My aunts and uncles used to bring me books; luckily I like to read. Once my Aunt Rosemary didn't realize that she'd accidentally left behind a cook book that she'd bought as a bridal shower gift along with the books she'd left for me, and since I was bored I read it. I got interested in food preparation in spite of myself. When I got out of the hospital finally, there was no holding me."

I was a bit nervous about the party itself, but I ended up having a wonderful time. I met members of his family that I'd never met before, and with the exception of Randi, they were all welcoming and friendly. Randi was still somewhat standoffish and just a trifle rude, but the rest of the family, both Ferguson and Whittaker, were so lovely to me that I could ignore her.

Over the next several weeks, I found life to be a bit different than it had been over the summer, but it soon took on a comfortable pattern. Kaitlyn was in school all day; Jeremy a half day. Lori had to be at school from eight to three and naturally Adam was gone all week. Two days a week Beth stayed home with me; the other three days she went to day care for the time Lori was in school. On those days Jeremy went to day care for the afternoon after his morning kindergarten let out. Tuesday was the night of my cooking class, which I thoroughly enjoyed. I rarely saw Joyce or Kenneth during the week, since both of them were in school full time and working full time, but I saw Josh several times a week. A few times his aunt Deborah, Kenneth's mother, invited me to dinner, and eventually I began to call her Aunt Deb and Mr. Aldrich, Uncle Scott, the way Josh did.

Weekends were when we traveled. Every other weekend, as soon as Joyce was through with her ballet class, she and I and Josh and Kenneth all piled into Kenneth's little red car and we headed off to some New England location that the others insisted I had to see.

"We'll wait till Columbus Day weekend to go to Bar Harbor," Kenneth promised. "That's just a bit too far away to do easily over a weekend."

"We can fly," Josh pointed out. "And rent a car there."

Kenneth nodded. "We could do that. But I'd still recommend waiting for Columbus Day. There's so much to do there, I sure wouldn't mind having the extra day."

Outside of Plimoth, which was only a short drive away and done in a single day, we generally stayed overnight to get the most out of our visit. Sturbridge, Mystic, Newport, Portsmouth... we saw them all.

It was in Bar Harbor that it finally happened. We had failed to make reservations in advance and, given that it was a holiday weekend, were having trouble finding three rooms. We were finally offered two, and rather than continue a search that might be fruitless, accepted the two rooms with a cot in one.

"Jillian and I can share," Joyce offered half-heartedly.

I shook my head. "You and Kenneth go ahead. Josh and I will manage." I couldn't bear the disappointment in her eyes, and I'd been tempted to go ahead and let my relationship with Josh progress to the next step anyway. If it was going to happen, it may as well be now as anytime.

She and Kenneth took off to their room, and Josh looked at me. "This isn't going to be easy," he pointed out. "It's been getting harder and harder to control myself."

I smiled at him. "We'll get through. It's only two nights." I wasn't ready to commit myself yet, even though in my own mind I was almost sure what I was going to do.

Josh shook his head but didn't respond. We went into our room and dropped our bags.

"A lot of places will already be closed," Josh warned me. "A lot of other places will be closing as of Monday. This is very much a summer resort. But Kenneth and I checked into things and there's still plenty of things we can do, and plenty of good restaurants open." He pulled out his mobile phone. "We're going to stick together most of the time," he explained. 'They'll be ready to go in about half an hour. We're going to take a dinner cruise around the harbor, if that's okay with you?"

"It sounds lovely. What should I wear?"

"Something nice but warm. It gets cool on the water in October. We'll be inside for dinner, but even just getting on and off the boat it'll be chilly."

I had brought a pair of winter white slacks in a light wool. I took them out of my overnight bag with a soft aqua sweater. I had a black belt with a gold buckle, a gold and white silk scarf, and black leather shoes. "Will this do?"

Josh nodded appreciatively. "Very nice. Do you have a windbreaker of some sort?"

"I have a raincoat."

"Bring it," Josh commanded. "You'll probably be all right before dinner, but you'll want it walking back to the hotel." He got out his own clothes for the dinner—a pair of khaki pants, a yellow button down shirt, a camel blazer and a navy tie.

We met Joyce and Kenneth in the lobby. Joyce wore an ankle length challis skirt the color of bluebells, with a paler blue jewel neck sweater and a string of multicolored beads. Kenneth was dressed much like Josh, except that his pants and blazer were navy and his shirt a blue and cream plaid. We looked at each other and nodded.

"A very good looking crew," Kenneth observed. "Come on, we're going to be late."

I had never spent much time on the water in England. Occasionally I had taken a water taxi down the Thames but that was about all. I was learning that in New England, traveling by water was taken for granted. I would have to do more of this when I got back to London. I was loving the relaxing feel of the gentle rocking.

"It can be a lot rougher," Josh cautioned. "We're in the protected harbor here. But if you really like it, one day we can have Kenneth drop us at the Hingham ferry on his way to school, and we can do a day in Boston. People commute to Boston by water every day—that harbor is protected too."

"A few years back they experimented with having one run out of Scituate," Kenneth added, "but that route took you out into the open sea; it was too rough and they dropped the idea."

Dinner was lobster bisque, a roast duckling with wild rice, a salad of mixed greens, and a light fruit custard for dessert. It was delicious and I found myself trying to break down the bisque recipe for later duplication. We could watch the sunset through the windows, and there was music. The air was thick with romance, and I knew that my final decision was made.

By the time we got back to the hotel, though, someone had come in and opened up the cot. I disregarded it. I was not about to let a random cot opening change my mind.

"You change first," I urged Josh, having decided how I was going to present myself. "I need a few minutes."

He came out of the bathroom ten minutes later, smelling of toothpaste and wearing sweat pants and a long sleeved tee shirt. "Do you want me to take the cot?" he asked.

"Of course not. You'd never sleep a wink on that, and your leg would be as stiff as a board tomorrow," I told him. "I'm five one. You're six four. I'll take the cot. You take the bed." I waited until I saw him climb into the king bed and went into the bathroom.

I took care of what needed dealing with, brushed my teeth and hair, and spritzed on some perfume. Then I walked naked out of the bathroom.

Josh sat up straight, his eyes wide. "Jillian..."

I pulled the covers back and got into bed beside him. "I'm ready, Josh."

He swallowed hard. "Good. Because I'm very, very ready." He reached behind him and turned out the light. Then he reached for me.

Long, long after that, I fell asleep on his bare shoulder, his arms holding me, happier than I'd ever been in my entire life.

I woke up in the morning to find him propped on one elbow, looking down at me. "Have I told you recently how beautiful you are?" he greeted me.

I considered teasingly. "I believe you may have mentioned it at one point or another."

"I don't think I can mention it often enough," he breathed into my ear. We made love again before finally getting up and taking a shower together.

"Well, it's about time!" Kenneth greeted us when we finally met up with them at breakfast. "What kept you?"

"Don't answer that," Josh said to me, even as Joyce commented, "Kenneth, really!"

I felt myself turning red. "What is it you all say? I refuse to answer on the grounds that my answer might serve to incriminate me."

Josh put a protective, or possibly possessive, arm around my shoulders. "So do I."

Kenneth smirked slightly and changed the subject. "What are we going to do today?"

Bar Harbor had a lot to offer, but as it appeared to be rolling up its sidewalks in preparation for winter, I took a number of mental notes of things to do next time. I had already decided to come back for a visit next summer, if school and/or job permitted. Josh and I were going to have to have a serious conversation about our future now, I realized, but I somehow wasn't worried about it. I knew that we were meant to be together. As Lori and Joyce had both told me, that meant there would be a way.

Almost before I knew it, we were into November, and a holiday we had no equivalent for in England—Thanksgiving. I knew it was a big family gathering, but just how big it could get I didn't realize until one day when Josh raised the issue. "What are your plans?"

"Just with Adam, Lori and the kids," I said. "Adam will be home Tuesday night and will have until Monday morning home."

"Thanksgiving is really a time for big family gatherings," Josh declared. "So my aunt has asked me to extend an invitation to you, your brother and sister in law, and the children to have dinner with us. She'll call your sister in law herself later, but she asked me to start the ball rolling."

"Why, that would be lovely!" I exclaimed. "I can't speak for Lori and Adam, but I'll definitely put the invitation to them. What can we bring?"

"We'll sort out who's doing what later," Josh suggested. "Most of the Ferguson family will be there. Aunt Rosemary and Uncle Stan will be there, and my cousin Lynne and her family, and my Ferguson grandparents, Russ, Kenneth, Joyce and her parents, and maybe one or two others. You met Aunt Rosemary, Uncle Stan, and Lynne at my party over Labor Day."

"It sounds lovely," I said. "I'll mention it to Lori this evening."

Lori was delighted. "I've wanted to get to know the Aldrichs better," she said. "Debbie and I were on the Music Committee at the church together a few years back, and she seemed like a delightful person. There's never much time at choir. I'm sure Adam won't have any objection."

Adam had no objection and we made our plans to join the Aldrichs for Thanksgiving day. I still wasn't entirely clear on Thanksgiving except that it was similar to our Harvest Festivals at home. I'd heard stories about Pilgrims and Indians (apparently called Native Americans here) and all manner of other tales including Days of Mourning, and had finally just given up trying to get a straight answer. There were parades, it officially kicked off the Christmas season, and Thanksgiving weekend was a retailers' nightmare, was about the best I could figure out.

Whatever it was, though, it was fun. The day before Thanksgiving I went with Adam, Lori and the children to a farm stand to get apples and a squash. Or that's what I thought we were going for. By the time we left we had not only the apples and squash, but corn, potatoes, leeks, and other vegetables as well. We'd gone apple picking, gone on a hay ride and taken the children to pet the animals at a petting zoo. It was a wonderful day and I wish that Josh had been able to come with us.

Thanksgiving day was a bit overwhelming. I knew that Thanksgiving was a day for family but I thought it might have been easier to meet those of Josh's family that were new, or newish, to me in smaller doses, not all at once. Still, I liked all of them on sight and I had a wonderful day in the kitchen with Aunt Deborah, with Lori and Ruth Ryan occasionally sticking their heads in and asking if we were sure they couldn't help, and Josh sitting at the kitchen table acting as sous chef, chopping and paring and doing other preparatory tasks.

When we were just about finished and the cooks were getting ready to start serving, Josh stood up. "I have something I need to do before dinner," he said casually, "and I need Jillian to help me. We'll be back in just a few minutes."

"Go straight into the dining room," Aunt Deborah instructed. "We can manage without Jillian for a few minutes. She's done a lot today."

Josh took me to the archway that led into a first floor bedroom. "Don't worry, I'm not going to try anything untoward," he promised with a teasing grin. "But I did want some privacy to talk to you about this. Have a seat."

I sat down on the edge of the bed, and he sat beside me and took my hands in his. "I know this is terribly sudden," he said. "I know that we've only really known each other since July—not even quite five months. But you're only here for a few more weeks and I feel as if we have to make the most of the time we have."

He looked into my eyes. "We'll have a lot of things to work out," he warned. "But we can do it together if…Jillian, angel, will you marry me?"

I couldn't breathe.

He continued, "I can't bear the thought of your going back to England and leaving me here alone. Will you, please?"

"Oh, yes!" I exclaimed and threw myself into his arms.

He kissed me deeply. When we came up for air, he laughed exultantly. "That's all I needed to hear," he said. "We can make everything else work as long as I know you love me. And Jillian, don't worry about where we'll live. Don't forget, I've lived in England already. I love it there. I'll happily get a visa and move there with you."

I looked at him in utter joy. He laughed and kissed the tip of my nose.

"Let's go join the others," he promised. "Are you okay with telling my family tonight? Because if so, let me do it. I have a lot to say and I want to do it all at once."

"You can do it any way you want," I promised. I was still shaking with joy at the very idea of being engaged to Josh.

We joined the rest of the family at the table. Lori, on my left, looked at me. "Is everything all right?" she asked. "You look a bit flushed."

"Everything's fine," I promised. "I'll tell you about it later."

When everyone was seated, Josh took a brief look at his Uncle Scott and stood up.

"We're too big a group today to do what we sometimes do," he said. "It would take forever for us to go around a table this large and say what each of us are thankful for. But I've asked Uncle Scott if I can say a few words anyway, since this has been such a vitally important year for me and I've never in my life had more to give thanks for.

"You remember the state I was in last year. I had fallen into a depressive state, depressed and lonely, afraid I'd never make it as a musician, and just generally as unhappy as hell. My personal life was non-existent. I was trying to sell my serious music and couldn't get anyone to look at anything. If anyone had asked me, I wouldn't have been able to come up with anything I was thankful for, other than maybe the fact that I was still breathing.

"But then my life turned around. I sold several songs, began getting regular calls to play backup keyboard, and even made a music tour. The BSO agreed to premier my concerto. But most importantly, I met Jillian, and fell in love with her." He paused as there was a ripple of applause.

"Jillian has made all the difference to me. She's the one who taught me that there was still love and happiness left in the world. I hadn't really been sure of that until I had her in my life. I can't imagine life without her. I love her more than life itself, and she loves me, and just a few minutes ago, she promised to marry me."

Lori looked at me, startled. I smiled at her as Josh's family applauded for real. Josh continued, "And that's what I want to thank God for today. Thanks to all of you for letting me blather on." He sat down again. There were cheers from the assembly.

Scott stood up and gave the blessing. Then the meal began.

"Is he telling the truth? Are you engaged?" Lori asked urgently.

"Yes, he just asked me a couple of minutes ago. We haven't made any definite plans yet—we haven't had time." I looked earnestly at her. "I know it's sudden. I know we haven't known each other very long. But we love each other, we really do."

"So you're going to stay in the US?" Adam asked from a couple seats down, leaning forward to hear.

I shook my head. "That's not certain yet. He's talking about moving to England."

Adam shook his head. "You know that Dad is going to blow his stack."

"I don't care," I surprised myself by saying. Never before had I deliberately gone against my parents' wishes directly. Even my failure to confront them with my desire to go to culinary school had only to do with not wanting a confrontation. "I love Josh and he loves me and we want to be together forever."

Lori smiled at me and patted my hand. "Don't worry, dear. Adam and I will tell your father that we approve of Josh."

After dinner we were surrounded by family and friends. I repeated that we had no immediate plans. We had a lot of decisions to make, I realized. We would have to decide in which country to be married, for one. My family was mostly in England, as were Pammie and Siobhan and Maggie. I couldn't imagine getting married without having them as bridesmaids. And yet, I'd rather like to have Joyce and maybe Rachel too. And with the exception of a grandfather I had yet to meet, all of Josh's family was here in America. Two ceremonies? One in each country? I shivered deliciously at the idea of all the fun it was going to be.

On the other hand, it was already late November. In only a few weeks I would be returning to England, and Josh would be staying here. I knew now that we would eventually be together forever, but the idea of leaving him even temporarily was painful. I wondered how long it would take for him to get a visa, and how we would manage the fact that we had significant family in both countries. I pushed that thought aside. Today I didn't want there to be anything but joy.

"You can't marry him," someone said at my elbow. I turned around. Sure enough, it was Randi.

"I can't?" I asked politely. "May I ask why not?"

"You're British!" Randi's tone suggested insurmountable difficulties with this concept.

"Yes, I know," I commented. "But thank you for telling me anyway. In what way does my being British preclude my marrying Josh? Has your Congress passed a law outlawing international marriages?"

"Well, you live in London." Randi had regained control of her voice and was back to her old, patronizing self. "And Josh lives in Boston."

"You still haven't told me anything I don't know," I pointed out. "Or why these facts are incompatible with my marrying him."

"Don't you see, dear?" Randi was at her most annoying. "You live in two different countries. How can you marry?"

I could be patronizing too, if I put my mind to it. "Obviously, one of us will have to move. I would have thought that a university graduate would be able to figure that out. Oh, that's right, you didn't go to university and dropped out of college, didn't you?"

As I'd hoped, Randi was temporarily distracted. "My certification is just as valid as your university degree!"

"I'm sure it is, dear." We had more "dear" in this conversation than there were cervidae in all of Scotland, I suspected.

"But that's irrelevant to the question," she hastily backtracked. "Are you saying that you'll stay here in the US?"

"Either that, or Josh will move to England. We—he and I—will decide that in the next few days."

"Obviously, Josh will have to stay here," Randi decreed. "All his doctors are here, and his family, and his support system."

"I'll be his family," I pointed out. "And it isn't that long ago that he was living in England anyway; I'm quite sure his doctors there haven't thrown his records away. We're quite well educated in England, or hadn't you heard? I'm sure the medical care there is sufficient to deal with Josh's issues."

"I don't think you quite understand…" Randi started, but I cut her off.

"No, Randi, it's you who doesn't understand. Josh and I don't need your permission to marry. I'm so sorry you ever got the impression that we did. I'm not sure how you got that idea but now that you understand quite clearly that we don't, we can put the whole issue to bed." I turned on my heel and walked away from her, not headed for anywhere in particular but determined not to let her spoil this moment for me.

Over the next couple of weeks Josh and I began to make plans. After studying the requirements for a marriage visa, we recognized that it would be far easier for me to move to the US, than for him to move to the UK. As an ex-patriot citizen, I could simply pull up stakes and move. Josh would have far more difficulty. "But I want to try," he insisted. "We want the right to live in either country. I can easily pass the financial requirements—we just need to convince the UK government that it's not a marriage of convenience."

To that end we decided not to marry immediately. We were luckier than many couples in our situation; Josh had the money for us to go back and forth across the ocean, visiting each other. Still, we would miss each other badly until we were able to be together forever.

Josh decided that he would come to London shortly after the first of the year and stay until March. I would make whatever arrangements necessary to leave what school or job I was in by then to come to the US for the premier of Josh's concerto. After that, we would regroup.

Adam, Lori and the children rotated Christmas. One year, they went to England; the next to Colorado to see Lori's family; the third year they stayed home. This was an England year, so it simply made sense for me to fly over with them. After Christmas, they would return and I would stay.

I had to admit Christmas, and the end of my time in the US, was coming when we went to see Kaitlyn and Joyce, in a community theatre production of The Nutcracker. Kaitlyn was adorable as one of the children at the party; Joyce was breathtaking as the Sugar Plum Fairy.

"I'm going to dance Clara when I'm bigger," Kaitlyn announced after the performance.

Joyce hugged her. "You certainly will, sweetheart. And when you're a grown up lady, you'll dance the Sugar Plum Fairy too."

"Joyce, you were just splendid," I told her. "I'm truly impressed."

Joyce blushed. "Thank you."

Kenneth didn't say a word but he took his fiancée's hand and squeezed it; the expression on his face said it all. I would be surprised if the two of them managed a two year wait to marry—I would spend most of that time expecting a call to come to the wedding.

Joyce gave a small dinner for the four of us, Rachel and Will, the night before we left. She refused to let me help this time. "You're a guest for this one," she announced. "I want to show you how much I've learned from you."

She wisely kept it simple; a roast beef, roasted potatoes, green peas, with an easy mushroom soup to start and an ice cream parfait for dessert. She did remarkably well for a beginner and we had a good time. We all exchanged Christmas gifts early, and I was touched at the thought and care that had gone into the choices. I had bought from Harrods's online store for my friends; a cosmetics bag for Joyce to take to the theatre with her; a shopper bag for Rachel; an iPad cover for Will; a wallet for Kenneth; a watch for Josh. In return I had received a diamond pendant from Josh; a Vera Bradley overnight travel bag from Joyce; a matching handbag from Rachel; a wallet and cell phone cover, still matching, from Kenneth that he admitted he had had Joyce choose. Will had broken the pattern and had a gift card for me that would allow me to load up my Kindle with books for traveling.

"You're all such good friends," I told them. "I hope you'll all come visit me."

At the end of the evening, before Josh walked me home, I hugged my hostess. "We'll keep in touch," I promised. "I have your mobile and your email and your Skype. And I'll see you in April."

"I'm going to miss you," she declared. "Come back soon."

Rachel refused to say goodbye. "I'm going to spend my spring break in London visiting my grandfather," she told me. "I just decided. I'll see you then."

Kenneth hugged me. "You're family now," he told me. "I won't say goodbye either. We'll see each other soon."

At the door, Josh reached into his pocket and pulled out two small boxes. "I want to give you a couple of extra Christmas presents now," he told me. He handed me the first of the two.

"Do I open it now?" I looked at him teasingly. My heart was breaking at the thought of leaving him, but I didn't want to ruin the little time we had left.

"Of course you do." He smiled down at me.

I unwrapped the red ribbon and folded back the holly paper. Inside the box that was revealed was a miniature of the type we had seen in Washington, of the two of us together. The artist had painted us with me standing in front of Josh, a head and shoulders shot of us both. I looked up at him in bewilderment.

"I got the one of you about two weeks after we got back home," he said. "I know I told you, I remember showing it to you. What I didn't tell you was that I was so pleased with it that I sent him a couple pictures of myself, and some more of you, and asked him to do this one of the two of us. He did two of them, so we each have one."

"I love it," I whispered. "This will be my talisman of the entire trip, not just the week in DC."

"I hope this will be too." He handed me the second box. I opened it to find a sapphire and diamond ring set in white gold.

"Try it on," he urged.

I handed it to him. "I want you to put it on me." I held out my left hand and he slid the ring onto my engagement finger. It fit perfectly. I threw myself into his arms.

"I love you," I told his shoulder.

He kissed me. "It won't be long, angel. Only a few weeks and we'll be together again."

Scott Aldrich offered to drive us to the airport in his van rather than have Adam pay for parking his car, or taking the children on public transportation. Josh went to the airport with us. "I won't be able to go to the gate with you," he told me, "but it will be a little longer that we have together. And I'll be there, angel, in just a few weeks."

Tactfully, Lori and Adam took the children up to the gate, leaving Josh and me at the security point together. "I hate to let you go," he said to me softly, as I nestled against him for the last time. "But we'll be together soon. I have my reservation for January 21st, and we'll be together for two months." He kissed me for a long, long time as we soaked up the feel of each other. "You do what you think best about telling your folks about us," he told me. "I'll go by your guidance. And love, text me when you arrive in London, just so I know you're safe."

"I will. And I'll Skype you when I get to my parents' house." I held tightly to him. "I'll see you soon."

"Goodbye, angel." Josh kissed me once more and let me go.

"Are you all right?" Lori asked me quietly when I joined them at the gate.

"I will be," I said. "Just, don't talk to me right now." I was fighting tears. Tactfully, my brother and sister in law let me be.

We landed at Gatwick where Adam decided to hire a car. "I just can't face taking the children on a four-hour train trip where we'll have to change trains twice," he said. "This will be much easier in the long run."

It was mid-afternoon by the time we reached my parents' home in Devon. For a couple of hours it was chaos as family members greeted other members they hadn't seen in months, if not years. My brother Nick, his wife Mariel and their children had come down from their home in the Lake District; my brother Phil and his wife Anna, who lived in St. John's Wood, were due the following day. Since three years previously Phil and Anna had gone to Anna's family, it was the first time in six years we'd all been together. Already I was missing Josh desperately. It would have seemed so right to have him here with the rest of the family. Yet at the same time it felt good to be back in England. It was almost as if something deep inside me stretched, relaxed and settled down comfortably with a sigh of, "Ah, home."

Suddenly I remembered that I had promised to contact him. I'd have to wait to have a conversation with him but I quickly pulled out my phone and sent a quick message. "Arrived in Devon safely. All kinds of family around. Will talk to you later when things quiet down." I pressed Send just as my sister in law Mariel came over. She was expecting their third child in March and I was delighted to see how happy she looked.

"Is everything all right?" she asked. "You're looking a little sober for a happy holiday occasion."

"I'm just missing Josh," I said softly. "I haven't told Mum and Dad yet, but we're engaged; we're going to be married. I'm wanting him terribly just now."

Mariel hugged me. "I want to hear all about him," she told me. "Why don't we sit down and you can tell me about him. Do you have his picture?"

I opened my picture files and showed her. "He's very handsome," Mariel commented. "And…oh my word, he's so big!"

"Six foot four," I told her. "I feel very small and cherished when I'm with him."

Her smile invited me to tell her more, so I did. I must have been talking for twenty minutes when my mother came over. "What are you talking about so intently?" she asked.

"Jillian is telling me about her boyfriend," Mariel answered, with a smile that told me she would keep my confidence. I had turned my ring so that the stone was inside and it was not immediately obvious.

"Oh, yes, the nice young musician Lori told us about," my mother commented. "You're surely not going to try to keep up a long distance relationship, are you?"

"He's going to come visit next month," I told her. "And I have to make a visit in April—I'll explain to both you and Dad later. Even if I only go for a weekend."

It was not till after dinner, when the children had all been put to bed and we were sitting around the living room when I had the opportunity to raise my issues. I'd told them all about my trip and how much I'd enjoyed my stay; then I took a deep breath and looked at Adam, who smiled encouragingly. Lori made a "Go ahead" motion with her hand.

"I promised that I would make a decision about what I wanted to do going forward, and I have," I said a bit hesitantly. "In fact, there are two things I want to do, and they're not mutually exclusive. I can do both." I stopped.

"Tell us," Mariel said with a smile.

"I want to go to culinary school and open up an event planning and catering business," I said all in a breath. "I know I'll probably have to take a couple of business courses too and that's all right. But that's what I want to do. Or one thing. The other thing I want to do—Josh and I are getting married. Not for a year or so. But we're engaged."

There was silence for a moment.

"Josh is a wonderful boy. Very talented. And he loves Jillian very much," Lori finally broke the silence.

"We can talk about the culinary school idea," my dad said. "It's an option to look into. But marriage to a boy you've only known a few months? Jillian, I thought I raised you to have better sense than that."

"I love him, Dad," I said. I could feel myself tensing. "And he loves me."

"I'm sure he's a very nice boy," my mother said. "But Jillian—no. Not so soon."

"He's not a boy, he's a man," I said, a bit irritated. "And I'm an adult."

"You're very young still," my mother pointed out.

"Hold on," Adam broke in. "Dad, Mother, Jillian's grown up a lot in the last six months since she's been with us. She's not a little girl any more. She knows what she wants, and I can vouch for Josh."

"I can too," Lori agreed.

"He's coming to visit next month," I told them. "So you can meet him."

"And one thing to remember," Nick added. "Jillian is over eighteen. In fact, she's over twenty-one. She doesn't need permission to marry. She doesn't need permission to go to culinary school or to open a business of her own. I know you'd like to see her in some branch of the law, Dad, and that Mum wants to see her teaching. Can you honestly say that you think she'd be happy in those fields? That's simply not where her talents lie. Cooking and event planning is."

Adam backed him up. "She's told Lori and me about her plans, and we support her. She's not asking permission, Dad. She's making an announcement. The sooner everyone realizes that and starts helping her plan instead of telling her she can't, the better."

It was almost another hour before my parents finally admitted that they couldn't stop me from either culinary school or marriage. "We're not planning to marry immediately," I assured them. "Josh is going to apply for a visa and we're going to live in England."

My dad sighed. "All right, Jillian. We'll meet him next month. We just want you to be happy, Princess."

"I know, Dad." I accepted his hug. "We haven't decided yet which country we're going to be married in, or whether we're going to have a ceremony in each country. We know that for purposes of Josh's visa, it's better if we wait. So we have time to meet and all get acquainted first."

"Do you know which school you want to apply to?" Dad asked.

"I've really only started looking," I said. "Ideally I'd love to apply to the Cordon Bleu, but I need to do a bit more research. And the Cordon Bleu is dreadfully expensive."

"Don't worry about the cost," Dad said. "If you have a definite plan for what you want to do, I'll help you with the tuition."

"Josh said when I had my culinary diploma he'd help me with the startup costs," I said shyly.

"Does he have the money for that?" Dad said, startled.

I realized that I'd left out quite a lot of information about Josh's history. "Yes, he does. I won't go into details now—we'll give you the full history when he's here. But he's able to do that."

"He's a fine young man," Adam said firmly. "I heartily approve him as a brother in law."

Later, when I was able to get Josh on Skype, I told him about the conversation. "I couldn't believe how easily they accepted the idea of culinary school," I said. "But they're not altogether happy about our marriage."

"Of course they're not," Josh soothed. "Did you expect them to be? They've never met me, and we've really not known each other long. They'll get used to the idea."

"It'll be better when they've met you," I realized.

"Of course it will. And I'll be there in just over a month."

Part Two

I WENT BACK TO LONDON shortly after New Years', after promising Dad to do my research on culinary programs and business school classes. It was good to be home; back in the city I knew and loved, where the cars moved on the correct side of the road and I could get myself to the Underground and I could buy the brands of food and shampoo and tea I was used to. America had been a wonderful experience; I had satisfied my longing to travel, I had made good friends, and I was glad I had gone. I would miss Josh desperately until he arrived and I hoped Joyce and Kenneth would come to visit. But all in all, it was good to be home. I placed the picture Josh had bought me in DC on the wall in the sitting room and the miniature of Josh and me together on the table by my bed.

Pammie, Siobhan and Maggie had a good time teasing me about the "giant" I'd become engaged to. "How do you fit?" Pammie asked me. "He'd make three of you!"

"We manage," I said, feeling myself reddening.

"Aha!" Siobhan pointed a finger at me. "So you are doing it with him!"

I stared at her. "How did you know?"

"The unicorn that's been following you around all this time is gone," Maggie said teasingly. She patted my hand. "Seriously, Jillian love, we know you too well not to realize when something of that magnitude happens to you."

I relaxed into the familiar teasing. "Do you know how much it costs to feed a unicorn?" I asked her. "Besides, I was afraid the landlady would be raising our rent to cover the costs of the hoofmarks on the floor."

"When is he coming?" Pammie asked. "And where is he staying?"

"He's coming the third week of the month," I told her. "His grandfather lives here in London, and he'll be staying there with him."

I looked over at Maggie. "But enough about me. Are you going to let us give you a baby shower?" Maggie and Jasper were expecting their first baby in late June, just a year after their marriage.

"That would be brilliant!" Maggie exclaimed, and we started planning.

I'd been in London for a week and was deep in comparing culinary programs when my mobile phone rang with Josh's ring.

I answered it, "Good morning, love!"

"It's Deborah Aldrich, Jillian," came the answer. "Jillian, dear, I'm afraid I have some bad news."

I sat down on the edge of a chair. "What's happened?"

"It's Josh. He was rushed to the hospital this morning with a bone infection. He'll be undergoing emergency surgery later this morning to clean it out but bone infections are very serious. If they're unable to contain the infection, he could lose his leg."

I gasped. "Oh no! I'll be there as soon as I can get a flight, Aunt Deborah! What hospital is it?"

She told me. "Let me know as soon as you have your flight information, and someone will pick you up at the airport."

"I'll be there as quickly as I can get there," I promised, and closed my phone. I got my suitcase out and began throwing clothes into it, tears running down my face.

I went into the bathroom to get my toiletries and ran into Pammie in the hall. She stared at my tears. "What's happened, Jillian pet?"

I told her, and she immediately took me by the arm and marched me back into my room. "You finish packing. I'll find you a flight."

"I don't know if I have the money for a last minute, international flight!" I wailed.

"I do," Pammie said. "I've been putting money aside. So has Siobhan. Between the three of us, we'll get you to your Josh. You can pay us back later." She clicked away at my laptop. "Here you go. It's a student discount, but it's valid for alumni too, up to age 25. Be sure you have your old student ID with you. You leave at 3:00 this afternoon and you get into Boston at 5:40 pm." At my startled look she reminded me, "There's a time difference, honey." She told me the price and I sighed with relief—I could manage it.

I handed her my credit card, the one my father had given me for emergencies, and she made the reservation. "Now, let's make sure you have everything you need. You're too upset to think straight right now." She helped me re-organize my things so that I had enough for an indefinite stay and finally closed my suitcase. "Oh, honey, he'll be all right. I'll pray for him, and you know Siobhan and Maggie will too." She hugged me. "You let Josh's aunt know that you're coming, and I'll call your parents and your brother and sister in law for you."

Siobhan took me to the airport. "I'll be prayin' hard, darlin'," she promised, hugging me. "Let us know what happens."

"I will," I swore, hugging her back.

The trip was uneventful, but it seemed to me to take forever. As soon as we landed I checked my mobile and there was a text—Waiting at the baggage carousel for your flight. I got through Customs finally, made my way to the baggage claim area, and threw myself into Kenneth's arms.

He hugged me and whispered, "I'm so glad you're here." I sobbed into his shoulder until he finally set me on my feet. "He's going to be all right," he told me when I could stop crying long enough to hear him. "They got all the infection cleared out in time, and he's not going to lose his leg. He'll be in the hospital for a week or so; he'll be going home on crutches and he'll have to take big-time antibiotics for several months. But he's going to be okay."

The relief was so great that I almost fell down. Kenneth caught my arm. "Let's get your bags and I'll take you straight to the hospital," he told me. "Josh will probably still be asleep off and on; bone infections are terribly painful and he's on heavy-duty pain meds that make him drowsy. But he's been asking for you during the times he was awake."

"Did you tell him I was on my way?" I turned to the carousel and watched for my bag, with the blue and green ribbons tied to the handle.

"We told him," Kenneth assured me. "But he's not retaining anything he's told very well. Which is normal," he added quickly when I turned to look at him in horror. "That's perfectly natural when he's coming out from under anesthesia and is taking pain medication. I'll get you to him quickly. Joyce will be there when she gets out of class, and my folks are there still."

I saw my bag coming and Kenneth took it from me. "Let's go, honey."

As before, we hit rush hour traffic, but about forty minutes later Kenneth pulled into the car park. "I'll take you right to his room," he promised. "Your bags will be safe enough in the trunk." It took me a minute, in my anxiety, to recognize that he meant the boot. He led me into the building and past the desk to the lift.

Mr. and Mrs. Aldrich, Russ, Joyce, Rachel and her parents, were already there. "Jillian, honey, I'm glad you're here," Aunt Deborah said, hugging me. "Josh was asking for you."

"I had to come," I said. "I couldn't have stayed away. Kenneth said the surgery was successful?"

"We hope so," said Uncle Scott. "If we've caught this in time, and we think we have, he'll be on crutches for several months but he won't lose the leg."

"Hey," came a sleepy voice from the bed. "Don't talk about me like I'm not here."

"You're awake!" I knelt by the side of the bed and took his hand. "How are you feeling?"

"Too sleepy to tell for sure," Josh admitted. "But I'm very glad you're here."

"Of course I'm here," I soothed. "I came as soon as I could." I took his hand but it was obvious he was drifting off to sleep again. I looked at Aunt Deborah. "What happens now?"

She explained, "He'll need three months of antibiotics and three months on crutches, and then he should be right as rain."

"No worse than before," came that sleepy voice from the bed again. "As long as there are no complications, and I don't intend to complicate." He yawned hugely.

"Well, well, what's this?" A nurse stood in the doorway, hands on hips. "A convention?"

"Just family," Mrs. Aldrich said. "But we'll go out to the waiting room if we're in the way."

"Let me just check a few things," the nurse said. "Then immediate family can stay." She began a check of Josh's vital signs.

"We're all more or less immediate family," said Rachel's mother.

The nurse nodded. "That's okay with me," she confirmed. "The doctor may have other things to say when he returns."

Rachel's Dad stood up. "I think we can go now," he said. "We know that he's all right and we've seen him. I cancelled class this morning and I have a lot of papers to grade. Come on, Julia, Rachel."

Rachel hugged me. "I'm glad you're home," she said. "He'll be all right now." I was still so shaken that I didn't realize at first that she had identified America as home for me.

Her mom hugged me too. "Welcome back, dear," she said. "We'll see you soon."

They left and suddenly I felt so shaky I couldn't stand up any more. Kenneth pushed me into a chair and Joyce put a cup of hot tea into my hand.

"Take it easy," Aunt Deborah urged. "He's going to be all right. Hang onto that."

"It's after midnight Jillian's time," Uncle Scott pointed out. "She's probably exhausted."

"Thirsty…" Josh mumbled suddenly. We all started and looked at him.

"I'll get you something," Aunt Deborah promised. She left the area and came back a few minutes later with a paper cup of ice chips, which she handed to me. "Just give him a few at a time. When he's a little more awake he can have some water, but right now ice chips are better, the nurse said."

I obeyed. Josh let the ice chips melt in his mouth and smiled. "Thank you," he murmured.

The Aldrichs and I kept talking to him and stroking his hair, until he was more awake. "Now, I'm in pain," he said. "Do you think you could call the nurse back?"

Kenneth, who was closest to the door, motioned to the nurse, who came over immediately. "I bet I know what you want," she said. "I'll get your pain meds." She injected something into his IV, and a few minutes later Josh smiled in relief.

"That feels better," he said. He looked over at me. "You really are here," he said. "I thought I'd dreamed you."

"Of course I'm here," I soothed him. He squeezed my hand.

"I'm too sleepy to talk now," he said. "I feel—floaty, if you know what I mean. But I'm very glad you're here." He closed his eyes and it was clear moments later that he was asleep again.

The nurse smiled at me. "He'll be doing that for the next few days," he said. "I take it you just arrived?"

"I'm his fiancée, and I live in England," I explained. "I just came back when I got a call this afternoon about him being in hospital."

"Fiancée, and living in England. That must be very hard on both of you."

"It is. But I'll be staying with him for now." I couldn't stop a yawn.

Uncle Scott stood up. "I think we should let Josh sleep, and Jillian has had a very long day."

I wasn't about to argue. "Would someone mind driving me to my brother's house, please? Do they know what's happened?"

"They know. I called them, but your friend Pam in England had already gotten through," Joyce promised.

"But you're not going there tonight," Uncle Scott said. "You're coming back to us. We'll be going back and forth to the hospital and you'll want to be here most of the time; if you stay with us it will make things easier. I've already spoken to your brother and he's fine with it."

"And we have plenty of room," Aunt Deborah said. "That's a five-bedroom house and there's only Scott, Kenneth and me in it."

I was too exhausted to argue. I kissed Josh softly and followed my someday-to-be-in-laws back out.

It wasn't a long drive back to the Aldrich's home in Cohasset, the next town north of Scituate. I went with Kenneth, since he had my bags, and we arrived only minutes after his parents. We went in the back door into a kitchen and at Aunt Deborah's insistence I went straight to bed. "This was Josh's room when he lived here, which granted wasn't long," she said, leading me up the stairs to the first door on the left. "There's a bathroom right over here." She opened a door in the corner. "It's all for you. Kenneth has his own too, as do we in the master suite. Sleep as long as you want in the morning. We'll take you over to see Josh whenever you get up. How do you like your eggs? And are you a tea or coffee drinker?"

"Any way is fine," I said. "Scrambled, I guess. And I'm a tea drinker. Thank you so much." I yawned again. I was going to fall asleep on my feet in a minute, as much as I would have loved ask many questions about the current situation. But I was too sleepy, now that the adrenaline had crashed, to understand the answers.

Aunt Deborah smiled. "Go to sleep," she said. "I'll see you in the morning."

Left alone, I changed into my nightgown, washed my face, brushed my teeth, and fell into the inviting bed. I was asleep before I could turn the light out.

When I awoke the clock on the bedside table told me it was almost ten o'clock. I started—I had wanted to be with Josh as early as possible. I took a quick shower, scrambled into my clothes and hurried downstairs. By the sound of voices I found my way in the unfamiliar house. Kenneth and Aunt Deborah were waiting for me in the kitchen. This was more familiar—I had helped here at Thanksgiving.

"Good morning!" Aunt Deborah said cheerfully. "You missed Scott; he's already left. You'll see him again tonight. But sit down and have a cup of tea and eat something, and we'll take you over to the hospital. I'm sure you must be anxious."

"I am," I admitted, sitting down across from Kenneth. "Can I help with anything?"

"Not this morning," Deborah said, breaking eggs into a bowl and whisking them with milk. "I'm sure that during your stay I'll be able to use your help any number of times, but this morning you sit. There's tea in the yellow pot; milk and sugar on the table. Ken, get her a cup."

Kenneth agreeably got up and did so.

"I'm sure you have a thousand questions," he said. "You were too tired last night. What can we tell you?"

"Just . . . what happened?" I asked, a little desperately, pouring tea into the rose-patterned teacup.

"I don't know how much detail Josh gave you about the nature of his injuries nine years ago," Deborah said from the stove. "He had what they call a compound, comminuted fracture of the femur, which is a pretty serious break. The femur is the thigh bone; a compound fracture means an open one that breaks the skin; comminuted means the bone was shattered, to put it all into layman's terms. I'll have you sit down with his doctor to get a better understanding. But the end result is that due to the nature of this break, he's now subject to bone infections, and not even the doctors can say what triggers them. It's called osteomyelitis, and this is the second time he's been hit with it. I'll let his doctor give you the full explanation.

"A couple of days ago, Josh was complaining of pain in his bad leg. At first, he tells us, he thought he'd just twisted it or bumped into something when he wasn't paying attention. It felt like a bruise, he said. But then he noticed some redness and swelling. The pain grew worse, and he realized that he had a fever, which suggested infection. He called us, and we met him at the emergency room, where his doctor confirmed that he was having an outbreak of osteo. That was when I called you. He had the surgery to clean out the infection on an emergency basis yesterday morning and the prognosis is good. He'll be in the hospital for several days; then he'll be released on crutches. He'll be taking antibiotics for weeks, and at least at first he'll have to take them on an IV basis. You'll see more about that later." She put a plate of scrambled eggs and bacon in front of me. "But I'm afraid he won't be able to travel for a while yet."

"That's not a problem," I said, taking a bite of eggs. "We'll postpone his visit to meet my parents until he can travel safely. The main thing is that he's all right, and he's not going to lose his leg."

"Not this time," Deborah said with a sigh, sitting down next to me and pouring herself a cup of tea. "As long as he recognizes it early, like he did this time, he should be fine. But if he ever failed to realize that it was osteo, he could face amputation at some point in future. It's something of a miracle, given his initial injuries, that they were able to save his leg at all at the time of the accident."

"What triggered the infection?"

"Hard to say," Deborah admitted. "Even the doctors can't say for certain. Sometimes it's a shard of dead bone flaking off, sometimes it's a minor injury that he won't even notice, sometimes nothing we can define. But whatever causes it, the infection has to be cleaned out surgically and the dead bone, if there is dead bone and there was this time, removed."

I shuddered. "Poor Josh." I ate for a few minutes. "Aunt Deborah, I wanted to ask, what's Josh's state of mind right now?"

"I'm not sure." Deborah frowned. "He's been asleep so much of the time, what with the pain meds. And he's been missing you badly."

"I've been missing him too." I finished my breakfast. "I don't want to be rude, but could we go over now? I really, really need to see him."

"Of course." Deborah stood up. "Are you coming, Ken?"

"I'll be over later," Kenneth said. "I have a class this morning, but I'll be by when it's over."

"We'll see you then, in that case," Deborah said. "Jillian, you might want to bring some reading material—Josh is likely to be asleep a lot of the time."

"I have a Kindle in my purse," I assured her. "I don't know how much I'll be able to read it, but I have it." I followed Deborah out the door to the garage.

At the hospital, the nurses were very glad to see me. "He had a bad night," the nurse at the main station told them. "He woke up screaming twice, even with the narcotics in his system. Does he always have such bad nightmares or is it related to being in the hospital?"

"Some of each," Deborah said. "He's had nightmares since his teens, but they relate to the accident that is indirectly responsible for his being here, so it's not surprising that the nightmares would be worse while he's here. Have they been that bad recently, Jillian?"

I blushed. "Not when I was with him. He was having them once or twice a month, he told me, but that was all. Certainly not twice a night. Though he tells me he used to have them that badly. Please, may I see him?" I was beginning to feel the same anxiety I had felt on the plane.

"Of course." Deborah took me down the hall to Josh's room. As we entered, Josh appeared to be asleep but as I sat down in the chair by the bed, his eyes opened and lit up at the sight of me.

"You're here!" he exclaimed. "I thought I dreamed you."

"Of course I'm here," I said. "I was here last night, but you were quite sleepy. And you said exactly the same thing, about dreaming me."

"What took you so long?" he asked, taking my hand.

His aunt laughed softly at him. "Josh, dear, I called Jillian to tell her about your surgery slightly more than 24 hours ago. She was on another continent at the time. And she was there to see you by last night."

Josh grinned sheepishly. "I'm sorry," he said. "I don't mean to push. I've just missed you so horribly."

I leaned over and kissed him for a long time. "I missed you just a little bit, too," I told him. Then, remembering where I was, I sat back, keeping his hand in mine. "How are you feeling?".

"Lousy," he admitted. "The meds are working so I'm not in a lot of pain right now, not like it was yesterday, but it's still throbbing. And I'm still feverish, I can tell. I just feel blah, if you know what I mean."

I nodded. "I'll take care of you," I promised.

"Good." He closed his eyes. Shortly it became evident that he was asleep.

After an hour or so Deborah left, promising to return later after she'd done some errands. I was quite content to sit where I was; just being in Josh's presence, asleep or not, was enough for me just now.

I'd been there about two hours and Josh had been asleep the whole time when Randi walked in.

"Don't wake him—he had a bad night," I whispered.

"How do you know? They won't tell you anything out there." Randi looked at me with evident dislike.

I gently released Josh's hand, tucking it back under the bedclothes, and stood up. "Let's go out in the hall," I said softly. "We can talk there."

Josh's room was just across the hall from a lounge area. We took seats across from each other.

"They won't tell you anything about his condition at the desk," Randi repeated. "Was he awake earlier, to tell you about his bad night?"

I looked confused. "They told *me*," I said. "But yes, he was awake for a short time when I first got here." I was to learn later that Josh had authorized the desk to give information to his foster parents, to Kenneth and to me, but to no one else. Some kind of US privacy law.

"When did you get in? Josh was asking for you yesterday." Randi's voice was slightly accusatory.

"I got in yesterday afternoon. Aunt Deborah called me about noon my time and I was on a plane three hours later," I replied.

"So, my Aunt Deborah is your Aunt Deborah now?"

"She asked me to call her that." I looked at her. "I am marrying Josh, remember?"

"I should have thought this would have shown you that I was right before—you can't still be thinking of marrying him!"

"If you think I'd drop him because of something like this…" I was suddenly so angry I couldn't see straight. "Randi, get this straight. I am marrying Josh and there is nothing you can say or do that will stop that."

Randi looked defiantly at me. "We'll see. Josh has been pursued by gold-diggers before."

"I'm sure he has," I said very stiffly.

"So, can I see him?"

"I'm not stopping you. But he is asleep at the moment."

Randi sighed with exasperation. "I'll just have to wait until he's awake, then."

"That's up to you." I stood up and walked back to my seat by the side of Josh's bed, taking his hand and stroking it. Randi followed me, and sat back down on the other side.

About half an hour of silence later, she stood back up. "I'll come back when he's awake," she announced, and strode back out without saying goodbye.

"Best of British to you," I muttered under my breath. Only a few minutes later, though, I had to grin as Josh's eyelids flickered and he woke up.

"I see you're back with the living," I commented.

"Isn't the beautiful princess supposed to kiss the sleeping prince?" Josh complained sleepily.

I considered. "I do believe you have that slightly backwards," I pointed out. "But since only the prince is sleeping, perhaps we could stretch a point."

Josh was in hospital for a week, and I stayed with Uncle Scott and Aunt Deborah the entire time. It just seemed to make so much more sense, when all of us would be going back and forth to see Josh. Adam came to pick me up one evening and took me back to have dinner with them and I tried to explain to Kaitlyn why I wasn't living at her house any more.

"In a year or so I'm going to marry Mr. Whittaker, only he wants you to call him Uncle Josh," I told her. "He's in hospital now and I need to be with him to make all the bad hurty things feel better."

'When you get married, can I be a flower girl?" Kaitlyn was easily distracted. "My friend Lisa was a flower girl when her Aunt Laura got married."

I hugged her. "Of course you can."

I had already realized that this was going to delay our marriage still longer. We needed to show the visa immigration folks that it was a marriage of love and not for immigration purposes; for that we would need to show a pattern of back and forth visits, and for friends and family on both sides to see us together. Josh would not be able to travel for months. I wondered if it wouldn't be easier for us to simply marry in the US and for me to stay there. I'd talk about it with him.

But Josh was adamant. "We might want to consider that at some point in future, angel, but if I heal properly this shouldn't delay our plans more than a few months. Unless you decide you *want* to live in the US, in which case all you have to do is say so. I'm comfortable in either country, so you decide where you want to live and I'll be happy."

When Josh was released from hospital he agreed to go back to the Aldrich's home for the first few days. "Just to get used to walking on crutches again," he insisted. "Then Jillian and I will go back to my place."

Uncle Scott and Aunt Deborah seemed to take it for granted that Josh and I would share a room. I was a bit concerned how my family would feel but since Adam was unlikely to inquire or care about the sleeping arrangements, I didn't worry too much about it. I was trying to remember that I was an adult and didn't need permission to do what I wanted to do, but it was an effort. I still had some growing up to do, I realized. It suddenly occurred to me that perhaps this was one reason my parents were still opposed to our marriage.

Once I was certain that Josh was all right, I decided there was no reason to postpone my educational plans. I found a well-regarded culinary school in Boston that I could reach by train and I signed up for a certificate program.

"Now I just have to worry about how to get to the train," I said ruefully to Josh as I reviewed the materials the school had sent me. "Kenneth's school times don't coincide with mine so I can't go in and out with him, and Joyce goes off in a different direction entirely."

"Not a problem," Josh said. "I'm going to rent you a car so you can get back and forth."

"Can you? Don't you need a drivers license to hire a car?"

"Oh, I have one," Josh explained. "I'd gotten my license in Connecticut just before the accident and I kept it up." His eyes shadowed and I quickly changed the focus of the conversation.

"Won't that be terribly expensive?"

"Not terribly. A smaller car will be easier for you to manage than that big one of your brother's and they don't cost much at all. It won't run more than a few hundred dollars a month to rent it for the length of your course. Or, for that matter, for your stay here. I don't want you driving into Boston; not alone. That's not easy even when you're used to it. But a car will give you freedom to go back and forth to the train station, or to the T if necessary, quite easily."

I was still not quite sure how to compare the American monetary system against the one I was used to so I didn't argue any further. I'd done enough driving during my first visit to be reasonably confident but I was glad that I was able to go into the city by train and didn't have to drive there.

I enjoyed my classes. They were three a week, two full days and one half day per week, for ten weeks. The initial few classes were fairly basic for someone trained by my mother, but I understood the importance of building blocks. I made casual friends with three classmates; Samantha, Brittany and Sabrina. Sabrina and Samantha lived on the South Shore as well and we sometimes took the train together.

It was Sabrina who asked me one day as we were walking out after class, "Are you going to watch the Olympics, Jillian?"

I'd almost forgotten about the Olympics in the rush of returning to the US, settling into Josh's condo with him, and signing up for class. "I love the Olympics. Particularly the winter Olympics. When does it start again?"

"The Opening Ceremonies are tomorrow," Samantha told me, turning towards the Red Line.

"Who will you be cheering for? England or the US?" Brittany teased.

"Great Britain, of course," I retorted. "Then for Canada and any other colonial nations. Then the US."

"You're living in the US now," Samantha said with a straight face. "You're obligated to cheer for the US."

"And so I will. For all the silver and bronze medals." I knew there was very little chance of my country winning much of anything, but I was still loyal to Britain.

When I got home that afternoon, Josh came to greet me, balancing on his crutches. "Hello, angel. Have a good day?"

"Very good. I'm really enjoying the class." I returned his kiss. "How are you doing?"

Josh would be taking antibiotics through a picc line for several weeks, before transitioning over to taking them by mouth. He was having a daily visit from the visiting nurse in the area to change the surgical dressings and to teach his aunts and me how to give him his medication. But he was moving around on the crutches fairly easily within his restrictions, was in much less pain, and had many close family members who would drop in at a moment's notice if needed.

"Just fine. Aunt Deb came over and made sure I got lunch, and I made some real progress on my new piece. She started dinner since I knew you wouldn't be back till late and I can't really do much on these crutches."

"Sounds fine. You'll be able to do more later when you get some strength back and are allowed to be up longer." I kissed him lightly. "What is dinner tonight, anyway?"

"Her famous beef stroganoff and noodles."

"Oh, that's so good!" I dropped into a chair. "When will it be ready?"

"She said to tell you to add the sour cream at 6:45, and start the noodles at about the same time."

"I can do that. Do you want a green salad with it?"

Josh nodded. "But only if you're not too tired. I know your full days are long days for you."

"I'm not too tired to make a salad. Just let me change my clothes.

Over dinner Josh said a bit diffidently, "Would you mind if a bunch of my cousins came over tomorrow to watch the Olympics?"

"Of course not! Your family is always welcome. What time are they coming? Should I plan food? I don't have class tomorrow afternoon so I'll have plenty of time."

"I thought maybe we could have a lot of stuff that we could eat just sitting around the living room. Finger food, maybe soups. Set up a buffet, would that work?"

"Sounds like fun." I got up and began to clear. "How many?"

"Probably about a half dozen or so, maybe a few more depending on who brings significant others. Kenneth and Joyce, of course. Russ and Colleen. Rachel and her boyfriend, I forget his name."

"Will."

"Will, that sounds right. Maybe Melissa. I know Lynne will be busy with the kids. The only thing is... Josh looked a bit uncomfortable. "I think Randi will be here."

I was silent for a minute. I was on excellent terms with all Josh's family except Randi, who so clearly resented my very existence that it was hard to stay polite sometimes. "I'll behave myself if she will."

"I can't ask more than that." Josh stood up, balanced on his crutches, and came over to the counter between the kitchen and the sitting room. "Angel, I know Randi's difficult. Try to ignore her when possible. I don't know what her problem is but I'll speak to her if you say so."

"No, that would only make it worse. Then she could be a martyr. I'll try to ignore her. You go sit down—you know you're not supposed to be on your feet any more than necessary yet."

The next day I prepared a large pot of shrimp bisque, several platters of roast beef, ham and cheese, chicken and egg mayonnaise finger sandwiches, and a slow cooker full of cocktail meatballs in tomato sauce. Realizing that I had something of a reputation to keep up, I also came up with several different starters.

"You don't need to go crazy," Josh said lazily from the sitting room. "It's only family. I'd help if I were allowed to spend more time on my feet, but it's just a family supper. I can promise you that everyone coming will bring something as well."

"Don't you know by now that this is fun for me?" I came over and kissed him lightly. "You wouldn't want to stop my having fun, would you?"

Josh groaned slightly. "I'm going to put on thirty pounds eating your good cooking without getting any exercise."

"Then you'll just have to watch what you eat." I touched his cheek and went back to filling tiny croissants with different fillings for dessert.

Family started arriving at about 6:30. Kenneth and Joyce were the first to arrive. "I brought contributions," Kenneth announced, showing me bags of crisps and pretzels. Joyce had a bowl of spinach and artichoke dip. It looked good, too. I tasted it. It was good.

"I'm learning," she announced proudly.

I thanked them and pulled out bowls for the crisps and pretzels, setting them around the room with small dishes of Joyce's dip. "Help yourself to any food that appeals to you," I told them. "There's wine, beer and soda in the fridge and there'll be coffee in just a mo." I had more beer, wine and soda in the pantry as I was still not used to the size of refrigerators in America and had over-estimated what it would hold.

Russ and Colleen arrived then, bearing hard cider and a bottle of wine. Rachel provided cocktail shrimp and sauce; Will had an aluminum foil covered plate of brownies which he admitted his sister had made. Josh's cousins Amanda and Melissa, on the Whittaker side, brought chicken wings and deviled eggs respectively; Amanda's fiancé Connor contributed to the beer collection.

Randi, however, had apparently decided to beat me at my own game. Or try to. She had brought a bowl of salsa with corn crisps, something called Buffalo wings which to me looked and smelled dreadful, a cheese ball and crackers, a crab dip, what looked like a very large sandwich on a roll chopped into slices, and potato skins.

"Why, thank you, Randi!" I said with forced cheer, though I was seething inside. "Let me just set this all up." I took it into the kitchen with me and began to set her contribution up on serving trays while she took a seat next to Josh on the couch. Joyce came out to help me.

"She's just trying to irritate you," my friend told me quietly. "Don't let her. Besides, you've already won."

"I didn't even know it was a competition," I pointed out.

"You watch. With the possible exception of the crab dip, most of her things will still be here at the end of the evening, and yours will all be gone." Joyce looked at my plates of miniature pizzas, chicken and shrimp skewers, bruschetta, stuffed mushrooms and multiple dips.

Amanda came out too. "Do you need any help, Jillian? Can I pass things, or anything?"

"I thought we'd just set everything out and let everyone help themselves whenever they were hungry," I said. "Other than Josh, of course. He can't balance a plate and his crutches too. Maybe you could put a plate together for him while I finish up here?"

"Of course, I'd be happy to." Amanda patted my shoulder and whispered, "Don't let Randi bother you," as she poured Josh a mug of soup and prepared him a plate of starters. I noticed that she took particular care to see that his plate was filled with things that I had made, ignoring Randi's offerings.

After Amanda served Josh, there was a general rush for the food before the ceremonies started. As Joyce had indicated, Randi's contributions did not appear to be general favorites. I took care to seat myself next to Josh while Randi was getting her food. She glared at me, waiting for me to get up and give her, her seat back, but I smiled blandly at her and remained seated. I'd eat later.

"Can I get you anything more?" Randi asked sweetly when Josh put down an empty plate.

"Thanks, Randi," Josh agreed. "Could you get me a couple of Jillian's little pizzas, a few shrimp skewers, and two ham and cheese sandwiches please?"

Randi didn't look happy but she got him what he asked for—up to a point. "There are no more ham and cheese," she reported. "I brought you some buffalo wings, instead."

"Thank you," Josh repeated, "but I'm actually not terribly fond of buffalo wings. Why don't you give those to Russ—you know he loves them—and give me a couple of Amanda's wings instead? Or if there are still roast beef sandwiches, those will be fine too."

"Sure, I'll take them," Russ agreed. "I love buffalo chicken. Hand them over."

Joyce winked at me. I got up myself at that point and served myself, returning to my seat just in time to regain the seat beside Josh. He put his arm around me and pulled me close. We watched the ceremonies for a while. When there was about an hour left to go, I served dessert, including Will's brownies, and coffee.

"This was fun," Melissa, the youngest of Josh's cousins, said as they left. "We should do it again."

"Sure!" Josh insisted. "Please do. Any night. Every night. We'll feed you, won't we, Jillian?"

"Any night you like," I said. "Please, feel free to come by any night at all. Or during the day! I have a class two and a half days a week but I know Josh would like the company."

I was already planning soups, stews and starters that could be made ahead and frozen for nights that I was getting home late. Mondays and Wednesday I didn't get home till almost 6:30. But Tuesdays, Thursdays and Friday afternoons, I had plenty of time to prepare meals for an unknown number of people. Amanda proved to be interested in cooking herself so we arranged for her to come in on my class days and set up things that I'd gotten ready ahead.

"Don't worry about Randi," Amanda told me when she and I were preparing things the following week. "I don't know what's gotten into her since Josh has been sick but she's always been a little goofy over him. She resents it any time he's dating someone. Now that he's engaged to be married, she's gone a little off the deep end. Ignore her."

"She's making herself pretty hard to ignore," I grumbled, but I accepted her advice.

Josh's cousins, and a couple of friends, accepted our blanket invitation and dropped by to watch the Olympics any time there was a hockey game. I didn't understand hockey very well but luckily Joyce insisted on watching figure skating and Alpine skiing as well, so there was something I could watch in which I wasn't totally confused.

It was during a skating competition one evening that a British skater took the lead. I cheered heartily for my home country. Josh put his arm around me. "Congratulations!" he said cheerfully. "Of course, you realize that I'll be cheering for the US competition during the long program, right?"

"I wouldn't have it any other way." This was quite a familiar situation to me, with my mother and me being British and my Dad American. While he used to tease me that I was his daughter too and should join him in cheering on Team USA, he never really expected me to cheer for the US over the UK, and Josh didn't either.

"I have to cheer for the US," Joyce told me, "but I'll cheer for England after that."

Kenneth nodded agreement, pointing to his cheek to signify that his mouth was full of chili. After he swallowed, he added, "I'll second that."

Randi looked thoroughly annoyed. "It doesn't matter," she said snidely. "Your skater hasn't got a prayer, Jill. It's only a fluke that he's gotten this far."

"Jillian, not Jill," Josh corrected her. "And don't be rude."

"I'm just being truthful," Randi said with a toss of her head. "How many medals has the US won, and how many British?"

"Torvill and Dean," Joyce suggested, getting up and serving herself a second bowl of chili. "I shouldn't be eating this, but it's just too good," she told me. "I'll just lengthen my work out tomorrow."

"Yes, against how many others? And that was how long ago? Face it, Jill, your country simply doesn't have what it takes."

"So I suppose we should just award all the gold medals to the US and not bother with the Games?" I asked. "I'd heard that Americans had an entitlement mentality, but that takes the biscuit, that does!"

"I never said that. Don't be childish." Randi looked inordinately pleased at having put me into what she thought was a bad position.

"Jillian's not the one being childish," Russ corrected her from his corner. "You're being incredibly rude, little sister."

"I'm being...." Randi sounded incredulous.

"Yes, you are," Josh chimed in. "And you need to stop it, right now."

Seeing that she was in the minority, Randi subsided, at least for the moment. But she started back up again when a British luger ran off the track. "I'm telling you, Jill, your countrymen are just not sports oriented."

I wasn't certain if I was going to explode or cry. I was no sportswoman myself, and my only interest in sports as a spectator was generally during the Olympics. But I had my share of national pride and the overwhelming attitude I was sensing from not only Randi, but my classmates and random conversations I overheard on the train was that the US was entitled to the lion's share of medals, just because they were the US. Not everyone; Josh and the rest of his cousins had been appreciative of good work done by other nations, and I knew that Samantha, Sabrina and Brittany had only been teasing me in a good-natured sense. I was pleased to accept it as such. But Randi's complete disrespect of my homeland—and my feelings—was getting under my skin more than a little bit.

"Randi, cut it out," Kenneth said wearily. "It's really getting old listening to you snipe at Jillian. Who, I will remind you, is American on her dad's side even if she did grow up in England."

"When she acknowledges US superiority, I'll stop," Randi declared.

Josh started to respond but I stopped him. "You want an acknowledgement of superiority? Fine, I will grant you that as far as sports are concerned, the US has certainly won a higher share of Olympic medals than the UK. But I don't know why you need my acknowledgement for that—anyone who can count is able to figure that one out.

"But as far as superiority in other areas are concerned, let me point out to you that the British Parliament never had to shut down the government because the House of Commons and the House of Lords were too busy playing "You Can't Make Me" to get together on a budget."

Kenneth began to clap, softly. Russ did likewise. But I wasn't finished. "We Brits abolished slavery a good generation or more before you lot did, and we didn't have to fight a war to do it—we just signed a paper. Your workers have no protection at all—someone can be fired because the day of the week, ends in Y. And shall we talk about gun laws? When was the last time you heard about a workplace or school shooting in the UK, Miranda?" Now that just might be childish. But if she was going to call me by the abbreviation of my name that I didn't like, I could call her by her full name, which she didn't.

Randi started to interrupt me but I kept going. "What percentage of the world's resources does America consume? A bit more than their fair share, or haven't you heard? Where do you all stand, world-wide, on education? And please by all means, explain to me what a first class job your country does with health care costs and efficiency, not to mention access? Sweet flaming Nora, the sheer and utter arrogance of you lot, only some of present company excluded! And if you want to discuss superiority, Miranda, I very strongly suggest that you consider the subject of etiquette towards visitors to your country before you begin!"

"Jeff Daniels, eat your heart out," Russ murmured as I stormed out of the room and slammed the bedroom door behind me.

I sat down on the edge of the bed and buried my face in my hands. A few minutes later I heard the door open and someone came in, sitting down beside me.

"Are you all right?" Kenneth's voice asked.

I looked up in astonishment. "Why…" I stopped.

"Why isn't Josh in here?" Kenneth finished for me. "He wanted to be. Russ and I practically had to tie him to the chair to keep him out." He touched my hand. "He's consoling himself by taking Randi apart, bone by bone. Meanwhile, I have some things to tell you that Josh would find very painful to hear. That's why I'm in here and not him." He smiled affectionately. "Don't worry. I'm not going to bawl you out."

"Is Josh mad at me?"

"Josh is absolutely furious—at Randi. The rest of us are all in awe of you. No one is mad at you. Even Randi—she's too stunned to be angry. She will be later, but don't let that bother you."

"I'm so sorry . . ."

"Don't be," Kenneth said firmly. "That was wonderful. It's about time you told Randi where to put it, the way she's been sniping at you for so long." He sighed. "Jillian, how much do you know about what happened to Josh?"

"I know that he was injured in the accident that killed his parents and sister, and that he was in hospital for a long time before he went to live with you and your parents in England." I thought. "You all went home after a year and he stayed to finish uni, living with your grandparents."

"That's more or less correct. Alex and Diana are—were—Diana has since passed on but Alex is still with us. Anyway, they're Josh's grandparents but not mine, technically. In practice, the Fergusons and the Whittakers have all grown up in each other's pockets and claim each other as relatives."

"The way you and Josh call each other brother, even though you're cousins?" I couldn't help asking.

"That started when Josh came to live with us," Kenneth explained. "I look like both my parents, but Josh is all Whittaker and doesn't look at all like any of us."

"You and he have the same smile," I pointed out.

He shared that smile with me. "People would ask us, are you brothers, and if we said no, we're cousins, we had to explain how it was that Josh was living with us. At the time, that was far too painful to talk about much. So we decided that we were foster brothers and began answering, Yes. It was hard for Josh—he resisted a bit because it seemed disloyal to Uncle Dan and Aunt Beth. But part of him desperately needed acknowledgement that he still belonged to a family."

"That must have been so hard for all of you," I whispered.

"It was." He hesitated. "Now that *you're* going to be a member of the family," he finally said, "there are some things I want to tell you that you should know, and that might help you make sense of what's going on with Randi. I'm not defending her—she's been incredibly rude and there's no excuse for how she's been treating you. But so you can maybe understand."

I looked at him silently, waiting for him to go on.

"The whole family was devastated," he told me. "You know what a close family we are, and suddenly we'd lost three family members at once. It was days before we knew for certain that Josh was not going to lose his leg, and weeks before we knew that he would walk again. And his leg wasn't his only injury—it was only the worst one. He'd also broken his shoulder and a few other lesser fractures, and had a bad concussion. It was the leg that took so long, though. He was in the hospital for close to a year, and when he finally came home, we were only a few months from a move to England for my dad's job. We were going to be gone a year, and we asked Josh if he wanted to come with us, or stay in Scituate with Aunt Rosemary or his Uncle James Whittaker. That's Amanda's and Melissa's family. I think Rachel's parents had offered too, but I'm not sure about that."

"And he opted to go to England," I said softly.

Kenneth nodded. "I think if Mom and Dad hadn't invited him to come, he would have asked to go. I remember him pleading with them to move up the departure—he wanted so badly to be free from the memories. He saw his folks and Janey everywhere he looked." He suddenly chuckled slightly. "And here I was pleading with them to put it off as long as possible; I couldn't bear the thought of leaving Joyce."

"You were already in love with her?" I asked sympathetically, momentarily distracted.

"I've been in love with Joyce since I was five," Kenneth declared firmly. "I didn't know how I was going to get through a year without seeing her. But for Josh it was a lifeline."

He stood up and began pacing. "Somehow it escaped Randi that Josh was going to England until only a short time before we left. She thought we were staying with the original plan—to have Josh live with her family while we were gone. He had finished high school while he was in the hospital, almost a term early since he had so much time to study. He'd applied to music schools in both countries just to hedge his bets, and was accepted everywhere he applied, so he had his choice. I don't know why she thought he'd decided to go to school in Boston, but she did. She had—something of a tantrum when she found out she was wrong. It was rather embarrassing."

He sat down again, in a chair across from me. "England was really good for Josh. It was so good for him to be in a new place. Since his whole old life was gone, it helped to be somewhere new to start the new one, he said."

"Josh said something once about Connecticut...?" I ventured.

Kenneth looked surprised. "We really have all assumed you knew things, haven't we? When Josh was just entering high school, Uncle Dan got a new job in Connecticut and they moved. Connecticut isn't too far away, though, as you learned when we went to Mystic in the fall, and about once a month they'd come up for a visit and spend a weekend with us or another member of the family. They were driving back to Connecticut after one of those visits when the accident happened."

"How dreadful," I whispered.

"Anyway," Kenneth continued, "Randi and Josh had always been close friends. I was in England with Josh and could see him improve. He found a therapist that he really liked that was able to help him make the adjustment. He had a girlfriend. He was angry, really, really angry at life, but the therapist said that was healthy as long as he learned how to manage it, and he was. Then our year was up and Mom and Dad and I went home. The senior Whittakers had moved to

England a couple of years earlier and Josh moved in with them for the rest of his music school course. By that time he'd made the adjustment and moved back to the US for grad school. Randi had only seen him once or twice in three years, just for short Christmas visits."

"I'd have thought she would be happy to see him so improved," I pointed out.

"Randi has always been very good at living in the past," Kenneth replied. "She seemed determined to continue to see Josh as broken and needing protection. Make no mistake, kiddo, Josh is still broken. You haven't seen it yet, but every so often he lapses."

"Josh told me," I admitted.

"The rest of us can see how much he's improved most of the time. Jillian, it's really a miracle that he didn't lapse with this outbreak of osteo, and it's probably due to him being so happy with you. He had the first outbreak not long after he first got back to the US, and he backslid a bit, and I think that's why Randi never really saw the new improved Josh. In her mind, he never really improved at all while he was over there, and she is absolutely terrified that he's going to lose ground if he moves back."

"Do you think so?"

"Heck, no. I think it's the best possible idea. I'll miss him, of course. Whatever relationship we have genetically, he's still my big brother and always will be." He stood up again. "But he is so happy with you, and England was so good for him before, I can't imagine wishing that away from him."

I stood up too. "So Randi sees me as the threat that's going to hurt Josh, and she's trying to push me away?"

"I'm no psychologist, but that's what it looks like to me."

There was a light tap on the door, and to my response Joyce poked her head in. "Josh sent me in to ask if Jillian is all right, and to tell you that Randi has gone home."

"I'm all right." I looked at Kenneth. "Are we done?"

He put a hand on my shoulder. "Yes, future sister in law, we're done."

We went back out into the sitting room. Josh and Russ were attempting to explain to Amanda and Connor, who had evidently just arrived, what had happened. I sat down next to Josh and he put an immediate arm around me.

"Are you all right?" he asked with obvious concern.

"I'm all right. I'm sorry I blew up."

"No need for you to be sorry," Russ told me from his corner. "My sweet little sister has been informed that she is not welcome back here until she has apologized to you. And I think she's being let off entirely too easily."

"I was thinking that I was being rude," I admitted. "After all, as one of my classmates teasingly reminded me, I am in the US now. And as Russ or someone pointed out, I am American on my dad's side."

"You've been here long enough to know what you're talking about, though," Russ said. "I've never lived abroad the way Josh and Ken have. I'd be interested in hearing more about how the US is viewed by Europeans. Could we talk about that sometime?"

"I can't speak for the French, or the Germans, or the Italians," I warned. "I wouldn't even presume to speak for the other nations that make up Great Britain. But I can talk about England."

"I wish you would," Amanda spoke for the first time. "I've visited there but I wouldn't say I really know what it would be like to live there."

"There are a lot of differences," I acknowledged. "Some of them are just—cosmetic, if you know what I mean. We have different brand names and different foods and different TV shows, although you import some of ours and we import some of yours. But those aren't the important things. That's just the visible stuff."

"So tell us some of the less visible stuff," Joyce encouraged with a smile. "I've never even visited England. I want to. But I haven't yet."

I thought carefully. "Russ asked about the attitude of the English toward Americans. It's something in the manner of a tolerant parent to a mischievous child. A bit amused, a bit protective. You're a very important ally, and you gender a lot of respect. But at the same time, we find your antics a bit amusing."

Josh tightened his arm around me.

Russ looked thoughtful. "Tell me some of the other things you find different."

"There are some things I think the UK could learn from the US, and vice versa," I said. "And there are some things that I think could go both ways. For example, there's no such animal as freedom of the press in the UK."

Kenneth looked astonished. "I was only a kid when I was over there. I didn't realize that."

Russ, the broadcast engineer, looked horrified. "That's terrible."

"Is it?" I asked. "Before he was captured, you don't think Osama bin Laden watched CNN? Or Saddam Hussein, in the Gulf War? You don't think that sometimes a bit of reticence is due? Just because you can say it, does that mean you should? Americans have a deep-rooted need to know everything about everything, but quite often it's either not a good idea to have the information in the public eye, or simply none of your business."

"She's got a point," Connor said.

"On the other hand, much of our journalism is of the tabloid style," I admitted. "So it cuts both ways."

"What else?" Kenneth asked. "No, I'm really interested."

"What about 9-11?" Russ said at the same time.

"That was a terrible thing that never should have happened," I said. "I was only a little girl, but I remember it vividly. It was the only time I ever saw my father cry. You truly did have the sympathy of the whole world, give or take a few countries in the Middle East." I paused, not sure how to say the rest.

"But . . ." Kenneth prompted.

"But we Brits are a hardy lot," I said. "We survived the Blitz, and even I can remember IRA bombings in London, as well as a few by Islamists. We learned to take it in stride, whereas for you all the entire world stopped. The sympathy, support and anger on your behalf was real. But I'd be lying if I said there wasn't even a small faction that wondered if it wasn't just as well for the world's policeman to get a small taste of what so many of the rest of the world's countries had already been living with for years."

"That's fair," Russ acknowledged.

"Are you saying we deserved it?" Connor challenged, leaning forward.

"Oh, no, not at all!" I insisted. "No one deserves that. I don't think anyone, anywhere, except supporters of the bombers themselves thought that. Just that you'd finally lost your virginity. You'd all been living in a bubble—you were the great and powerful United States; no one could attack you. But there's no immunity out there. And if there is, it probably belongs to the Swiss."

"Okay, I see what you mean." Connor relaxed back into his chair.

"I haven't been here long enough to know whether you've assumed the position of the world's law enforcer; if it's been forced upon you; or, what is most likely, if it's a little of both," I continued. "But that is truly a no-win position for you all. If you take any kind of action against, whatever it is, then you're interfering in other nations' affairs. But if you don't, then you're a rich and powerful nation turning your back. There's no way for you to win. And that is truly sad." I smiled at them all, a bit teasingly. "The UK knew what they were doing when they got out of the super-power business."

"Were you a political science major?" Russ asked admiringly.

I'd been in the US long enough to translate that. "No. History. But my brother, the one who lives here in Scituate, read political science at Cambridge before he came here for his post graduate degree, and another of my brothers is a solicitor. And remember that my father worked for the Embassy for years."

Joyce smiled shyly at me. "Are there good things about Americans?"

I returned her smile. "Lots of them. Americans are the most generous people in the world, I think. They're honest, and they're sincere. When there's a disaster, Americans are the first to offer aid, and it comes from not just the government, but individuals as well."

"What should we be addressing that we're not?" Josh asked me.

I was ready for the answer to this one after living with Adam and his family for several months. "Education. You lot rank shockingly low on the global scale. That's not just my opinion, that's documented—you can look it up. The end result is that as a nation—don't take this personally, it doesn't apply to any of you specifically—America is about as informed as the average adolescent, and you—again, as a nation, not you all specifically—make your decisions on the same level as a teenager would."

"Now hold on," Connor said. "More Americans have a college education than . . .

I held up a hand. "I'm not talking about how much education you have. I'm talking about the quality of education you receive. You have some exceptional schools in this country—really world class. Right here in Boston you have some schools anyone anywhere in the world would be honored to attend. But the average American doesn't get to attend those schools. Right? And tell me honestly—overall, how good is the high school education that most Americans get?"

Connor was silent.

We talked for over an hour, exchanging views and opinions. I felt that we all understood each other's positions much better by the end. Finally everyone left Josh and me alone. I sighed as I returned to the couch after seeing them out the door.

"Was I out of line?" I asked him, snuggling into his comforting arm.

He shook his head. "No, angel, you had every right to get upset and I told her so. She's been nothing but rude to you every time we've gotten together. I don't understand it, but then I'm a guy; I guess there are girls' undercurrents that I'm not picking up from what Joyce said."

"What did Joyce say?" I demanded, sitting up and looking at him.

He looked astonished. "Something about how I shouldn't worry about it, it was a girl thing."

I relaxed, realizing that I didn't need to be concerned about Joyce or Kenneth. They had been nothing but supportive. Josh held me close.

"You know I love you more than anyone, don't you?" he reminded me. "You are the most important person in my life. If Randi can't deal with that, it's her problem."

I didn't press the issue.

By the middle of March, Josh's leg was improving. He was still on crutches, but he was taking his antibiotics by mouth now and no longer needed the daily visit from the visiting nurse. If he continued to improve at the rate he was going, he would progress from crutches to a cane just about the time that the BSO played his concerto at the end of April. After that, I assumed, I would be returning to the UK and we would plan for him to visit me over the summer.

Josh's cell phone rang one afternoon, and he answered it. "Talk to me," he commanded. "Hey, little brother, that's great! I'm proud of you. Wouldn't miss it." He dug into his pocket and pulled out a notebook. He scribbled something inside it and put it back in his pocket. "Formal? Okay, sounds good." He handed me the phone. "Joyce wants to talk to you."

"Isn't it exciting?" Joyce demanded. "You will come, won't you?"

"What happened?" I asked, leaning back in my chair. This sounded like it was going to be a long conversation. "I couldn't tell what was going on from Josh's end."

"Kenneth won an award!" Joyce squealed. "He entered a contest for all architecture students in New England, New York, Pennsylvania, and a few other states too—the whole Northeast and I think Mid-Atlantic."

I decided to ask Josh later what this encompassed.

"And he won! We don't know if he won the grand prize or a lesser prize, only that he won something. But there's an awards dinner for all the winning students and their families, and it's even in Boston, which is nice although it would have been fun to go to New York or Philadelphia. Anyway, Kenneth has to tell them how many family members are coming and he wants you and Josh to come—you will, won't you?"

I looked at Josh and he nodded at me. "Of course we will. Tell Kenneth congratulations. Does Josh have the where and when?"

Josh nodded again and pointed to his pocket.

"Jillian, please come dress shopping with me," Joyce pleaded. "I want to find something really spectacular to wear that night, and you always have such beautiful clothes."

"I'd love to, when?" Since I had been mentally reviewing my wardrobe as we'd been talking, I thought perhaps I would join her in buying something new.

We arranged a date and time and I hung up the phone. Josh was beaming.

"I'm so proud of my kid brother," he repeated. "He used to hang over my dad's shoulder when he was working, when he was only three.

He's always said he was going to be an architect just like his Uncle Dan." His face shadowed for a moment and I knew he was missing his father.

"Joyce and I are going to go shopping for new dresses," I told him to distract him. "Any particular color that's your favorite?"

"You look lovely in every color," Josh told me. That wasn't much help.

I had expected that Rachel would be joining us. After all, she'd been Joyce's best friend since they were children, and she was tangentially related to Kenneth anyway. I was not expecting Randi to be there. But then, Randi was Kenneth's cousin too, more closely related than Rachel. I sighed and got into Joyce's little blue car.

"Have you been to the Braintree mall before, Jillian?" Joyce asked as she started up.

"I don't think so," I replied. "We went to the Hanover mall before Christmas, but I don't remember the Braintree one."

"You'll love it," Randi said enthusiastically.

I wasn't so sure. I wasn't a big fan of malls even in the UK. But this was Joyce's trip and if she wanted to go to the mall, so be it.

"Do you want long or short?" Rachel asked.

"I'm open to either," Joyce said thoughtfully. "I'm limited on colors because of my hair and skin—I don't want to start out with any other pre-determined limits."

I saw what she meant. Because of her copper hair and milky skin, most reds, pinks, oranges, some yellows, blacks and most whites would be right off her list. Not that there weren't still plenty of blues, greens, aquas and lavenders that she could wear.

"Let's try Nordstrom's first," Joyce suggested, pulling into the car park fifteen or so minutes later.

"That's expensive," Randi warned, getting out of the car.

"I know," Joyce said cheerfully, "but my dad gave me some extra money for the dress and shoes if I need them since it's such a special occasion."

"Do you have Nordstrom's in England, Jillian?" Rachel asked.

I shook my head as Joyce locked the car and we started for the store. "I've ordered from them online but we don't have any of their stores."

"What about Lord and Taylor?" Joyce asked. "If I don't find something at Nordstrom's that's where I want to go next."

"You're going for the classic look then?" Randi determined.

Joyce nodded. "I think that suits me best. Do you have them, Jillian?"

"No," I admitted. "We don't have any of the stores you have as anchors here."

We entered Nordstrom's and found the right department. Randi found what she was looking for almost immediately—a short, sapphire blue lace dress with a V neck and cap sleeves. It didn't take me long to find something either, but I was quite pleased with the tea length black, turquoise and gold abstract print. Joyce, however, was harder to please.

We'd gone through Nordstrom's, Lord and Taylor and Macy's and now were checking the various specialty shops. "I'll bet this is a lot of fun for you, Jill," Randi said suddenly. "You don't get to do this kind of shopping in England, do you?"

"What makes you think so?" I asked, feeling the now-familiar anger at her snobbish assumptions beginning to stir.

She looked surprised. "Well, you just said you didn't have these big anchor stores. Do you have malls at all?"

"Oh, yes, we have malls. It may surprise you to know, though, Miranda, that not everyone enjoys mall shopping."

She scowled. "I don't like being called Miranda."

"And I don't like being called Jill. My name is Jillian." I looked her square in the eye. "Why should I stand for being called an abbreviation that I don't like and never use, if you don't have to stand for being called by your full name?"

"Sauce for the goose," Rachel chimed in. Randi glared at her.

"As for shopping," I continued, "I said we didn't have *these* anchor stores. We have others, though. Perhaps you've heard of Marks and Spencer? Or Selfridges?"

"I wouldn't be surprised if England had stores that we'd never heard of in the US," continued Rachel, who seemed to be enjoying herself hugely.

"Debenhams?" I offered. "House of Fraser? Sainsbury? John Lewis? British Home Stores?"

Randi looked blank. "I've never heard of any of them, except maybe Sainsbury, and I associate them with sausages."

"They began as a grocer's," I informed her, "but they're much more than that now. As you would know if you knew as much about British stores as you expect me to know about American ones."

"It's not that I expect you to know about them," Randi attempted. "It's just that…that…"

"That you expect her to be impressed by the American stores," Rachel finished for her.

"There are those of us who are not impressed with consumerism for consumerism's sake," I informed Randi. "I'm sure it's all very nice to have such a display of excess, but some of us remember what the man said—Less is More."

"But are your stores as completes as these?" Randi continued to insist.

"I'm sure the good folk who run Harrods will just roll over and die once they've seen photos of the Braintree Mall," I said scornfully.

At that Randi seemed to collapse. "I am sorry, Jill...ah, Jillian," she said, in a seemingly sincere voice. "I don't know why I keep forgetting that you lived in London. For some reason I keep thinking of you living in a small village."

"*You* live in a small fishing village," I pointed out. "But you can get into the city to shop. And I'm not quite sure I'd classify Braintree as a city. Boston, yes. Braintree, no."

"You're right," Randi admitted. "I'm sorry, Jillian. I don't know what I was thinking." But I could hear the syrup behind the words.

"I don't think you were thinking at all," Joyce said. "And frankly, Randi, Jillian isn't the only one who's sick of it." She turned to me. "And you. How many times did we tell you just to ignore her?"

"I'm sorry, Joyce. This is your day. I didn't mean to spoil your trip."

Joyce shrugged. She was clearly annoyed but I wasn't sure with which of us. "You didn't. But Randi, it seems to me, looking at it from Jillian's eyes, that you typify what's wrong with the US."

Randi looked astonished. "Me?"

"Yes, you. You've made it abundantly clear that in your mind, England is a third-world country that must be awed and amazed at the glory that is the US. And that nothing England has to offer could ever match what we have here. Well, I've never even been to England; I'm a loyal American, but I know that's not true. No wonder Americans have such a bad name abroad if they behave the way you've been!"

"I never...is that really how I've been coming across?"

"Oh, please," Rachel commented. "Don't give us the innocence act now. You know perfectly well what you've been doing, and you've been doing it on purpose. I've known you my whole life, Randi, and you can't fool me even if you can fool Jillian and Joyce. Though I don't think you're fooling them, either. Give it up. You've been trying to put Jillian into a bad light and a bad position because you're jealous of her place in Josh's life. Your family knows that even if you refuse to admit it to yourself."

"Please, stop!" I said, surprising even myself. "There are other shoppers staring at us. If we have to do this, let's do it later. But we don't have to do this on my account. I know I started it, but please, let's finish it."

"Agreed," Randi said hastily. "Maybe Jillian and I can talk later. But she's right that this is not the time. Let's find Joyce her dress."

We did, about half an hour later. It was short, with multiple chiffon skirts, and a halter style top. The mint green color did marvelous things to her hair and eyes and skin.

"Silver shoes?" she asked, whirling around and letting the skirts settle around her.

"No, gold," Randi and I said in unison. We looked at each other and she smiled a little. After a moment, I smiled back.

"Gold shoes and a gold purse," I said. "You're going to look absolutely lovely."

Joyce beamed. "I'm so proud of Kenneth," she said. "He's going to use the design that won, whatever he won, as part of his graduation project."

"What was his design?"

"His graduation project is to design a green, eco-friendly home," Joyce explained. "For the competition he entered the kitchen design. It's wonderful; he's used recycled materials for the countertops and the sink, and the kitchen has a wood-burning fireplace with a brick oven that can be used for cooking, and all kinds of wonderful ideas."

"It sounds wonderful," I said. I had always wanted a brick oven. "I can't wait to see it."

"Let's find Joyce some shoes," Randi insisted. "And a purse. I want to hear about Kenneth's design too, but maybe when we're done shopping."

When we had completed Joyce's outfit, right down to the dangling earrings and choker necklace, we retired to a Starbuck's for coffee. Seated at the table with our paper cups in front of us, I looked at Joyce.

"Tell me more about Kenneth's design," I requested.

Joyce happily described her fiancé's vision in detail. Built in compost bins with biodegradable liners; recycled materials; it sounded as if Kenneth had considered every detail. I hoped there would be a model available to see during the dinner. I loved model kitchens. When Joyce had run out of things to say about the kitchen design, Randi looked at me.

"Are you going to be here for Josh's premier?" she asked.

" I wouldn't miss that for anything," I declared. "I won't be going back to England before that, no matter what happens."

"When are you going back?" Rachel asked, sipping her mocha.

"I'm not sure yet. Not before Josh is off crutches, and not before his premier," I promised. "We haven't really discussed it yet."

"I think Josh is expecting you to stay indefinitely," Randi warned me.

If that were true, Josh and I needed to have a talk. "Well, I am staying indefinitely, in the sense that we haven't set a date for me to go back home," I pointed out. "I will definitely be here until his premier, and I will definitely be here as long as he's on crutches. When he graduates to a cane, he and I will discuss it."

It was none of Randi's business, was what I hoped to get across to her. She subsided, and we talked about other things.

That night at home I went online and looked up malls. The Braintree Mall, though not quite making America's top ten malls in size, was very slightly larger than the largest mall the UK had to offer. Since I wasn't sure if that supported Randi's point or mine, I decided to leave the entire topic alone.

Kenneth's awards dinner came three weeks later. He had placed third, which I could see in his expressive dark eyes was something of a disappointment, but still netted him what Josh assured me was a significant amount of scholarship money. His advisor, Walter Conroy, came over to join us after dinner and the ceremony, when we were still congratulating him over coffee.

Kenneth introduced us all and Mr. Conroy sat down in a chair that Owen Sawyer, Lynne's husband, pulled over for him. "You've got a very talented young man here," Mr. Conroy told the Aldrichs'. "There's no question that his interests lie in design rather than the engineering aspect, but I expect him to go far."

Joyce beamed with delight at hearing her Kenneth praised. Kenneth himself reddened and Aunt Debbie and Uncle Scott looked pleased.

"Thank you, sir," Kenneth responded. "I'd like to open my own design firm someday. Once I'm properly licensed, of course."

Mr. Conroy looked at him with approval. "I think you'll do very well."

"Kenneth's second major was structural engineering," Uncle Scott objected.

"Dad, I took that major because I *knew* I wasn't as good at it," Kenneth pointed out. "Uncle Dan had been teaching me design since I was about three. I've always known I could do that part."

"Uncle Dan?" Mr. Conroy asked.

"My godfather," Kenneth answered after a moment. "He's the one who first got me interested in architecture."

"Is he here?" Mr. Conroy looked around.

After an awkward pause, Aunt Debbie answered, "My sister and brother in law were killed in an accident about ten years ago."

"Oh, I'm sorry," Mr. Conroy said.

That was when it hit me. This would be the ten-year anniversary of the accident. Josh's concert was in late April, which was also approximately when his doctor expected him to be able to discard the crutches in favor of a cane. The accident had happened in May. Perhaps I should consider staying a little longer than I'd initially anticipated. Josh would need me. Inwardly I sighed. I loved Josh desperately and I loved his family. But I had now been in the States for the better part of a year and I was homesick. Still, I couldn't leave him when he needed me, and he would need me for this. Anniversaries were hard.

I realized I'd lost the thread of the conversation going on around me and brought my attention back to the present.

One night at the beginning of April, I was up to my elbows in tomatoes and basil leaves when I heard the buzzer that someone was requesting entry. I called out to Josh, who pulled himself out of the music long enough to respond. He came back to the kitchen a moment later, looking a little puzzled.

"He says his name is Pete Chapman, and that you probably don't remember him but that he's an old friend of your dad's, and he knew you when you were a little girl," he reported. "He'd like just a couple minutes of our time. I let him in; he's on the way up."

"I vaguely remember the name," I admitted, dropping my paring knife and going to the sink to wash my hands. "I can't really say I remember him, though. Did he say what this was about?"

"No, only that he wanted to talk to us both."

There was a knock on the door and with a confused look at Josh, I went to answer it.

"Jillian? I'm Pete Chapman. I'd have known you anywhere; you look just as you did when you were five, only taller. Do you remember me at all?"

"I do now that I see you," I said, smiling and shaking hands. "This is my fiancé, Josh Whittaker."

The two men shook hands and I led them into the living room. "You worked with my dad, and you and Mrs. Chapman used to come to dinner. How is she?" I indicated that we should all sit down.

"Susan's very well, and she sends her regards. How are Mark and Phillipa?"

"Quite well. I'll be sure to tell them that I saw you. Can I get you some coffee?"

"That would be great, thanks." Mr. Chapman smiled. "Black, please."

It only took me a moment to get three cups of coffee and bring them back.

"How are your brothers?" Mr. Chapman asked.

"They're all well, all married. Phil is a lawyer in London; Nick is a software engineer in the Lake District. Adam teaches political science at university. He and Lori have three children; Kaitlyn, Jeremy and Beth. Nick and Mariel also have three; Michael, Violet and Dylan. Dylan's just a few weeks old—I haven't even seen him yet. Mum and Dad went up to take care of the other two for a couple weeks. Phil and Anna don't have any children." I took a deep breath.

There was a pause. Josh coughed. "Is there something wrong, sir?"

"Call me Pete, please."

"Yes, sir. Is there something wrong, Pete?"

Pete looked at me with an unreadable expression. "First, I want you to know that I didn't realize you were here until quite recently, or I'd have contacted you to say hello sooner. I keep in sporadic touch with your dad but it wasn't until I got the Christmas card from them that I knew you had been in the US, let alone that you'd returned."

"That's all right," I said curiously. "Dad didn't mention that you were in the Boston area, either."

"I left the State Department some years ago," Pete explained. "For the last ten years or so I've been with what is now called the ICE."

I looked at him, a bit startled. I had no idea where this was going.

He smiled at me again. "A few weeks ago, a member of my staff received a rather odd report. A non-profit agency that takes reports of illegal aliens and fraudulent marriages had an anonymous tip claiming that you were in the country illegally."

Josh slammed his fist into his thigh and swore, almost under his breath but not quite. Pete looked over at him.

"Does that say something to you, Josh? I can call you Josh, can't I?"

"Of course you can, sir. Yes, that says something to me. What happened?"

"The agency is required by law, once the report is made, to submit it to ICE," Pete admitted. "The report came to my staff member. An individual, anonymous report is a very low priority for our office so it sat on his desk for a while, but he did eventually run a routine criminal check just to be sure there was nothing we should be taking further. He was rather surprised to learn not just that you were legal—we get quite a few reports on folks who turn out to be legal—but you had qualified for a diplomatic passport while your dad was with State. That was sufficiently unusual so that he mentioned it to me, and I recognized your name. I didn't let him know that, of course.

"Your presence in the US is quite legal, naturally. Your father registered your birth with the Embassy when you were born, just as he did your brothers. You are unquestionably a US citizen, with every right to be here. While some of my higher-ups would frown at my saying this, you are also a British citizen. That does not change your rights as an American. There isn't any issue for my office to take up. But I did call your father."

"You called...." I half stood in panic.

"I didn't tell him anything about the report," Pete assured her. "I made it sound as if I was just checking in to say hi, but was able to confirm with him that you were engaged to an American and living in the Boston area temporarily."

"Then why…" I stopped. I was completely numb. That Randi would go so far as to try to get me thrown out of the country….

"Why am I here at all?" Pete reached across and gave my hand a fatherly pat. "Two reasons. First, to see if you had any ideas why someone would make such an easily disproved report."

"Oh, I know why," Josh said grimly.

"I do too," I admitted. "Josh's cousin—she doesn't like me very much." I held onto my coffee mug with both hands, as if the warmth offered some kind of protection. Josh put an arm around me, and that felt much better.

"Is it really necessary to pursue it?" Josh asked. "It's a family matter. I promise to put a scare into her that she won't forget in a hurry."

"Pursue what?" Pete asked. "My office has already filed the report in the Take No Action file, I was never official notified of it, and anyway, I was never here."

I sighed with relief.

"The second reason, of course, was just to touch base with you; I haven't seen you in so many years and I wanted to meet Josh. Maybe the two of you, and maybe your brother and sister in law, could come to dinner some evening? I know Susan would love to see you all grown up. You were such a pretty little girl."

"She still is," Josh said, giving me a one-armed hug. "I don't know what I'd do without her."

"I don't like to ask but…" Pete looked at his crutches.

"I had surgery on my leg in January," Josh explained without going into detail. "That's why Jillian flew back here, instead of my flying to England for a few months."

"You have the time to travel overseas for months?" Pete looked curious.

"I'm a self-employed musician," Josh explained.

"Oh, that's right. Mark mentioned that. You're a composer, aren't you?"

"A very good one," I said shyly. "He's having a piece premiered by the BSO."

"Oh, yes, your piano concerto," Pete said. "Mark mentioned that too. Susan and I have tickets. We're looking forward to hearing it." He stood up. "I'll leave you to your family matters. Susan will call you about dinner, Jillian. Thanks for the coffee."

I went with him to the door and saw him out, then returned to Josh. He sighed.

"What am I going to do about Randi?"

"I know what I'd like to do with her," I grumbled, deflating all over again at the realization that Randi hated me enough to try to get me deported.

"So would I." Josh sat down on the sofa and pulled me into his lap. "I'm trying to think what would hurt the worst, if I were to call and tear strips out of her, or for us to completely ignore the whole thing."

"Josh—don't tell the rest of the family what she did," I requested, laying my head back on his shoulder.

He shook his head. "I won't. No point upsetting everyone. But I am going to make sure she hears about this." He picked up the phone and dialed.

"Randi? Josh. We just heard today. It's the oddest thing; someone filed an anonymous report with the government claiming Jillian is in the country illegally. Of course it took ICE about a minute and a half to disprove it; after all, her Dad is State Department and she has a US passport. She's a dual citizen—she has every right to be in the US. The fellow from ICE was ripping mad—if he ever finds out who filed that false report he's going to press charges—whoever it was could end up in jail. You don't have any ideas, do you, Miranda Rose?"

He listened for a minute. "No, I didn't think you would. Be sure to let me know if you think of anyone—we'll tell the guy from ICE so whoever did such a reprehensible thing can get what's coming to them. Of course, it goes without saying that if I ever have evidence of it, I'll break both her arms and all ten fingers before I drop her in a vat of boiling oil. Which is nothing compared to what I would have done to her if Jillian had had to so much as submit to an interview. Comprende? Good. Bye, Randi. See you at Aunt Rosie's tomorrow."

He ended the call and put it back in its charger. "That should take care of that," he announced. "Oh, she knows I know, love, if you'd heard the change in her voice when I told her there was potential jail time, you'd know that. Jillian? Oh, angel, don't cry."

Suddenly it was all more than I could take. "Why does she hate me so much?" I sobbed into Josh's comforting shoulder. "What did I ever do to her?"

"I don't know, love," he soothed, rubbing his face in my hair. "But don't worry about it. We'll be back in London soon and you won't have to deal with her. Right now I'm so angry with her that I don't care if I ever see her again."

"She's your family," I protested.

"Yes, but that doesn't give her the right to try to hurt you." Josh stroked my hair and back. "I'll talk to her again tomorrow, but you won't have to be there."

"Is it really a crime?" I wanted to know, snuggling into his shoulder for comfort.

Josh shrugged. "Who knows? If it isn't, it should be. But if she doesn't have any issues with lying to the government, I don't have any issues with lying about the potential consequences." He kissed my cheek. "Don't worry about it, angel."

The following day the Ferguson side of the family gathered for Stan's birthday. After dinner, Josh crooked a finger at Randi and said, "Follow me, cousin," in a tone that brooked no argument.

"Is something wrong?" Randi said innocently, following him to Stan's study. I followed. I knew Josh had said I didn't need to be there, but I couldn't let him fight my battles.

"You know damned well there is, and you know damned well what it is," Josh growled, shutting the door behind us. He pointed to a chair. "Sit."

"You sound like Kenneth when he's mad." Randi tried to make light of it, but she sat. I sat too, across from her. Josh had told me that Kenneth got mad about once every five years but when he did, the entire family ran for cover. Josh sounded even madder than that. He did not sit.

"I'm madder than Kenneth ever thought of being," Josh informed her, standing over her. "Right now I'm so angry that I don't even know what to say to you. So instead, you tell me—what in holy Hades were you thinking? And don't you dare tell me you don't know what I'm talking about."

"But I don't . . ." Randi started to say, but the look on Josh's face stopped her. "I'm sorry."

"Sorry doesn't even come close to cutting it," Josh said grimly. "Sorry isn't worth damn squat today. Sorry is an insult after what you tried to do. How dare you? What in hell were you thinking? What do you think gives you the right to control my life?"

I broke in. "Josh, you don't have to do this," I said. "This is my fight. I can't let you fight it for me." I stood up, took hold of Josh's hand and squeezed it.

"It's mine too," Josh told her. "I'm the one she apparently thinks is so feeble-minded that I can't make a move without her supervision. She tried to do a terrible thing to you, angel, but she's not blameless with regards to me, either." He backed up and sat down on the arm of my chair. I sat back down, continuing to hold his hand in a solidarity move.

"I don't think you're feeble-minded . . ." Randi started, but a look from Josh stopped her.

"Are you seriously going to try to tell me that you didn't take this step in an attempt to prevent me from going to England with Jillian?"

"Yes, but not because you're feeble-minded!" Randi cried. "Just vulnerable. I don't want you alone when she . . . I mean, if she eventually leaves you."

"I see. I'm such a pathetic loser that no woman will stay with me for long." Josh gave her a look of disgust. "It's nice to finally know what you really think of me." He stood up. "If you want to talk to her, angel, go ahead. I've heard enough." He looked once more at Randi. "Since I'm such a sad character that I'll lose every woman I'm with, you don't have to be with me either. I haven't said anything yet to the rest of the family about what you tried to do, and Jillian has asked me not to, so I won't. However, beyond the bounds of all-family gatherings, you are no longer welcome in my home. I'll pretend in front of the aunts and uncles that everything is fine, but you and I will both know that it isn't, and it won't be for a long, long while. I might be able to forgive you some day, but that day isn't now. Jillian, love, I'll see you later."

The door shut behind him. My gaze caught Randi's and held it. In my anger it took everything I had not to look away, but I eventually had the satisfaction of seeing Randi look down.

"Well?" I demanded.

"Josh hates me now," Randi said in a whisper. "Just like you've always hated me. It's all your fault."

"No. It's not." I was firm on that. "I came here wanting to be friends with all Josh's relatives. But from the very first time you and I met, you had already decided that I wasn't good enough for Josh. You'd made up your mind before you even met me that I was a gold-digger; that was your word. You weren't even polite about it, even if you stopped short of accusing me of it outright. You knew that I was legally in the country. I wasn't trying to marry an American citizen so that I could stay in this country—I can stay in this country if I want to whether I'm married to a US citizen or not. The fact is, I *don't* want to—I have a life that I love in the UK. If Josh wanted to live here, that would be one thing—I'd be happy to relocate here if that was what he wanted. It was Josh's choice to live in the UK and his decision for us to live there. What's more, and both Aunt Debbie and Aunt Rosemary agree with me on this, that may even be what turns out to be better for him; to be somewhere where he can make new memories instead of being mired in the old ones."

I stopped to breathe, with one part of my mind utterly astonished to hear myself talking to Randi this way. I took a deep breath and continued before Randi could say anything, "So don't tell me it's my fault. It's not my fault. I don't hate you—I feel very sorry for you. You've let your world get so very small; I can't hate you, I can only pity you. But you don't care what I feel about you; you only care what Josh feels. And yes, he probably does hate you, at least for now. That's your doing. It's not mine."

"I never wanted him to hate me," Randi whispered.

"No, you just wanted me out of his life," I said bitterly. "Tell me, Randi, who would be good enough for Josh? What girl would meet your standards and expectations of a suitable wife for Josh?"

"I just want him to have someone who loves him." Randi still was not speaking above a whisper, her eyes on the ground.

"And when did you get your Silks? Who made you the Queen's Counsel, deciding who loved him enough to satisfy you? Why are you the one who gets to say if I love him enough or not?"

Randi had no answer to that. It was my turn to stand up.

"You're pathetic." I started out the door, but Randi stopped me. "Jillian—wait."

I turned. Randi didn't say anything else.

"I'm waiting," I reminded her.

"How can I make this right?" Randi asked in a low voice.

All in a minute it hit me so powerfully that I couldn't believe that I'd never seen it before. "You're in love with him."

Randi looked at her, shocked. "He's my first cousin!"

"That makes him off-limits, I grant you," I acknowledged, "but it doesn't mean you're not in love with him. It's the only thing that makes sense, Randi, unless you're just causing trouble for the sake of causing trouble. And somehow, that doesn't feel like what you're doing. You're doing it for a reason, even if you don't know what the reason is."

"I love him." It was clearly the first time she'd ever admitted it to herself. "I love him in a way I shouldn't love my first cousin. I wanted him for myself, and I knew I couldn't have him. I was being a dog in the manger; if I can't have him, no one else can either."

"Finally the truth," I said with satisfaction. "Now we're getting somewhere."

"I'm so ashamed," Randi whispered.

"Look at me," I ordered. "No, don't look at the ground. Look at me!"

With obvious reluctance, Randi did.

"Understand this. I am Josh's fiancée. I'm going to be his wife. I love him and he loves me. That is not going to change, none of it. He and I together will make the decision as to where we live and for now, that decision is that we will live in the UK after we're married. If we ever decide to live in the US we will make that decision together with no input from you. I asked Josh not to tell the rest of the family what has happened and he has agreed. The last thing I want is to be even the inadvertent cause of a rift in the Ferguson family. But I won't do it again. The next time you take it upon yourself to try to manipulate either his life or mine, all bets are off. I think I can persuade Josh to forgive you, if and when I decide to do so. But when and whether I do depends on you and your behavior from now on. Is that clearly understood?"

"I get it, I get it. I'm at your mercy. The rest of the family would never forgive me, either, so do your worst."

"I'm not out to hurt you, Randi," I pointed out. "That's your line of country. As long as you stop trying to interfere in Josh's and my relationship, I have no reason to do anything. Just leave us alone."

The door opened and Kenneth poked his head in. "Aunt Rosemary sent me to get you," he said. "Dessert and coffee are on the table."

"We'll be right there," I promised. I looked at Randi. "Are we through?"

Randi nodded. "I'll behave."

"See that you do."

Time passed quickly and before I knew it, my class was over, Josh was off the crutches and using a cane, and it was the week before his concert. Josh was on the phone when I came into the flat one afternoon, after buying a few necessities. He held a finger to his lips as he listened, so I simply blew him a kiss and started putting my purchases away.

"Yes," he was saying. "We could... when?" He listened. "Certainly. We'd love to. Thank you very much; we'll see you then."

"Who was that?" I asked. "Which aunt wants us to come for dinner?" I tossed him a box of tea, which he deftly caught. "Could you put that in the cupboard, please?"

"Sure." He walked to the cupboard but instead of putting the tea inside, he stood in front of it, tossing the box up and down. He appeared distracted.

"Josh?" I prompted.

"Sorry." He put the box away and turned to face me. "That was Gregory James, the pianist, on the phone. He wants us come to his Boston condo this afternoon. He says he's very excited about my music and wants to discuss my concerto with me!"

I had never seen Josh so elated. "That's wonderful!" I exclaimed. "When?"

"He said we should come to their condo around four." Josh was practically bouncing with delight. "I'm so glad I'm off the crutches."

I did my best to finish unpacking my groceries, but it was hard with Josh tripping over himself in his excitement. "I'm so glad, my love."

Somehow, I managed to finish unpacking and putting away the few items I had bought, shooing Josh out of the kitchen and telling him to play the piano to get into a musical mood. I wondered what one wore to meet a minor celebrity, who was likely to be a major celebrity within a few years.

I finally dressed in a pair of winter white slacks and a blue-green tunic sweater with a gold thread. I added some jewelry to dress it up a bit and slid my feet into low heeled blue pumps. Josh had also dressed up slightly, wearing khakis instead of jeans, with a dark red shirt. I drove us to the train station—we would have to be returning the car Josh had hired for me soon but for now it was handy to have.

When we got to Boston he called for a taxi; it wasn't a long walk but even with his cane, it would be too much for his weak leg so soon.

I stared when the driver let us off. The building was right on the water and I could only imagine the view. I stopped and stared some more.

"Come on," Josh urged.

I realized how eager he was to meet the pianist who would premier his work, and thus essentially usher Josh into his career as a classical composer. "Of course," I said, smiling, and took his hand as we walked into the lobby.

The door was opening as we got off the elevator. "Joshua?" called the man in the doorway, with an enormous grin. "We're down here."

"Josh," Josh corrected, following the welcoming gesture. "This is my fiancée, Jillian Munroe."

"Josh," their host repeated, shaking Josh's hand and ushering them inside. "And I'm Gregory. Welcome. Jillian, very nice to meet you. This is my wife, Christie."

Christie James was small, only an inch or so taller than I, and with the same small frame. She had very, very dark hair, almost as curly as mine, and I couldn't decide if her eyes were blue or grey. She held herself with a quiet confidence that I envied. "I'm glad to meet you," I said.

"And we're both very glad you're here," Christie said. I realized with delight that there was a trace of British in her voice. "Come in and sit down."

"What a lovely room!" I exclaimed as Christie led us through the foyer and a short hallway into a living room that faced the water. The room was dominated by a beautiful grand piano on a dais by the window, open and ready to be played, but the rest of the room was comfortably furnished and decorated in a style that made me feel immediately at home.

"Thank you. This was Gregory's condo before we were married," Christie responded, with a teasing glance at her husband. "I had to completely redecorate it."

I looked at him, too, as we all sat down. Gregory James was head-turning handsome; in his early thirties; tall, but not as tall as Josh, perhaps six feet against Josh's six-four. He had broad shoulders, but not at broad as Josh's—he had a medium frame as opposed to Josh's large one. He had blond hair, but not as blond as Josh's; it was perhaps two shades darker.

But the force of Gregory's exuberant personality immediately drew your attention to him and held it. He had an energy that made him stand out, and I was sure that even in a crowd he would be noticeable. One couldn't help but like him, his smile was so infectious, so friendly, and so obviously sincere. He was the positive, Josh the negative of the photo. Knowing that I was biased, I honestly thought that Josh was the handsomer, not that there was much to choose from; they were both drop-dead gorgeous. But Gregory fairly took one's breath away.

"Have we met before?" Gregory asked Josh. "You look familiar."

"It was years ago," Josh said, almost shyly. "You spoke to my advanced keyboards class my first year of grad school. I had a conference with you afterwards, and you were the first one to suggest that I go into composition instead of piano. It's all due to you." No wonder Josh almost worshipped this man, I thought.

"That was you?" Gregory said with a pleased smile. " I remember that well but I didn't recall your name. I don't think I ever heard your last name that day. I've thought about you often and wondered how you were doing. I've been so excited to meet you." Gregory's pleasure in this meeting was obvious. "This is a wonderful opportunity for me. What I'm hoping that you'll do, is play the piano part of your concerto for me. May I ask that of you?"

Josh looked at little uncomfortable. "I'm a bit out of practice on the piano," he said. "I had surgery on my right leg a few months ago, and just got off the crutches last week. It made it hard to practice."

Gregory laughed. "I won't be listening to your playing," he assured Josh. "I'll be listening to the music. You see, you'll be giving me an opportunity that few classical pianists ever get; to hear how the composer himself interprets the music. Chopin and Beethoven and Liszt were all long gone by the time I came on the scene. Their music remains to speak for them, but how can I know if I'm saying what they wanted to say?" He leaned forward, holding Josh's gaze earnestly. "But in your case, you can show me what you intended the music to mean. It's a wonderful chance."

"I don't know what to say," Josh said, a bit overwhelmed.

"Say you'll play for him," Christie said, laughing a little. "He's talked of nothing else for the past month. Do it, Josh, just to give me a little peace."

Josh bowed slightly towards her. "Your wish is my command, m'lady," he said, smiling. He took his seat at the piano and, after a few warm up exercises, began to play.

I loved listening to Josh play his own music. I was absorbed in watching him until Christie gently tapped me on the shoulder and pointed to Gregory. The pianist was playing right along with Josh, silently, on his own knees, absorbing what Josh was "saying" with the music, internalizing it. He did not appear to be aware of what he was doing.

When Josh had finished, Gregory said one word, "Again." His voice was short, but Josh appeared to understand that it was not meant that way. Instead, Gregory was still absorbed in the music. Josh understood that all too well. He began to play a second time. Christie caught my eye, stood up and motioned me to follow.

"They'll go through it three or four times," Christie explained, settling the two of us on a couch in a smaller den. "We don't need to stay, though I was glad to hear Josh play it once. Unless you wanted to stay?"

I shook her head. "I liked listening once, but I'm not the musician that Josh is. I'll be hearing it again in a few days, at Symphony Hall. That will be enough."

"That's my feeling as well," Christie agreed. "But Gregory has been very excited about this. We've been up in New Hampshire and just got in today, and Gregory couldn't wait to call Josh. He hasn't even unpacked yet."

"Josh was thrilled to come," I said. "He admires Gregory so much. He was honored that Gregory would be willing to premier his first classical work."

"The feeling was mutual," Christie said. She put her feet up on an ottoman and sighed with relief. "Gregory and Josh have the same agent. And Gregory loves folk music—it's one way he relaxes. Neil Donovan is Gregory's best friend and he heard Neil singing one of the pieces Josh wrote for him. Neil told him that Josh was writing a piano concerto for the BSO and Gregory went straight to the Symphony and asked to play it."

I stared. "I don't think Josh knows that," I said. "He thought he was lucky that it happened that Gregory would be playing that night."

"Oh, no," Christie assured her. "Gregory wanted badly to do this. He's very much in the Symphony's good graces right now and they like to try to please him, so he didn't have to ask very loudly. But it was very definitely Gregory's idea. Don't get me wrong—the Symphony was going to premier Josh's piece anyway. I think those arrangements were made through the conservatory. But having Gregory play it was Gregory's idea."

"So Gregory knows Neil? I've never met him, but Josh thinks a lot of him."

"Even in Boston, the music world is a small one," Christie said. "Gregory even considered partnering with Neil as a folk musician, but he loves classical piano too much. Sooner or later, Gregory and Josh would have met. They have friends in common, and as I mentioned, they all three share an agent." She smiled at me. "Tell me about you," she said. "When are you and Josh planning to be married?"

"Not till next year, probably," I answered. "From everything we've learned, the longer we wait, the easier a time Josh will have getting his visa."

"So you're going to live in England?"

"That's been the plan." I explained about Josh's prior time in the UK.

Christie asked, "You haven't been in this country very long, have you? Your accent is making me homesick."

"Only since this past summer," I agreed. "And I was home at Christmas for a month. I'll be going back probably sometime in May or early June, and Josh will come stay with me for a few months."

Christie looked disappointed. "We're just getting to know you and you're already going away," she said, but I could tell she was teasing. "I miss England. Perhaps we'll come and visit you."

"I hope you will. And I mean that sincerely," I said. "Are you British? I can hear the accent."

"No, I'm American. But I lived in England for much of my childhood. My father's job had him traveling all over Europe, so they parked me in a British boarding school so that I could have some consistency in my education, instead of running all over the place."

"Was he State Department?" I asked. "My mother is British but my father is American—he was with the American Embassy in London."

Christie shook her head. "He was the international Sales manager for a big manufacturing firm," she said. "State Department, that must have been interesting. So you're a dual?"

I nodded. "I'd never lived outside Britain until I came to visit my brother's family last summer," I said. "My parents have retired to the south coast of England, near Plymouth. I'm British in every way that counts."

"Of course you are. I know how that feels." Christie took my hand. "I hardly remembered the US, it had been so long. I felt British too. In many ways I still do." She squeezed my hand, and released it. "So many little things, that all add up to a lot of strangeness, right?"

It all came spilling out. I hadn't realized how much I had been holding back until I found a sympathetic listener who really understood. Lori and Joyce tried but they couldn't know all the differences. Josh would understand but I hadn't wanted to burden him with my insecurities; he had enough to cope with right now. Christie had been there. She knew. She knew about all the little oddities and strangeness; the growing list of unfamiliar things; all adding up to a series of landmines that I had to maneuver in order to survive in a strange culture. She knew about never completely being able to relax because there'd be something else new and unfamiliar coming along every minute. Unfamiliar brand names, currency differences, cultural changes; so much to adjust to.

When I was finished, almost in tears, Christie gave me a hug. "Didn't know there was so much, did you?"

"I really didn't," I admitted. "I love Josh so much, and overall I'm happy as long as I can be with him. I don't dislike it here, but it's so foreign to me. It just backs up on me every once in a while. It will be such a relief to get home."

"Where Josh will be in a foreign country," Christie said quietly.

"It was his idea to live in England," I reminded her. "His brother Kenneth says he's better over there. He's prone to depression."

"I was going to ask you, but I didn't know if it would be indelicate. But I noticed that he limps—is that just a bi-product of the surgery you mentioned?" Christie asked.

I shook my head. "He was in an accident when he was sixteen, and his leg was seriously damaged. He'll never walk without a limp and he's subject to bone infections. That's what the recent surgery was about—clearing out a bone infection."

"That poor man," Christie said. "He's so big and handsome and looks as if he should be an athlete."

"He was playing high school baseball when the accident happened," I said. "He had wanted to be a professional ball player. He'd like to join a neighborhood baseball team but his leg will never be strong enough for that. He'd love to learn to ski but that's out of the question—he can't balance properly. He can walk for moderate distances, but he has to be careful about hiking, and he can swim. He can bat a tennis ball around with me but he can't really give me a good game. He can live a relatively normal life but it can't include athletics." I stood up and walked to the window, looking out.

"It's a good thing he's got his music," Christie said. We stopped and listened for a moment. The music had changed; it was still Josh's concerto but the handling of it was different.

"That's Gregory playing now," Christie said.

"I can tell," I said. "Josh is a good, competent pianist, but that's a master playing now." I came back and sat down again.

"You have a good ear to tell the difference," Christie commented. "Most people can't."

"It's obvious," I said, surprised. "How could they not be able to tell?"

"You'd be surprised," Christie said, shaking her head. "The average Joe or Josie doesn't understand enough about music to hear the differences in style."

I listened carefully. I'd heard Josh play this many times, but it sounded different under Gregory's masterful hands.

"It's a wonderful piece of music," Christie said. "Josh is very talented. Gregory is going to want to premier any other pieces he may write as well."

"You'd better let Gregory say that," I said, a bit nonplused.

"Gregory did say that," Christie insisted. "He's going to tell Josh that this afternoon." She leaned her head back and closed her eyes. She was obviously tired and I hoped we weren't being an inconvenience.

"No, not at all," she assured me when I tentatively asked the question. "It's not you and Josh at all. I guess you can't tell yet that I'm pregnant—about six or seven weeks."

"That's wonderful!" I exclaimed. "I'm so happy for you. Is it your first?"

"Our third," Christie said. "We have a daughter, Stephanie, who's two and a half, and a son, Ian, who's a year old."

"Do you have pictures?"

She did. They were both adorable. I admired them. "Josh and I want children. I hope ours are as cute as yours," I told her.

"I'm sure they will be."

We listened as Gregory played the piano part through twice. Then the two men, both of them laughing and smiling, came to join us.

"This is one talented guy," Gregory said, motioning to Josh. "He's working on his second piano sonata now, and I'm claiming the honor of debuting both of them."

"I'm the one who'd be honored," Josh insisted. He sat down in the chair next to me and gave me one of his one-armed hugs. "Hello, angel. How did it sound?"

"Wonderful," I insisted, and Christie nodded agreement as Gregory rubbed her shoulders.

"Of course, it will sound different with the orchestra part," Josh reminded us.

"I'm rehearsing it with the orchestra tomorrow," Gregory said. "If you have time, I'd like you to come. It's a closed rehearsal so the girls can't be there, if I can call our ladies girls without offense, but I can get the composer in, no problem."

"I'll be there," Josh said immediately. "Just tell me where and when."

"Symphony Hall, 2:00," Gregory said. "Come to the stage door and give my name. And now, I am taking all four of us out to dinner. What's everyone up for, steak, seafood, Italian, French?"

We decided on a steak house with widely varied menu. Gregory apologized for having to call a taxi. "We brought my car, and it's a two seater. We left Christie's for her parents to use; they're watching the kids for us. Normally I'd suggest we walk but if you just got off crutches, Josh, you probably shouldn't be walking a long way. And Christie…" He hesitated.

"I told Jillian," Christie admitted. "It's okay. I know we weren't going to tell people yet but it just seemed right. Josh, I'm pregnant, due in November."

"Congratulations! Then Gregory's right," Josh declared. "Neither of us should be walking that far tonight. Don't worry about the taxi; I don't even own a car. We keep the taxi services, commuter rail and car rental places in this city in business."

"You don't own a car?" Gregory asked.

"Not everyone does," Christie said dryly. "Certainly, my love, not all people who live in a city with an advanced public transportation system. I didn't own a car when I lived here full time."

Gregory looked embarrassed. "I'm sorry, of course you're right."

"I'm a bit phobic about driving," Josh explained. "It's a reaction to the accident I was in when I was a teenager."

"Were you hurt badly?" Gregory asked with sympathy.

"It's why I limp," Josh said. I reached over and took his hand in silent support. "I was in the hospital for months. And both my parents were killed, as well as my younger sister. I lived with my aunt and uncle after that."

"I'm sorry. I shouldn't have said anything." Gregory put his hand on Josh's shoulder. "That was rude of me."

"No, it wasn't," Josh said. "You had no way of knowing. I know how to drive, I have a license, but I have difficult time making myself do so."

The taxi driver buzzed and we went downstairs. It was only a short drive to the restaurant and we were seated quickly. The waiter came over and offered drinks. "Jillian, what will you have?" Gregory asked.

"I'd like a daiquiri, if that's all right."

"Of course it's all right. Josh, what about you?"

Josh, finally finished with his antibiotic therapy, ordered a vodka gimlet, his favorite drink on those occasions when he allowed himself one. Gregory had a scotch over ice. Christie stuck with fizzy water with lime.

The drinks came. We toasted Josh's premier. Then Gregory took a deep breath.

"I don't want to make matters worse," he said. "But I lost both my parents early, too. I was in my mid-teens when my father died of a defective heart. He and my mother had both known he was likely to die young, but they didn't tell me, so it came as a complete surprise. My mother died of cancer eight months later."

Christie took her husband's hand.

"I was engaged when I was in music school," Gregory went on. "That ended very badly, and I was deeply hurt. That was before I met Christie, who is the best thing that ever happened to me."

Christie smiled and blew him a kiss.

"I'm telling you this because I see so much of myself in you," Gregory continued, looking at Josh. "I'm not all that much older than you are, but when I see you and talk to you, it's like looking into a mirror—a mirror of my past. You're a very talented musician, Josh. I'm not sure you realize how talented. You're very intense, very focused, very driven when it comes to your music. Am I right?"

I answered for him. "You're spot on."

"You've gone through a personal tragedy—more so than I did. But you can make this work for you, Josh. If you're as much like me as I think you are, sometimes you let that overwhelm you."

"You don't do that anymore," Christie objected.

"But you know I used to. It wasn't until I had you that I was able to fight it successfully," Gregory said. "And Josh has so much more to overcome than I did. I lost my parents and had a failed love affair…oh, I see by Josh's face that I've missed part of the story?"

Josh glanced at me. "Not exactly. Not in the way you're talking about," he said softly. "But there was a girl when I was in grad school, Natalie. I was just trying to decide if I was ready to ask her to marry me when she dumped me on my ass. It wasn't her fault. I can be very hard to live with when I get into one of my depressive moods. Jillian doesn't know yet what she's getting into." He smiled at me. "It didn't really hurt for very long. I was more in love with the idea of being in love than I was in love with Natalie. That, I realized as soon as I met Jillian."

Well. This was news to me. Why had no one, not even Joyce, mentioned Natalie to me before? Kenneth had mentioned that Josh had a girlfriend in England, but that was all. Then I realized that it didn't matter; she wasn't important enough to mention. Josh loved me. That was all that mattered.

Gregory shook his head. "You've gone through an emotional roller coaster," he said. "But Josh, this is the important part. Don't fight it. Use it."

"Use it," Josh repeated wonderingly.

"Yes, use it. Put it all into the music. Make it work for you, instead of letting it define you. I may be all wrong—you may have already learned that. Certainly the piece of yours I'll be playing in a few days is a very mature work for a man only in his twenties; you may not need this advice. But I'm offering it anyway, man to man, musician to musician."

"And I'm accepting it as such," Josh said. "Thank you, Gregory. You've given me something important to think about. I can already hear how I need to revise the first sonata. I . . . damn, I need something to write on."

Gregory pulled a small notebook out of his pocket and handed it across the table. "Help yourself."

Josh scribbled frantically for several minutes. By this time, I knew that he wouldn't hear anything that was said while he was composing, and both Gregory and Christie seemed to understand, so the three of us chatted idly while he took frenzied notes. The waiter approached; Gregory silently signaled for a second round of drinks and the waiter retreated.

Finally Josh looked up and handed the notebook to Gregory. "What do you think?" he asked anxiously.

The pianist studied the notation for a few minutes. "Excellent," he proclaimed. "I'm looking forward to playing this when you have it finished." He tore off the pages in question, handed them back to Josh and tucked the notebook back in his pocket. "I ordered you another drink," he pointed out. "We're one ahead of you."

Josh took a sip and sighed deeply. "I can't thank you enough, Gregory," he said. "That was exactly what I needed to hear."

"That sonata is going to be a masterpiece," Gregory promised. "Are you sure you're set for now? I don't want to interrupt the creative process."

"I'm fine," Josh said. "I'm starving. Did you order?"

"No, we waited for you," Christie said, as Gregory signaled the waiter. "Gregory was sure you wouldn't be long."

"I know how it works," Gregory said. "I've done my share of composing."

"I'd like to hear something of yours sometime," Josh declared, picking up his drink and taking a long swallow.

"Tomorrow. I'll play my graduation piece for you."

"I thought you were a keyboard performance major." Josh looked confused.

"I was. But I minored in Theory and Composition. Shall we order now?"

I chose a seafood casserole; Christie the lamb chops. Both men ordered steaks. Between us we opted for a variety of salads. The men chose appetizers; Christie and I abstained. We talked about everything over dinner. Gregory and Josh discussed professors at music school. Christie and I compared notes about living in England. We shared stories about families. Christie showed Josh the pictures of their two children. We were becoming good friends.

When dinner was over, Gregory offered to share their taxi home, but Josh shook his head. "We can walk easily from here, even me," he said. "I have to get used to walking, and we're only a few blocks from South Station. But I'll see you tomorrow at Symphony Hall."

We walked the rest of the way holding hands. "Did you enjoy yourself?" I teased, seeing the glow on Josh's face.

"I had a marvelous time," Josh admitted. "I feel like I've had a major breakthrough with my music, just hearing him play and listening to what he said about using my history. Did you like Christie?" We entered South Station and checked the time of our train; we still had twenty minutes to go.

"She was wonderful," I exclaimed. "She really understood what I've been going through. She's American, but she lived in England most of her life until university, so she knew in a way that no one else, not even you, really understood."

Josh sat down on a bench and pulled me down beside him. "Has it really been that difficult?" he asked softly. "I'm sorry, my love.."

"It wasn't your fault," I said, snuggling into his shoulder. "You couldn't have helped needing surgery—you'd have been in England with me months ago if it weren't for that. But yes, I have to admit I'm somewhat homesick. I'll be very glad to be back home where things are familiar. On the other hand, Christie reminded me that you'll be on unfamiliar territory then."

Josh waved a hand in dismissal. "I lived in England for three years and I've spent probably another six months there overall, off and on, visiting Granddad. It's not as unfamiliar to me, as the US is to you."

"Still . . ."

Josh kissed my neck. "I'll be fine, sweetheart. I wouldn't have suggested we live there if I didn't think I could manage it long term."

"We can come back and visit," I suggested.

"And we will." Josh kissed me deeply, oblivious to other travelers passing by.

They called our train and we made our way home. It was after eleven by the time we reached our condo.

"Angel, I am still so wound up about the music. Can you stand it if I play the guitar for a while? I won't try to play the piano; I don't want to disturb anyone above or below us. But will the guitar bother you?"

"Of course not. I'll read for a while and then just go to bed if you're still up."

I had been asleep for almost two hours when Josh finally came to bed. He pulled me close and nuzzled against me. "Are you awake?" he whispered.

"I am now." I turned in his arms. "I can tell what you want." I snuggled close. "Just give me a few minutes to wake up a little more, and I'll let you use up that energy."

It didn't take me long to start responding to his loving.

Josh spent much of the next few days with Gregory, either at rehearsals or working on his new sonatas. Gregory, who seemed to have appointed himself Josh's mentor, let Josh bounce ideas off him. "I feel as if I ought to give Gregory co-composer credit," Josh told me one evening. "He won't hear of it; I tried. But I feel as if he's done a lot of the work."

"I know how hard you've worked on that piece," I said loyally. "Don't you dare try to give credit away."

For my part I spent the time getting ready for my move back to England, which Josh and I had agreed would take place mid-May. I somehow neglected to mention to him my reasons for wanting to stay well into the month. I spent one long afternoon shopping with Rachel and Joyce, looking for a dress for Josh's all important concert. Randi did not go with us this time. We finally found an outfit that satisfied us all; a white lace bodice with ruffles edged in blue silk ribbon cascading down the front, and a long velvet skirt in Wedgewood blue, with a narrow waistband and tied with long satin ribbons the same color. I found low heeled blue satin shoes to match, with lacy stockings that I immediately coveted as soon as I saw them.

"You're going to blow Josh away," Joyce insisted.

I waved that away. "He'll be so excited about the music, he won't even see me. The Boston Symphony Orchestra is premiering a piece that he wrote—that's exciting enough to take all his attention."

The afternoon of the concert Josh was almost too excited to talk. Just about every family member, as well as Joyce and several of his friends from music school, all called to wish him congratulations, but finally I took the phone away from him. "Go sit down at the piano and play," I ordered.

He did so, playing out his excitement until it was time to go. We were driving in with Uncle Scott and Aunt Deborah and they arrived right on time to pick us up. "Are you ready?" I called.

Because we knew how late we were likely to be that night, we were spending the night at a Boston hotel. Josh took the garment bag with his tux and my dress; I took the small overnight bag with the incidentals, and we went down to where the Aldrichs' were waiting.

"Aren't Kenneth and Joyce coming?" I asked as I climbed into the back seat with Aunt Deborah. Josh, so much bigger and needing extra room for his bad leg, took the front passenger side.

"They're coming in Ken's car," Uncle Scott explained. "Don't worry, they won't miss it."

Josh was almost silent on the way to the hotel. I knew he was listening to the music in his head. Mercifully his foster parents seemed to understand and did not ask him to interact.

We'd timed it so that we had just enough time to dress and get to Symphony Hall without having to wait around a long time. I was dressed first and waited in the tiny sitting room attached to our much larger bedroom. Finally Josh came out of the bedroom in his tux. He looked so good I had to swallow hard. I'd never seen him in a tux before. "You look wonderful," I said softly.

"Thanks, so do you." He clearly wasn't seeing me. I smiled. He'd see me later when the whole thing was over.

"Uncle Scott and Aunt Deborah are waiting; let's go." I led him by the hand out the door.

All the family had expected to attend the first performance of Josh's concerto. Most of them were already seated when we came in and took our seats next to Kenneth and Joyce. Several of them waved.

Josh clearly couldn't think of anything but the music, and was totally unaware of what was going on or who was there. I squeezed his hand and settled back. I knew he'd be oblivious till after the concert.

I looked over the program. Josh's piece was the second one played; just before the intermission. There were bios of both he and Gregory provided and I was interested to see that I was mentioned briefly. Then the lights were lowered and the music began.

I was so nervous on Josh's behalf that I hardly heard the first piece, which was a Beethoven overture for just the orchestra. Then Gregory was introduced and he came out on stage, bowed, and sat down at the piano.

I had never heard the concerto with the orchestra part before and I listened, enthralled. Josh had so tight a hold on my hand that his knuckles were white, but I barely felt it, I was so totally involved in the music. It was almost a shock when the movement ended. A brief pause, then the second movement started. This was a powerful movement, tugging at my emotions, and I felt tears starting in my eyes. The playful third movement began and suddenly I felt myself smiling, tapping my foot to the music. It swelled to a joyful climax; the conductor's baton came down, and it was over.

There was applause. Wild applause. Then people began standing, until the entire hall was on their feet in a standing ovation. The conductor indicated Gregory, who bowed with a huge grin on his face, then the orchestra, then Gregory again. Gregory whispered something to the conductor, then extended his hand towards the area of the hall where Josh and I were seated. The spotlight picked him up, and

Gregory motioned for him to come forward. The conductor did likewise, and I put a hand on Josh's back and pushed. He went forward and joined Gregory on stage, so proud he could burst. The applause got louder as the audience realized that the young man on the stage was the composer. Josh and Gregory bowed again, the conductor standing aside with a smile on his face. Finally, he led the two younger men off stage as the orchestra filed out. The applause continued. The conductor, Gregory and Josh returned to increased applause. After a second curtain call, it became clear to the audience that they would not be returning and the applause died down. The lights came up.

I was so excited that I could hardly sit still. I turned to Aunt Deborah and almost exploded with pride. "Wasn't it wonderful!" I exclaimed.

"It was absolutely wonderful," Aunt Deborah agreed. "He's a very talented young man. I'm very proud of him."

"Have you met the pianist?" Uncle Scott asked.

I nodded. "We've spent a lot of time with him the past week or so. You can meet him at the party after the concert; he's wonderful too."

Josh returned to his seat, grinning ecstatically, to receive the hugs and kisses and congratulations from his family, friends, and even a few strangers. "Gregory says we should come backstage after the end of the second half," he whispered to me. "He wants us to go over to the party with him."

I nodded. "I am so very, very, very proud of you," I told him, leaning against his shoulder for a moment.

This was perhaps the proudest moment of Josh's life, I knew. From this moment on he could consider himself a classical composer, rather than just a song writer. Not that there was anything wrong with being a song writer, but he had so badly wanted the recognition in the classical genre, and now he had it. One of the premier orchestras in the world had played one of his pieces, and it had been played by a master pianist who *wanted* to play his work—who had asked to do it. I was thrilled when he was brought back out for another curtain call at the end of the concert despite the fact that he had written nothing played during the second half. I never wanted this evening to end, and from the expression on Josh's face, neither did he. But of course eventually it did, and he returned to his seat to collect me. We went backstage to meet Gregory.

"We'll stay back here as long as you like. There will be a lot of people who want to congratulate you," Gregory promised. "This is your night, Josh. Enjoy every minute of it."

"It should be partially your night too," Josh insisted.

Gregory waved that away. "I've been playing off and on with the BSO, and with other orchestras, for eighteen years, ever since I was fourteen, and I'll undoubtedly continue playing with them for another eighteen—or more; I have no intention of ceasing to play when I'm only fifty. This is the only first premier you'll ever get. You'll have more premiers, and you'll have them with the BSO if I have anything to say about it. But this is your first one, and you should enjoy the hell out of it."

Gregory was right; a great many people did want to come back and talk to Josh. We stayed as long as we could, enjoying every minute of it and completely overcome by how many people wanted his autograph. But eventually, even with the support of his cane, Josh came over and whispered to me, "I'm sorry, love, but I have to sit down."

Gregory overheard. "Wait here," he commanded, leading us into his dressing room. "I'll make sure the limo is ready."

"Limo?" Josh asked, sitting with relief on the edge of a chair. I stood behind him and rubbed his shoulders. Christie, draped in silk the color of ripe raspberries and with a single strand of pearls around her neck, stood up from the stool where she had been waiting and went to join her husband.

"We've got a limo to take us over to the hotel where the party is to be held," she explained, taking Gregory's hand. "We wanted to make this very special for you."

"My foster parents are here; at least, they were here a few minutes ago. So is the rest of my family. We should make arrangements for them . . ." Josh began, starting to stand up. I pushed him back into place.

"Stay off that leg until we're ready to go," I said firmly. "Christie and I made arrangements to get everyone there days ago."

Josh relaxed at that. Seeing the strain in his face from the ache in his bad leg, I found some ibuprofen in my handbag. There was a water cooler in the hall and I got him a cup of water. He swallowed the pills gratefully.

"I'll be fine in a few minutes," he said. "I think the adrenaline kept me from noticing that I'd been on my feet too long."

"Just relax," Christie said as Gregory left the room. She sat down in her own chair. "No rush. The party isn't going anywhere without you."

Gregory came back a few minutes later. "It's all ready," he said. "Josh, are you all right?"

"A little overwhelmed," Josh admitted. "Just don't take my cane away and I'll be fine."

The party was held in a function room of one of the local hotels, catered by one of the city's finest restaurants. "The owner is a friend of mine," Gregory explained. "He'd be hurt beyond measure if I had a party and didn't let him cater it."

I was almost too excited to eat, but what little I did have was indeed superb. There were dozens of people there, all of Josh's family, Adam and Lori, friends of Josh's from music school, friends of

Gregory's, members of the orchestra. I overheard snatches of conversation about the concert, about Gregory, about Josh.

"Wasn't the cane a bit pretentious?" I overhead one comment.

"It's not an affectation," someone else answered. "I know one of his uncles. He had surgery on his leg this past summer."

"What happened?" It was the first voice.

The second voice was unsure. "I don't know. A sports injury, probably."

I smiled wryly, not missing the irony. If only.

The music director of the orchestra came up to me, shook my hand, and told me what a talented man I was engaged to.

"Thank you, sir," I said, a bit shyly. "I've very proud of him."

"You should be. If he has other pieces he'd like to have played, he should let me know. Young James over there is champing at the bit to play more of them, and we're happy to give local musicians a chance. That goes for composers as well as pianists."

"I'll tell him, sir. He's currently working on two piano sonatas, and I believe one of them is almost finished."

"Good! That will please my young friend Gregory. I'm a pianist myself, and we need more good piano composers. Even without the orchestra, we can use them as showcase pieces. You tell him to call me." The director patted my shoulder. "I fully intend to tell him myself, but you make sure he remembers."

As if Josh would need reminders to make such a call. "I will, sir. I promise."

Kenneth came up behind me, awe spread all over his face. Joyce, in a blue green silk that brightened her beautiful red hair still brighter and made me instantly envious, clung to his hand in the crowd.

"Josh wrote that?" Kenneth asked incredulously. "That was incredible! I had no idea my big brother had so much talent!"

"Wasn't it wonderful?" I responded with pride. "I'd never heard it with the orchestra part before. I'm so very proud of him."

"I can hardly believe it," Joyce said shyly. "That someone I know wrote a piece of music like that!"

"Did you like it?" Josh asked, approaching from where he had been talking to Gregory. "What did you think?"

"I'm in awe," Kenneth declared. "You're incredibly talented, Josh. I can't wait to hear what you come up with next."

"Thanks, little brother." Josh put a hand on Kenneth's shoulder. "That means a lot."

I quietly backed out of the way and let Josh have his moment. This was entirely his and I didn't want to steal a moment of his thunder. Even when Randi tried to appropriate his attention I pretended I didn't see her and went on talking to Lori. I was pleased, however, when Randi's own father diverted her attention and led her away. No one, not even a member of his family, not even me, should be monopolizing him tonight.

It was almost half one by the time Josh came over and indicated to me that he was ready to go. "I've had the time of my life but I'm exhausted," he admitted. "Gregory and Christie have offered us a ride to the hotel; are you ready?"

I was more than ready. But when we were back in our hotel room, Josh turned to me. "I needed to get off my feet," he told me. "But I still have a lot of adrenaline left in me."

"I have an idea how you can get rid of that," I breathed.

Josh, naked, stopped me when I hadn't removed more than my shoes. "Let me," he whispered.

He took the rest of my clothes off slowly and stopped when I was wearing only my stockings, the lacy ones I had fallen in love with, and garter belt. "I don't know why I find those so exciting," he said with some urgency, "but I do."

"Do you want them on or off?" I asked with a certain urgency of my own.

"On," Josh said firmly. "Because I don't want to wait long enough to take them off."

His lovemaking was passionate. I responded ardently, so much so that Josh finally whispered, "Wow. I should premiere a concerto every night."

I'd have been perfectly happy to have that happen.

We attended every performance of the concerto that weekend, finally returning to Scituate on Sunday. It was on Tuesday that there came a buzz that someone was seeking entry. Thinking it to be Joyce or a family member, I buzzed them in.

I had never seen the man at the door before. He was about five nine, fiftyish, skinny to the point of emaciation, shaggy greying dark hair and haggard dark eyes that looked up at me from a slump that made my shoulders hurt.

"I'm looking for Joshua Whittaker," he said in a creaky voice that sounded as if it had rust in it.

"You've found him," Josh agreed, looking curiously at him from behind me, leaning on his cane. "And you are?"

"I didn't realize you were…disabled," the stranger said, still avoiding the question.

"I had surgery on my leg last winter," Josh explained. "The cane is the final step before I'm pronounced recovered. And, I ask again, who are you?"

The stranger took a deep breath. "My name is Gabriel Murtree."

Josh's face froze. "Get out," he said coldly.

"Please, just let me explain why I'm here, and then I'll leave," Murtree promised.

"I thought you were in jail."

"I was. I was released two years ago."

Josh laughed sharply. "It's a pity my family can't be released from being dead. Or that I can't be released to have full use of my leg again, without having to have painful surgery every few years."

"I'm in AA now," Murtree said. "I'm going through the 12 step program. And part of the 12 step program is seeking out the people that you hurt and doing what you can to make amends. I know how badly I hurt you; as part of the program I have to admit that and do what I can to make amends."

"Unless you've got a time machine in your back pocket, there's nothing you can do to make amends," Josh said in that uncharacteristically hard voice again. I had never heard it so cold. "You can't bring my family back to life; you can't take away the permanent limp I'm left with; you can't change the fact that I'm probably going to need to have surgery on my leg every few years for the rest of my life. I don't know what amends you think you can make."

"At the very least I can apologize," Murtree insisted.

"Fine, you've apologized. Please leave now. Jillian, come inside." Josh picked up his cane and, barely waiting to see that I was inside the condo, slammed the door shut with all the force he could muster. Then he walked past me and into the bedroom, shutting the door behind him. I stared at the door. I could only imagine what pain he must be feeling right now.

At a soft knock on the door, I stalked back to the door and flung it open. Of all things to happen right after his musical triumph! "Well?" I snapped at Murtree, still waiting there.

"I'm sorry again. I didn't mean to upset him."

"How did you find him anyway?"

Murtree stared at her. "Are you kidding me? Both the Globe and the Herald, and the Ledger too for that matter, have had stories splashed all over them about the fancy music he wrote. It wasn't difficult to track him down from there."

"And you thought this would be an appropriate time to appear out of the blue and knock all his emotions on their arse." I could hear the bitterness in my own voice.

"My sponsor said this probably wasn't a good idea," Murtree said ruefully.

"So now you can go back to your sponsor and tell him he was right," I pointed out.

"I'm sorry, but in all conscience I couldn't . . ."

"I hope your conscience is happy now," I exploded, suddenly so furious I couldn't be polite. "He was getting over it. After ten years, the emotional damage was being repaired. I can only hope you haven't caused as much new damage as I'm afraid you have, but I suspect we're back to square one. I hope easing your conscience was worth it."

I put my hand on the doorknob. "Please leave now. Don't come back. And don't forget to tell your sponsor how much additional damage you did today. I thought that it was part of the program that you were excused from "making amends" if to do so would hurt someone else?"

I stood there pointedly until Murtree turned and, with a final, "I'm sorry," finally left.

I immediately went to door of the bedroom and opened it. Josh was sitting on the bed, his face buried in his hands. "Are you all right?" I asked softly.

"I'm all right. But I don't want to talk now," he replied, his voice muffled.

I went to him and rubbed his shoulders. "You don't need to." I continued to rub him. His shoulders felt as if they were carved out of granite.

"I love you, Jillian, but please leave me alone for a little while," he pleaded.

I kissed the top of his head and went back out, closing the door behind me. I thought I heard a soft sob, but wasn't sure.

I could only imagine what he must be feeling. I paced about the room, not sure what I should do. Finally I realized that I should let the rest of the family know what had happened, and called Aunt Debbie. She listened quietly and then said she would let the others know. She rang off more suddenly than was her usual wont.

When the silence from the other room had reached the point that I was getting worried, I quietly opened the door. Josh was stretched out on the bed, staring at the ceiling.

"I miss them so much," he said, as I sat down beside him. "I look like my dad, big and blond. My mother was smaller, with dark hair and blue eyes. Ken looks like that side of the family, but he gets his brown eyes from his dad. I wonder if that's why I'm attracted to small, blue eyed brunettes; Natalie was that type too, and so was Deanna, my girlfriend in England." He squeezed my hand. "So would Janey have been if she had lived. She'd be through college now, or maybe in grad school; she was just a few months younger than Ken."

He was silent for a minute, and then went on, "My mother used to sing. All the time. She had a beautiful high soprano. I can hear it in my mind's ear today. Randi sounds a lot like her."

He sighed. "I don't actually remember the accident itself," he acknowledged. "I was left with a concussion among my other injuries, and the doctors say that's more or less normal. I remember my mother screaming, and my dad shouting, and then the next thing I remember is the paramedics working on me." He could not control the tears that he'd held back so long. "I never saw any of my family again."

"Oh Josh." I put both arms around him and let him cry. How long had he needed this release?

"I couldn't even go to the funeral; I was in traction and couldn't be moved." Josh clung to me for several minutes.

"Why did they have to die?" he whispered. "Why was I spared when they all died?"

"God had something He needed you to do," I replied, hoping against hope that I was saying the right thing. "Maybe because He needed your music and you were the only one who could write it. Maybe something else. But He did, and you're here, and I love you."

"Jillian, don't leave me," he begged into my shoulder.

"I won't. I never will." I thought achingly of going home to England, but I couldn't leave him in this condition. I'd have to put it off again. He needed me.

"I love you. I couldn't bear to lose someone else. I've already lost so much, so many people...."

"I'll never leave you," I promised. "I'll be with you forever. For the rest of our lives, we'll be together. We can face anything as long we we're together."

"I guess so," he said. He reached into a drawer in the night table, pulled out a handkerchief, wiped his eyes and blew his nose. "Okay, I think I'm done making a fool of myself now. I thought I was over all that survivor guilt."

"There was nothing foolish about your reaction," I declared. "You backslid for a few minutes. That's understandable, under the circumstances. There's no need for you to feel guilty."

"Yes, there is." His voice was almost too low to be heard.

"Why?" I regretted saying it the moment the word was out of my mouth.

"Because I was driving!" The words exploded out of him with the force of ten years' pressure. "I was driving. I killed them."

"Josh! You did nothing of the kind!" I was horrified. "The accident wasn't your fault—Murtree was drunk and out of control!"

"I didn't have enough experience." Josh was almost talking to himself. "I'd just gotten my license the month before—you can get it at sixteen in Connecticut. Dad thought that even so I needed more experience with highway driving, so he suggested I drive home. I was pumped; I was the man—I was going to kick some highway ass. But I wasn't fast enough—I froze when I saw the truck coming at me. Dad shouted, 'Josh! To the right!' but by that time it was too late. They all died, and I lived. It's my fault. If I'd been faster..."

"You can't know that." Kenneth and Rachel between them had told me enough about the accident to know that almost nothing could have stopped it. I didn't think either of them knew that Josh had been driving. They'd never mentioned it, if they did. "No one else blames you—why should you blame yourself?"

"Most of the family doesn't know, at least I don't think they do," he admitted. "Uncle James does. The Division of Motor Vehicles in Connecticut does, and so do the State Police in both states. We were still in Massachusetts when it happened."

"And the barrister who prosecuted Murtree for manslaughter? Or the one who negotiated the wrongful death suits? Do they know?"

"Yes," Josh admitted. "And I suppose more of the family may know than I realize—the only one I told was Uncle James. He was the one who was with me when I first woke up in the hospital, and he was the one who told me what happened. But he may have mentioned it to others. I haven't driven from that day to this. I've renewed my license periodically because it's a good form of ID, but I haven't driven."

"And the Division of Motor Vehicles in Massachusetts allowed you to transfer your license, or whatever one does, when your Connecticut one expired, did they not? That's quite a lot of official personnel who don't hold you responsible, or there'd have been some action taken. Am I right?"

"You're right," Josh admitted again. "But I hold myself responsible."

"You shouldn't." I was adamant about that. "You need to stop. Right now."

"I'll try." Josh hesitated. "Angel, I really need to be alone right now. Don't worry about me, but I just can't be personable right now."

"You do whatever you need to do," I assured him. "I'll be fine right here."

I wasn't quite sure what to do, but whenever I was upset, cooking soothed and centered me. I began putting together one of Josh's favorite dinners, relieved to have something to do. It took me all afternoon to meet my own standards; I wanted everything to be perfect for Josh tonight. Finally I put the meal on the table; a roast leg of lamb with gravy and a mint sauce; potatoes whipped with sour cream and cream cheese; spinach au gratin; freshly baked rolls with herb butter; a mixed green salad with a champagne vinaigrette. I had a shrimp bisque to start and a peach cobbler with whipped cream to finish. I lit lavender scented candles; turned on a Mozart piano sonata CD, and went to the door.

"Come out with me and have dinner," I suggested.

He shook his head. "I'm not hungry, angel."

"Please?" I coaxed. "Even if you don't want to eat, won't you come down and sit with me? I worked all afternoon on this dinner."

He smiled sadly. "All right, love, I'll come sit with you. But I really don't feel like eating."

He came out to the dining area off the kitchen and sat down in one of the chairs. I went into the kitchen. "How about just a cup of soup?" I suggested. "You need to eat something, Josh, and that might go down easily."

He nodded wearily. I got the impression he was going along with me only because he couldn't raise the energy to argue. "All right. Just a cup of soup."

I ladled out two cups of my sherried shrimp bisque and set one in front of him. "Get yourself on the outside of this and see if it makes you feel better."

He took a spoonful and swallowed. He took another spoonful and smiled gently at me.

"It's good," he said.

"I'm glad," I told him. "I made all your favorites."

"That was sweet of you," he said. "I know you're tired."

I was, in fact, fairly dropping on my feet. It had been a long afternoon after a hectic weekend. But I knew it was really more emotional exhaustion than physical, and I had to do whatever I could for Josh. This had been a horrible day for him, bringing back memories he'd tried to bury, waking all his nightmares. I did not doubt that he would have nightmares tonight; he always did when he was upset. It occurred to me that this meant I, too, would have an interrupted night. No matter. I'd take a nap tomorrow, if Josh didn't need me. Right now, his needs were more important. Mine would come later.

I poured him a glass of wine. I knew wine was a depressant but he needed all the artificial relaxation I could find for him tonight. I poured another for myself and sat back down again. When Josh had finished his soup, I got up again.

"Stay still," I said. "But will you try just a small slice of the roast?"

He smiled gently at me. "All right, darling. Just a small slice. I guess it won't do either of us any good for me to refuse to eat."

"I know you're not hungry," I said gently. "But you need energy."

He ended up having two platefuls before I got up and served him a large helping of peach cobbler. Of course, the three glasses of wine didn't hurt. "I honestly didn't realize I was so hungry," he said, finishing his cobbler.

"You're a big man, and you used a lot of emotional energy today," I said. "You need fuel."

We went into the living room and he sank into a chair. Usually he sat on the couch next to me but he was holding himself apart from me, and, I suspected, everyone. I tried a couple of times to start a conversation but since he was less than responsive I eventually stopped. But when he stood up and said, "I'm going to bed, angel," I held up a hand to stop him.

"Will you do something for me tomorrow?" I asked.

He looked at me expectantly.

"Will you give Mitch a call?" Mitch was the therapist Josh had gone to when he first returned to the US.

He thought for a minute and then nodded. "I guess you're right. I will; I promise."

Despite twice weekly visits to Mitch, Josh remained silent and withdrawn for the next two weeks. He ate when I put food in front of him; he spent hours silently staring into space, and he almost never spoke. When he did, it tended to be of the, "Please pass the sugar," and, "Thank you, angel," variety. The date I had intended to return home came and went; I didn't dare leave him alone. I couldn't put this burden on the rest of the family as I had learned through Joyce that Murtree had attempted to contact other members as well, until James Whittaker, Josh's lawyer uncle, had threatened him with a restraining order. Everyone was upset and out of sorts.

Finally, in desperation, I called Christie's cell phone and told her what was going on. "Let me get Gregory," she told me. "He'll want to help."

A moment later I heard Gregory's voice. "We'll be there as soon as we can," he told me. "By the time we drop the kids with Christie's parents and drive down there, it'll be about an hour and a half, two hours. Are you okay till then?"

"I suppose so," I agreed. "He's just sitting there."

"Chin up, kiddo. The cavalry is on its way."

I decided if they were going to drive down to Scituate from Boston, I should offer them a meal, so once again I used cooking to calm myself down. By the time they arrived I had a roast in the oven and preparations made for the rest of dinner. I hurried to the door and let them in.

They each hugged me as they entered. "It's going to be all right," Gregory assured me. He had a small CD recorder which he set down on a table against the wall.

"There's an outlet behind you if you need to plug that in," I told him, though not quite sure what its purpose was going to be.

"Thanks." Gregory smiled at me and plugged the recorder in. "Now, call Josh for me, would you please, honey?"

I went to the bedroom door and peeked in. "Josh, Gregory and Christie are here."

I saw the first flash of light in his eyes that I'd seen in two weeks. "Gregory, here?" He stood up and straightened himself. "I'll be right there."

He came out of the bedroom a few minutes later; he'd even changed his shirt and combed his hair. He hadn't shaved in several days but his beard was thick and it looked deliberate rather than neglect. He shook hands with Gregory and hugged Christie. "It's good to see you," he told them.

"It's good to see you, too, but what's this I hear about your hiding away from life?" Gregory's tone was that of an affectionate older brother. I'd heard Josh use the same tone, talking to Kenneth.

Josh looked at me. "Are you telling tales out of school?"

"I'm worried about you," I told him. "I know you've been riding the emotional roller coaster recently." I deliberately borrowed Gregory's phrase from the night we'd had dinner together. "But you don't seem to be able to get past it. I thought Gregory might be able to help. He's been through it."

"And I know the best way to fix it," Gregory said earnestly. "Sit down at the piano and play it out. Let that rage out. You've been holding it inside you much too long, and you need to get rid of it."

With no hesitation at the order of his hero, Josh stood up and limped over to the piano, leaning heavily on his cane. I'd noticed that since Murtree's visit, his leg seemed to be weaker. That more than anything else worried me—I knew from Rachel, the physical therapist, how tightly the mind and the body interacted with each other. He sat down at the piano and began doing some warm up exercises.

Gregory let him get away with that for a few minutes, then came over and stood behind him. "Play it out," he ordered.

Josh began to play, starting out with some chording and then putting a melody to it. He'd only been playing for about fifteen minutes, though, when Gregory interrupted him. "That's not going to do it," he informed Josh. "Play the anger. Let it out."

Josh began again, but he'd only just gotten started when Gregory stopped him again. "You're still holding back," he said sternly. "Let it all out, Josh."

Josh started still again, but Gregory only allowed him to play a few minutes before he broke in again. "Damn it, Josh, you're not even trying. Put some muscle into it, man."

Josh scowled and increased the volume, but even that wasn't enough for Gregory. "What do I have to do, hit you?" he said coldly. "You're wasting my time here. Give it some emotion! I know you know how—why are you giving me such crap? Play the anger, man! Give me *something* here!"

I was horrified. What was Gregory doing? Where was the warm and compassionate friend, the gentle mentor? Who was this man with the cold steel blue eyes and why on earth had I called him?

Christie put a hand on my shoulder and pulled me back beside her. It was only then that I realized I'd moved forward, instinctively moving to protect Josh. "Gregory knows what he's doing," she said in a barely audible voice, into my hair so that only I could hear. "Trust him. There's a method to his madness." I nodded slightly, my eyes never leaving Josh.

Josh let more of the anger to come through as he played, but Gregory wasn't having any of it. "Let it out, man!" he shouted. "Damn you, let go of it and let it all out!"

Josh glared at him. "I am!"

"No you're not! You're wimping out on me! You coward, *let go of it!*"

"Listen, you bastard," Josh shouted back. "I can't do any more!"

Gregory's blue eyes blazed. "Yes. You. Can. *Now do it!*"

Josh started to shout back, but then he suddenly let go and let it all out. Suddenly the music had in it all the horror and shock of a sixteen-year-old whose world had turned upside down. It had the grief and pain he felt at the loss of his parents, of his sister's life cut short after only thirteen years. It had the fear of not knowing what the world contained, of the loss of everything familiar. It had the aching loneliness of a young man wanting his father's guidance, his mother's love. It contained the frustration of the teenager doing his lessons alone in his hospital bed. There was the horror and guilt of having been driving the car at the time of the accident; wondering if a more experienced driver could have saved his family. It held all the baseballs he never was able to hit out of the park, the tennis games he never could play, the hills he never was able to ski, all the exercise his otherwise healthy and athletic body demanded and was denied due to the limits of the weak leg. It included the pain he knew his grandparents still felt at the loss of their children, his parents; the sense of losing a part of herself that his foster mother, his Aunt Debbie, still felt at the death of her identical twin; the sadness he saw in his Aunt Rosemary's and his Uncle James' and his Aunt Julia's eyes on birthdays and anniversaries. It had the desperate fear that he might lose me too, somehow, sometime. It even had the frustration at the over-protectiveness of Randi and his aunts, the rebellion of his masculine soul as he strove for more independence from their shelter. It had the black despair of his sometime depression. Finally, it had the rage at the man who had caused it all.

Every time he tried to stop, Gregory said calmly from the chair he had retreated to, "No, Josh. Let go of it all." So he continued until he was exhausted, until his hands simply wouldn't play anymore, and he was shaking with the release of all the emotion that had been pent up for a long, long ten years.

As he sat there, breathless, trembling, Gregory stood up and walked over to him. Putting a hand on Josh's shoulder, he asked, "How do you feel?"

"Empty," Josh realized. "It's gone. All the anger, all the fear. I left it all on the piano keys."

"Good for you," Gregory declared. "It can't hurt anyone there. That was good work. I'm sorry I had to hit you so hard, metaphorically speaking, but I couldn't make you let go until you got mad enough at me, to forget to hold back."

So that was it. Now I understood Gregory's motives. I loved him for it and was ashamed of my earlier feelings. He caught my eye and smiled, and I knew he understood. He took the CD out of the recorder and handed it to Josh. "Here. You may want to use that in some future work."

"I'm sorry I called you a bastard," Josh replied shakily. "I didn't mean it."

"Yes, you did!" Gregory laughed. "But that's all right. You're forgiven, if I am." He held out his hand, and Josh shook it.

"I feel like I've been playing for hours," Josh commented. He stood up and made his way back to an armchair, sinking weakly into it.

"You have been," I pointed out. "It's almost six. And dinner will be ready in half an hour."

Josh looked at his friends. "You're staying, of course?"

"If we're invited," Gregory said, looking questioningly at me.

"Of course you're invited," I insisted enthusiastically. "I planned for you to stay. I just need a few minutes to finish up."

Christie stood up. "I'll help you." She followed me out to the kitchen and left the two musicians alone.

While Christie and I between us mashed the potatoes, made the gravy and the Yorkshire pudding, and wilted the spinach, the two men talked. Josh never told me what they discussed, but I was amazed, and very relieved, at how much better he appeared afterwards. Josh's respect and admiration for Gregory was so great that I knew he'd pay attention to anything Gregory told him. I wasn't fool enough to think that this was all there was to it; he'd need to work very hard with Mitch to get past this. But if he could be gotten to start looking forward again, and not back, he'd be fine. Eventually.

We had a lovely dinner together, the four of us, before the James's left to retrieve sleeping children and take them home to bed. For the next few days, Josh was back to his normal self, at least on the surface. I wasn't sure what was going on inside. He was sharing that only with Mitch, if he was sharing it with anyone. Meanwhile, I was torn. I couldn't bear the thought of leaving Josh, even for a little while. I loved him and wanted to be with him, and I knew Josh loved and needed me. But at the same time, I was desperately homesick.

Christie was the only one who truly understood. "When I first came to America," she confided, "I used to stand in the drug store and stare at all the choices. There's no question that the US has a wider selection of choices than the UK has. I occasionally question if that's always a good thing."

"Me too," I admitted.

"But I longed for real English bacon and sausage rolls and Scotch pies," she continued.

"And M&S foods," I added. "Whelks. Marmite. Real British sausages. Carbonated lemonade. Kippers."

"And when you can find those things, they're horrifically expensive," Christie commented.

"But it's so much more than that," I insisted. I told her a little of my conversation with Josh's cousins during the Olympics. She nodded gravely.

"Every time we go back to visit," she said, "when I return to the US my first thought is that this is not a civilized country. We think we are; we're the richest and most powerful country in the world. But we're still savages in many ways."

"Not savages," I objected. "Just—undisciplined adolescents."

"Same difference," Christie said with a grin. "But Jillian, honey, you and I have fallen in love with American men. I had lived in the US before I went to England to live, and I've been here much longer than you. I've assimilated. I had even before Gregory and I met. But you haven't, and I get the sense that you're fighting assimilation."

"I probably am. I don't know what to do, Christie. Before this all happened, Josh had said he was happy to live in England with me, but I don't know if this is the best time to uproot him. I don't want to leave him; I *can't* leave him. I love him too much to leave him. Even for just a few months. But I want to go home, Christie! I miss my home so much. And if I go home without Josh..." I shuddered. "That's unthinkable. That's not even on the radar."

Christie covered my hand with hers. "Then you have your answer, don't you? Hon, you need to talk to Josh."

"I will," I promised. "But not till he's better."

It was early June and I had now been here for close to a year, with just those few weeks at Christmas at home. I decided to make up my mind to the fact that I was going to be here a while, and enjoy it. I didn't hate it here; I quite liked some parts of it. I was just homesick, and I could get over that. Being with Josh was worth homesickness. I put the idea of going home out of my mind. I needed to start thinking of Scituate as home, until Josh was ready to move on.

Which was all well and good, until about a couple of days later, when I inadvertently mentioned "when we go home" and Josh turned to look at me strangely.

"You promised not to leave me," he said.

"I'm not leaving you," I said, surprised. "But we always planned to live in England eventually."

Josh was still lost in his own head. "I might have known it was too good to last. You don't want to be here, do you?"

"I never said that."

"But you don't," he challenged.

"I want to be wherever you are," I told him. "I want to be with you. Eventually, yes, I do want to go back home, but only with you. I don't ever want to be anywhere that you aren't."

Josh's eyes were cold. "I'm not going to keep you somewhere that you don't want to be," he said. "I love you too much to hold you here when you're not happy. You can leave."

"Josh, I don't want to..."

"Leave!" he shouted suddenly. "Pack your things and leave! Now! I don't want you here if you don't want to stay."

I made one more attempt. "Josh, please, I don't want to leave you…"

"I'm going to walk down to the waterfront for a few minutes," Josh announced. "When I get back, I want you to be gone." He picked up his cane and stalked out the door, slamming it behind him.

With tears running down my cheeks, I went into the bedroom and began to pack. I only needed my clothes and my laptop; the little things I'd bought for the house could stay. It took about forty-five minutes to collect everything and have it ready; then I called Lori.

"Can you come and get me?" I sobbed. "Josh and I…well, I guess it's over."

"Oh, honey!" She was immediately sympathetic. "I'll be there in five minutes."

I took out my key to the condo and put it on the table, along with the keys to the car Josh had hired for me. Kenneth and Joyce, or Russ, could help him return it. I twisted the little sapphire ring on my left hand but couldn't bring myself to take it off. Maybe later I could send it to him. For now I couldn't quite bear the thought that I wasn't going to be spending my life with him after all.

I was downstairs with my suitcases and laptop bag when Lori arrived. She helped me load my things into the boot and hugged me. "You poor thing. What happened, did you have a fight?"

I explained what had happened. "It was as if he didn't even hear me when I tried to tell him I didn't want to leave—not unless he was coming with me."

"I think Josh's emotions are still pretty raw after meeting up with the man who killed his family," Lori said tactfully. "I think he's still looking to protect himself from more hurt and is pushing you away because that hurts less than having you leave of your own accord, and right now he can't make himself believe that you won't eventually leave him. It's more survivor syndrome—he doesn't feel as if he's entitled to be happy."

Now that Lori had explained it, I could see it. "What should I do?"

"I can't tell you that. But if it were me, I'd leave him alone for a day or two and let him recover; then I'd call him and let him know how much I love him."

"But right now," she said, turning the ignition of the car, "I'm taking you home and letting you have a good cry. I know you need it."

I did. But I managed to control myself until I'd participated in an enthusiastic greeting from Kaitlyn and Jeremy, with a shy kiss from Beth. Then I hid in my old room and cried till I had no tears left.

Joyce came over the next day and hugged me. "I'm so sorry," she said. "I'm sure Josh didn't mean it and he'll come around. I've known him all my life and I know he loves you terribly."

"Has he said anything to you since I left?" I asked hopefully.

Regretfully she shook her head. "Kenneth called him yesterday and Josh wouldn't even talk to him. This happens periodically—he goes so deep into his depression that it takes him while to find his way out. But he's keeping his therapy appointments; Russ saw him coming out of the doctor's office this morning. So at least there's that."

I stayed with Adam and Lori for five days, after which I tried calling Josh. He didn't return my call, answer my text or respond to the message I left on his Facebook page. That night I sat down with Lori and Adam.

"I love you both," I told them. "But at this point, the only reason for my being in the US would be to be with Josh. If I'm not going to be with him, I may as well go back home to England."

Adam nodded. "You're welcome to stay with us as long as you want, but I have to agree that you're not really accomplishing anything here. When do you want to go?"

"I may as well go tomorrow, if I can get a ticket I can afford," I said gloomily. I searched the internet, found a flight with two stops that was within my budget, and booked myself a ticket.

Joyce and I had a long talk that night, but there were some things I couldn't tell even a friend as close as she had become; not when she was going to be Josh's sister in law in a little over a year. But we hugged, promised to keep in close touch through Skype, email and Facetime, and I promised to return in a year for her wedding to Kenneth. Joyce was still insistent that she wanted me in the bridal party, and I wanted to do that for her.

"By that time I should be more or less able to think of him without crying," I said.

"You'll be with him by then," Joyce promised gently. "I'm sure of it."

I hoped she was right, but I didn't have much faith.

The flight was a long one, stopping in New York and again in Dublin. Adam had upgraded me to first class when he'd realized the length of the flight so by the time we landed at Heathrow I wasn't too uncomfortable, only slightly stiff from sitting so long. I had the little portrait of Josh and me in my handbag and I pulled it out periodically to gaze at it, but it made me cry. The American woman sitting next to me had been so kind, listening to my troubles and sympathizing, but by the time I was ready to deplane I wanted nothing more than to be left alone to cry some more. My plans were made; I would go from the airport to the London flat where Pammie and Siobhan were loyally keeping my bedroom for me, and I had every intention of crying my heart out into Pammie's loving shoulder. Tomorrow I would go down and spend the weekend with my parents, whom I hadn't seen since Christmas. Finally I would return to London with my brand new certification from the cooking school, and start calling caterers looking for a job until I could save enough money to open my own event planning company in a year or two.

I cleared Customs and headed for the baggage claim area. My heart skipped several beats as I realized how much a man standing by the carousel looked like Josh, from the back. He was tall and broad, like Josh, with the same blond hair. Josh even had a shirt like the one this man was wearing; black and grey plaid with a silver thread in it. Worn with black jeans, just like Josh did. Then he turned, and I saw the cane.

This wasn't someone who looked like Josh.

This was Josh.

I was in his arms before I knew it, and he was holding me so tightly I couldn't breathe, whispering my name over and over. "I'm so sorry, Jillian, I'm so sorry. I was crazy to let you go."

"It doesn't matter," I gasped. "As long as you're here, and you want me."

"I'm here," Josh agreed. "And I want you forever."

Oblivious to the curious stares around us, he kissed me deeply and I reveled in it.

Later, after collecting my luggage, we found a quiet restaurant and went in for a cuppa, which by now I sorely needed. We also needed to talk, and would not be able to do so once we went to wherever we were going to be tonight.

"I was so scared," Josh acknowledged. "I've known how homesick you've been. Had things gone according to plan, I was going to go back with you when you left in May, and stay for the summer. Then Murtree came, and I suddenly couldn't get out of my own head. The session with Gregory helped, and so did my talks with Mitch, but I still wasn't fully out of the depression pit. I was so afraid of losing you that I ended up pulling away from you."

So Lori had been right.

"I knew the same day I told you to leave that I was being stupid. I was hoping against hope that you would pay no attention to me. When I got back to the condo and you had really left, I didn't know what to do. I was so depressed I couldn't talk to anyone but Mitch, and I could barely talk to him. Finally Gregory called to find out how I was doing, and he really let me have it. He told me what an idiot I was, and ordered me to do whatever I had to do to get you back. I was shaking by the time I got off the phone, but I knew he was right. Man, I don't know what it is about him but when he speaks, I listen." I kept my mouth shut.

He stopped to sip his coffee. "I called your cell, but you'd turned it off. I never thought to check Facebook until later, but when you check your page next you'll see my message. It finally occurred to me to call Adam, and he informed me in the coldest voice I'd ever heard that he'd just dropped you at the airport. I called Kenneth and offered him anything he wanted up to and including his last year of grad school paid for if he'd get me to the airport in time to see you."

"But then..."

Josh grinned. "We didn't quite make it. Adam had told me your flight information and your flight took off about fifteen minutes before we got there."

"Then how..."

"I can act like a fool often enough," Josh said with a grin that looked like his old self, "but I'm not quite one. While I was waiting for Ken to pick me up I grabbed my passport and my iPad and a duffle bag of clothes. I managed to get on a nonstop flight that was leaving more or less immediately so that I arrived about two hours before you did. As soon as the captain allowed us to turn on our electronic devices I found myself a hotel room online and made a reservation. I thought we'd want more privacy tonight than we'd get at your flat or my grandfather's. I dropped my things off at the hotel when I arrived and got back just in time to catch you at the baggage claim."

"How long are you here for?" I asked.

"That depends," he said, holding my eyes steadily. "We have to make some decisions. I can stay on a tourist visa for up to six months, but I can't apply for a marriage visa while I'm inside the UK; I have to go back to the US for that. So you and I have to make some decisions about when and where we want to be married. That will determine when I need to go back. But I'll only go back as long as it takes to deal with the red tape that will allow us to be married and live here, in England, for the rest of our lives. We'll have to figure out whether it makes sense for you to come with me or not. But this is it, angel. We're going to be married and I know you'd rather live here than there. I can deal with selling my condo from here if I have to, and I have more than enough relatives to help with things like shipping furniture."

"I was going to go down and see my parents tomorrow," I told him. "You can come with me and we can decide these things then. What are you going to do about Mitch?"

"I only left England five years ago. I'm sure Ron, my therapist here, is still in practice."

"What did Kenneth hold you up for?" I teased.

"Well, he didn't actually fulfill his part of the bargain," Josh chuckled. "So we settled on a romantic weekend for two, he and Joyce, on the coast of Maine sometime this summer. And we're going to each be the other's best man for our respective weddings, not that that wouldn't likely have happened anyway." He finished his coffee and stood up, holding out a hand to me. "And now, my love, where to? Shall we retire to your flat so I can meet Pammie and Siobhan, or would you rather we spend tonight together at my hotel?"

"Your hotel," I said shyly. "We'll see Pammie and Siobhan next week."

"The hotel it is, then, my lady. Your wish is my command. But there's one last thing we have to do." He stopped a young couple passing us. "Excuse me, would you mind taking a picture of the two of us together?"

"We'd be happy to," the girl said, reaching out her hand to take Josh's iPod. She and her boyfriend or husband or whatever he was took several shots of Josh and me, with a sign pointing the way to Heathrow Terminal Three prominently behind us. Then the two of them continued on and Josh emailed the picture to Gregory and Christie, with a message, "Thank you—call you soon!"

"And now, angel," he said, "I want you all to myself for a while. I'm going to rent a short term flat while I'm here . . . do you want to continue sharing with your friends or come in with me?"

I answered him the most effective way I knew how.

About the Author

CATHERINE BANNON WAS BORN IN CANADA and lived there until her family moved to the United States while she was in middle school. Despite living in the US for most of her life, she still finds the mix of cultures confusing, which is why she wrote this book in the first place.

Catherine likes to travel but doesn't have the time to do as much of it as she wants. She also is fond of classical music, which drives her classic-rock husband crazy. Catherine likes to cook, and her idea of hell is being stuck somewhere with nothing to read. She likes cats, but doesn't have any at the moment because her husband is allergic to them. Occasionally she borrows a friend's cat or dog just to get her "furry friend fix".

Catherine is a Christian and sings in her church choir. The church that Jillian, Josh and their families attend is the same one she went to for many years before she got married and moved out of town. Catherine works in the Employee Benefits office of a university in Cambridge, MA. She is married to Brad Bannon, a political analyst and adjunct political science professor. They live in Marshfield, MA, which is just south of Scituate.

CPSIA information can be obtained at www.ICGtesting.com
Printed in the USA
BVOW08s0312011016
463887BV00001B/14/P